Changeling Press. LLC

ChangelingPress.com

Roanoke River Omegas

Will Okati

Roanoke River Omegas
Will Okati

ISBN: 978-1-60521-854-0

Publisher:
Changeling Press LLC
315 N. Centre St.
Martinsburg, WV 25404
ChangelingPress.com

Printed in the U.S.A.

Editor: Margaret Riley
Cover Artist: Bryan Keller

The individual stories in this anthology have been previously released in E-Book format.

Table of Contents

Conceivable (Roanoke River Omegas 1)
Will Okati

Omega Jory's in love with his best friend, Alpha Darius, and Darius has no idea. Darius's in love with Jory, and Jory has no idea. But when Jory asks Darius to father his baby, everything's about to explode. Jory's body burns with the need to conceive. He's so hot to be bred he's insatiable, demanding everything Darius can give -- and more. And the more Darius gives, the more Darius wants.

But it's not all fun and games. Jory's body wants all the sex it can take, but it isn't cooperating with conception. And the fluctuating hormones are making Jory a little crazy. Darius's got to figure out how to save the day and to tell his best friend he wants to be more than friends, for keeps.

What do you do with a drunken sailor? Take him home, build a nest, and get him pregnant... if you can.

Chapter One

What *did* you do with a drunken sailor?

Why, anything you wanted, that's what. You could tie him up tight with a crimson ribbon, dip him in a pool of melted butter, run him through a room of screaming fire alarms, and when he got done with all that, then you could tuck him in bed with an Alpha's lover. And every last bit of it sounded *fine* when sung at the top of three dozen-odd throats at Happy Hour on a Friday evening in MacInnes's pub.

Better still when Darius could raise his mostly empty glass and swing it in time with the song. Best of all when tucked into a booth with his best friend beside him, warm as toast and smelling faintly of Omega and largely of burnt-sugar whiskey.

As weeknights went, this was a good one.

The last lines of the chorus were still echoing off the ceiling when someone who fancied himself a soloist stood on top of a table and started belting out a boozy version of "Danny Boy." He got a few catcalls and the occasional coaster tossed at him, but he had a decent deep tenor, and most of the rowdies settled down to listen. Darius included.

Still laughing, still warm, he slid back into the booth he shared with Jory and kicked his legs forward to tangle their feet together. Best friends -- closer than blood since they'd met in another bar on weekend passes five years back -- they'd always been in each other's space ever since. Didn't bother them any that Darius was an Alpha and Jory an Omega. Darius was Navy and Jory part of the Peace Corps, sure, but the military kept everyone on hormone suppressants to cut down on hanky-panky in the ranks, so what did it matter?

"Another round?" Darius asked when their impromptu soloist paused to drown his own thirst.

Redheaded and usually fair as cream, Jory's cheeks were cherry pink tonight from the two whiskies and a pint of Guinness he'd already downed, but he gave Darius a blazing grin and raised his empty glass. "You're on. And I mean it, you're on. Last round was mine."

Was it? Darius shrugged, not bothered either way. They always took turns. He halfway stood to wave at their waiter -- a friendly Beta who could pull pints fast as lightning strikes -- then thumped back down in a comfortable slouch. Jory, still grinning, made him laugh. Made him content. Being around him made something inside Darius feel... satisfied. Good.

"So," he said, after tipping back his empty glass in search of just a few more drops. "You were saying, about the kids, before that racket started up?" Jory had gone into teaching kindergarten after getting out of the Reserves, and taken to it like a duck to water.

"That they're adorable. Today I had to teach one of them not to lick the drinking fountain because that wasn't how it worked. Also? 'Racket' my hindquarters, you love it." Jory's smile shone softer, warmer, teasing. "As if you weren't singing along."

Darius bent his head, only a little sheepish and only for half a second. He came up with a glint in his eye and clinked his glass against Jory's. "Shut up."

Jory clinked back. He knew this game. "You shut up."

"Bite me."

"Needs ketchup."

"Kiss my ass."

Jory laughed. "Bend over!"

Their pert, pretty little Beta waiter -- what was

his name… Adam? -- rolled his eyes as he swung by their table with two full glasses. "Drown yourselves in these, would you?" He softened his words with a gentle love tap on the back of Darius's dark head and a rustle through Jory's auburn tangle. "Drink up, boys, order some more, and leave a good tip. I've got bills to pay!"

"Good thing I have a steady job," Darius remarked as Adam sped away. He'd left the Navy a year after Jory mustered out and would have settled where his best friend did regardless, but he thanked his lucky stars Jory had picked Roanoke Rapids, North Carolina. Made finding work on the water easy, and Darius had settled into a good hands-on position at the lake. Solid work that left him aching with sore muscles every day, but satisfied down to the bottom of his soul. "Or I wouldn't be able to afford taking my best friend out for booze-ups at fancy joints like this."

Jory wrinkled his nose. "Speaking of kids, how are the new hires *you* were talking about?"

"Eh, there's a few bright stars," Darius said with a shrug. "Some better than others. Time will tell. But they do already know how to use the water fountains. Probably."

"They're not as cute as a baker's dozen of toddlers, though."

Darius waggled one hand to and fro. "They probably think so, especially when they're out looking to score some tail, but nope."

Jory nodded in satisfaction. Darius had always liked his friend's face, not exactly handsome but friendly and open but with fine, well-shaped bones. Very dissimilar to himself, with his tall leanness, his longer features and darker complexion. His general attitude was sharper-edged, more serious. But whenever Darius got too stuck in his head, Jory pried him out, and whenever Jory's warm heart got a little too bruised, Darius was there to pick him up and settle him down.

What he'd do without Jory in his life, Darius didn't know. And he didn't want to know.

Darius downed his drink and wiped the Guinness foam away with a sigh of satisfaction. "So did the kid wrap his head around how water fountains work, in the end?"

"Hmm?"

Darius cocked his head. "I said…"

But Jory's attention had drifted. He did that sometimes -- wandered off in thought and lost himself in daydreams. Darius didn't worry about it, as he always came back, but every now and again it was interesting to try and track what'd caught Jory's fancy. He let his gaze go slightly out of focus, turned toward Jory's line of sight, and…

Ah. There it was. Courting couples. Of which there were plenty, no matter where you went, but especially in MacInnes's when the beer was flowing and the whiskey bit back. Darius followed Jory's regard, jumping from pair to pair.

First an Omega couple -- interesting, you didn't see that too often -- in their, hmm, mid sixties? Yes, and comfortable with each other in a way that said they'd been an odd couple for decades. Nice. From there, a couple of Betas who were plainly just friends, but with a few saucy benefits like the hands tucked in each others' back pockets. A thirtyish Omega buying a jar of spicy brined pickles for a laughing Alpha who rode him piggyback and kissed his ear, and a widower Darius knew who always drank one Long Island iced tea with a picture of his mate on the table with him.

Humanity, in all its infinite variety.

And then, something Darius knew Jory would zero in on as special. An Alpha with an Omega on his arm, the two of them so in love it almost rang from the rooftop and echoed in everyone's ears. Total hearts in their eyes, and eyes only for each other. Young, maybe on the uphill climb to twenty-five, but the Alpha had a toddler on one hip and the Omega's stomach was proudly curved, maybe six months gone with a second cub. He rested one hand on the swell, an unconscious gesture but one that spoke of pleasure and pride. His Alpha glanced down and wrapped his free arm around the Omega's shoulders, giving him a cuddle.

Darius shook his head, but with a lopsided smile. The whole effect was so sweet it'd give a man diabetes, but he wouldn't complain too much about it. He glanced at Jory to see that Jory had noticed him in turn. "Busted?"

"Nosy," Jory said, giving his shin a gentle nudge under the table.

"Look who's talking."

"But that's all right," Jory continued, undaunted. "You can buy the next round. Again."

Darius snorted. "Anyone ever tell you you're not a cheap date?"

"Every now and again." Jory checked his watch. "Actually, make it a cup of coffee instead. It's getting late, and I need to sober up."

"Why? We've walked home three sheets to the wind before."

"I have my reasons," Jory said without further explanation, leaving Darius to wonder what he meant by that. It seemed to be something that made him a little nervous. He pushed his glass back and forth in the circle of condensation it'd left on the table, but didn't drop any handy clues. "Did you see the couple with one in arms and one on the way?"

Darius nodded. Of course he had. *Ah.* Two plus two came together. "Is that the water fountain kid?"

Jory's smile blossomed, warm and pleased. "It is. He's adorable, huh? He wants to name his baby brother Mr. Ed."

A swallow of beer almost went down the wrong way. Darius coughed. "He wants to what, now? How does he know Mr. Ed? I don't even remember where *I* heard of Mr. Ed."

"No telling." Jory laughed too. "His parents are just hoping he'll come around to plain old 'Corey' when he's born."

He fell quiet again, but Darius could tell he was still watching the couple. Darius had to admit they made entertaining viewing. The baby must have been awake, inside. The Omega patted his belly, trying to soothe him, and the Alpha tracked his movements with one palm, fascination written across his face. *Little judo master,* Darius thought the Alpha said at one point. He winced in imagined empathy, and -- the strangest thing -- a flicker of jealousy.

Jealousy? Darius frowned down at the remnants of his Guinness. He'd been a bachelor since he presented as Alpha, and hadn't really minded. When he needed company or he went into rut he knew where to find what he needed. Aside from that, it didn't seem so important. He had Jory, and they kept each other busy. Besides, Jory had decided to stay on military-grade suppressants when he went civilian to keep himself level and lower the risk of getting pregnant by accident, so it'd never been an issue. But now, Darius wondered.

No. He knew. He'd seen that look on Omega

faces before, and it surprised him to see it on Jory's, but then again it wasn't a shock. It looked... natural. Nice. Darius tapped the back of Jory's hand with one finger. "I see. You've been thinking about it."

Jory, still captivated by the scene, raised his shoulder a fraction of an inch. "On and off." He shook his head and focused, looking back at Darius. "No, that's a lie of omission. I *have* been thinking about it. I can't stop thinking about it. I *want* that, and I can't stop wanting it."

"A baby?"

"Enough that I stopped taking my suppressants," Jory said, simple and clear. He settled his hands around his glass. "Three days ago. You know suppressants. They start working fast, and they stop just as fast. Should be gone by the weekend."

Darius blinked. Jory really meant business, then. The thought fascinated him in a way that surprised Darius. The mental image of Jory as round and curved and full as that Omega gave him a jolt like electricity applied deep down inside, something that sparked too much heat to ignore.

He stamped that down carefully, tightly, and securely. Darius had never been immune to Jory's charms. He'd had dreams, fantasies. Wishes. Desires. But he'd refused to let himself take one single step past plain and simple friendship. Nothing that'd start them down the road to a messy breakup. He'd seen it happen before -- too many times -- when friends hooked up. Hell, he'd encouraged Jory to date other people. He'd been glad that Jory was living with Alpha Whateverhisnamewas when he moved into town so the question of sharing an apartment couldn't come up.

Darius realized he was staring. To cover his

reaction, he cleared his throat and hurried on. "Fertile. No kidding. Who're you going to get to be the father?"

"That's the thing," Jory said, his gaze fixed calmly on Darius. "I was hoping it would be you."

* * *

Well. If he'd wanted to surprise Darius, he'd certainly done it.

Jory cocked his head and regarded his friend from a foot, foot and a half away, with only a tabletop and the weight of some significant questions between them, and waited for the shock to wear off. If pressed to it under torture, he might admit he didn't mind. Darius had the most endearing way of blinking like a stunned owl when you took him off guard. You could almost hear the Tex Avery cartoon noises as his eyelashes whipped up and down.

"You're staring at me," Darius said after a moment, eyes still wide as silver dollars, and almost the same shade of summer-storm gray, such a striking color. Fringed with those thick, sooty lashes of his, he'd brought far more Omegas than he knew of to their knees with lust.

You're worth staring at, Jory thought, but kept his smile easy and teasing. Jane Austen had it right: there were certain inalienable truths in this world. He didn't know about the man in possession of a fortune needing a wife, but the truth in *his* life? He'd been in love with Darius since the day they'd met.

Another truth, one he was positive of: Darius had no idea.

So, this right here? Walking a tightrope. Walking the thinnest, finest of tightropes. He resisted the urge to hold his breath, because that surely would tip Darius off about something odd being up, and folded his hands instead. "You look like I hit you on the head with an iron skillet."

"Are you sure you didn't?" Darius leaned back in the booth and took Jory's beer with him, draining the glass. He held it against his chest, as if enjoying the leftover cold, and Jory wondered if Darius's heart might just be pounding as fast as his own. "Say that again. Just so I know I heard you right."

Ah. Well, it wouldn't hurt. Jory hoped. "I want to have a baby," he said, simply as he could. "I want you to be the father." True, and true again. Nothing but the truth. If not the *whole* truth.

Darius's eyes narrowed thoughtfully. He glanced down into his empty glass, and Jory knew he was wondering if he'd had too much or not enough. If the guy on his third repetition of "Danny Boy" was affecting his hearing, or if someone had slipped him a Mickey Finn. It wasn't that Darius would doubt Jory, but he might be wary of himself. And he was -- Jory could tell -- on the verge of saying no.

"I didn't make the offer on impulse," Jory said quietly, catching Darius's baffled gaze and keeping it. "This isn't a whim. Understand that."

Darius's frown shifted from almost-denial to consideration, and then he shook his head, but it wasn't the flat "no" Jory had worried about. He put his beer mug down and crossed his arms. "I get that. I know you, don't I?" He raised one shoulder. "If you want a baby, that's out of the blue as far as I knew, but okay."

He stopped. Jory waited a minute before nudging Darius's calf under the table. "But?"

"But I don't get it," Darius said. "There's half a dozen Alphas in here you could lead out by the nose and have them thank you for it. You could pick anyone, Jory. So why do you want me?"

He meant it, and Jory could tell. The bless-his-heart Alpha had no idea.

Okay, fine. Jory made a split-second decision. Moving forward was all about adaptation, improvisation, and overcoming, right? Good old survivalist Bear Grylls hadn't steered anyone wrong yet as far as he knew. Except maybe when it came to the drinking your own piss to survive thing. There were lines Jory refused to cross.

And he was drifting again. That wouldn't do. "Come on," he said decisively, slipping out of the booth and standing up. "We've had too much beer for a talk like this."

"More like not enough."

"Nope. We need coffee." Jory offered Darius a friendly grin and a hand up. "Two coffees, and some fresh air. And don't sweat it. These are on me."

* * *

MacInnes's made surprisingly good coffee for an Irish pub -- or maybe, on second consideration, it wasn't that surprising at all. They needed something quality to put the Irish in for early customers who took their day drinking seriously. Also, something strong enough to melt spoons in to sober up the late night clientele before they poured their way home.

Jory took a long sip, relishing the deep, dark complexity of the smoky French roast. Better enjoy it now. With any luck, he wouldn't be able to drink caffeine for a good few months to come. He crossed his fingers and tapped his heel on the pavement three times for luck.

Darius walked beside him, quiet and thoughtful. He did that, always had. Went *me-big-tough-Alpha* broody, Heathcliff-on-the-moors, whenever he had a problem to chew over inside his head, and was never more serious or reserved than when his world had tilted sideways. Jory *was* sorry for that, but only that part of it. Darius didn't know he did it, as it happened. Nor did Darius realize what a big heart he had, under that distancing act. Wouldn't have believed it if he'd been told, but Jory knew. He *knew*.

"Why you?" Jory asked at last, lightly. He slipped his hand into Darius's coat pocket, and at his curious sideways glance, said, "Cold. I have my reasons as to *why you*. Let me start at the beginning and explain it all. It'll make more sense that way."

Darius considered that a moment, then nodded.

Good! Jory cleared his throat as he guided them left, down a side street away from MacInnes's to a park walk they'd taken countless times. Familiarity always soothed Alphas when they were in this kind of mood.

"I started thinking about babies, oh... five months ago? Six?" he started, sure that Darius was listening to every word. "Casually at first. Then, more and more often. I wondered if it was that biological clock everyone seems to talk so much about. You know, the one I was pretty sure I didn't have?"

Darius chuffed quietly, the humor touching his eyes. Also good! "I recall."

"Turns out I was wrong. There's just something in me that's hungry for it, that's *ready* for it. Maybe it's in tune. I'm making good money, as good as a kindergarten teacher can expect. I have friends in daycares and preschools who can cut me deals on childcare, and I have a good, steady home that's big enough for one little baby and me."

Darius listened, only giving the occasional nod, but that was good enough to go on with. Jory pressed forward. "So, baby. Fine. Next logical step from there is who do I want to be the father. I thought about a hookup for maybe five seconds. That's not me."

Darius wrinkled his nose in agreement.

"Then I thought about in-vitro fertilization, or donor sperm, or a volunteer Alpha, but that's not me either. Too much of a business arrangement. It works for some, but I need more."

Darius cleared his throat quietly. "Why not an ex-boyfriend? There've been a few."

Because no one else could ever compare, Jory thought. Then said, "Didn't seem fair."

"How so?"

"Because all I'd want from him was a baby, and how would that make him any different than all the other options?"

Darius gave a sideways nod, conceding the point. His fingers flexed, rosy from the cold, before he slipped his hand in his coat pocket with Jory's and knocked their knuckles together. "But I'm different? Really?"

"You are," Jory said. "And I'll tell you why." He licked his lips. His heart beat a little faster. *Now* they were getting to the meat of it, the crux of it, and he had to tread carefully if he was going to have a chance at a taste of everything he'd ever wanted. He knew Darius wasn't in love with him, and if he wasn't by now then he probably never would be. But there was a way to still have it all, all the same.

Darius had never gone on the hunt for an Omega to pop out cubs for him, but he knew Darius loved babies. He watched them as if their antics were endlessly fascinating, held them as if they were made of glass until they were old enough to roughhouse with, and the joy on his face when he did...

"You've been in my life longer than anyone else I know, at this point," Jory said, choosing his words carefully. "I don't think I could ever care for someone any more than I care for you. You're brilliant, you're kind, and you're a good man. Who could I pick that'd be a better dad?"

He watched Darius chew that over a bit, coming to a meditative stop as he did. His fingers toyed with Jory's in the coat pocket, absentmindedly twining around Jory's and lacing together with his. Finally, he looked up at Jory, searching his face. "And is that it?" he asked. "Is that all?"

Ah. "No," Jory said, bold and simple. He gently untangled their fingers and moved so that he stood in front of Darius, right there on the street corner in sight of God and man and who-knew-who else, because that didn't matter and Darius did. "No," he said again, taking his coffee and Darius's and tossing them in a handy trash bin. "There's this." *The biggest risk of all.*

He stood on his tiptoes and pressed his mouth to Darius's in a kiss.

Their first.

Chapter Two

What do you do with a drunken sailor? Kiss him on a corner with your eyes wide open…

Jory's were. Open, that was. Darius couldn't have shut his if he'd tried, and he didn't. He needed to see this. Jory, sweet-smelling, gentle-hearted Omega Jory, was in front of him, chest pressed to his, arms around his neck, and his mouth against Darius's, moving slow and careful, but his lips so warm Darius thought they'd both burst into flames.

What. The. Omega. Fuck, Darius thought, dazed -- but somehow not at all willing to move. This was absolutely everything he'd fought against for years, and here he was crumbling like a pillar of salt. But he couldn't stop. Not even when Jory nuzzled against his mouth as he ended the kiss and took a step back, staring up at him, waiting for him to react.

Darius licked his lips, tasting coffee and bitter hops and Omega, and… lost his mind, just a little. He blinked, and Jory was back in his arms, staring up at him in surprise.

Another blink, and Darius's mouth was against Jory's again, moving hot and insistent this time, coaxing his pretty pink lips apart and tasting anew the flavors that clung to his palate. Feeling the ripple of firm Omega muscle pressed tight against him, the flex of Jory's arms and the way Jory knotted his fingers into the back of Darius's sweater. The heat of his breath on Darius's chin when the kiss broke for half a second, the sound of his small moan.

Darius looked, listened, felt, and went a little crazier still.

Bending Jory backward, arms at his waist to keep him from falling, Darius pressed his mouth to the soft, sweet spot where neck met shoulders and nibbled lightly. Then not so lightly, driven by something he couldn't put a name to. Not a bite, but not far off, and something that would leave just a shadow of a bruise. Maybe for the sake of Jory's Omega scent, which sprang up rich and heady as molasses in a distillery, burnt-sugar-sweet. One of Jory's legs came up, knee digging into Darius's hip in the very first hint of offering the crux of his legs to Darius, and that made Darius groan, clutch him tighter, almost break skin with his teeth.

There's this, Jory had said. Good lord. He hadn't been kidding. *This*. How long had *this* been bubbling under the surface without his even knowing it was there?

Darius let go, wondering if he looked half as stunned as Jory. Probably more so. What did you do with a drunken sailor? Kiss him till he took the Omega to his home and to bed. But... he sniffed the air, tasting Jory's Omega scent. There was something different.

Oh. Yes. The lessening of suppressants. Faint disappointment tempered his lust. No wonder, then. Jory's hormones were out of control, poor man. He'd probably have humped a light post if he thought it'd given him the come-hither. He needed help, didn't he? And of course he'd ask his best friend for it. What else were friends for?

"You'll do it?" Jory asked, his arms still around Darius's neck. "Say you'll do it. Please. There's no one else I'd want to ask. No one but you."

And there was only one answer Darius could give. "I will," he said, his voice rough from kissing. He cleared his throat. "But not because of this." Not *just* because of this, he meant, and hoped Jory understood what he meant. "Because you're my best friend, man.

And I'd do anything you asked of me. So. When? Where?"

* * *

"When? Where?"

"Not now. Not here. Friday night. Your place. I'll be there at eight."

Darius blinked his way out of the memory and back into reality. His lips still tingled with the ghost of Jory's kisses, but there was nothing quite so grounding as the smell of a lakefront work trailer. Nothing in the world smelled exactly like that. Spilled diesel, the ghost of shitty corned beef sandwiches from a thousand lunches, and rubber from boots, slickers, Sou'Wester hats. And maybe -- was that a hint of illicit nookie lingering in the corners? Someone's lunchtime delight?

"Contemplating, or just constipated?" A tenor, faintly Southern, too-smartass-for-its-own-good voice.

Darius lifted one hand to wave without looking. He didn't need to. He knew that voice. He and Grant had been friends since he'd moved into Grant's neighborhood when he'd first arrived in Roanoke Rapids. Upstairs/downstairs neighbors. They'd fought like cats and dogs over parking spaces and rooftop access, joined forces when they realized they did better on the same side, and dished out as much shit as they could shovel in each other's direction. An Alpha, same as him, Grant loved raising a middle finger to anything that tweaked his sense of right and wrong.

Grant sauntered over to poke at Darius's shoulder and get his attention. A cinnamon redhead with a spray of nutmeg freckles, he didn't look Alpha, but one word out of his mouth and everyone knew. "Something's up. Spill it."

"Something has to be?"

"That's the best you can do?" He cocked his head at Darius. "I can tell when there's something on your mind. Not that I'll push too hard. Oh, no. I'll wait and ask you again later when you least expect it. Which is a comforting thought, I know, so I'd go ahead and tell me now."

Darius laughed despite himself. "God, you're a pain."

"I know," Grant said with a grin and without a drop of shame. "Come on. What's up?"

Darius chewed it over for a moment. Grant would get it out of him one way or the other, and it wouldn't hurt to have a sympathetic -- or at least willing -- ear on his side. He might need one.

And it'd be fun as hell to surprise Grant for once.

"Jory wants to have my baby. We're going to have sex on Friday," he said baldly. "Your turn. What's up with you?"

Silence. When Darius turned to look, Grant's jaw had dropped and stayed there, and his eyes gone perfectly round.

"Now that's interesting," he said. "Jory tells me that's almost exactly how I looked when he asked me if I'd be up for the job."

Grant carefully put a finger under his chin and pushed up, closing his mouth with a faint *click* of the jaw. He did not, however, blink for another ten seconds or so. "I -- what? Come again?"

"Haven't even come once, yet."

Grant made a lemon face and popped him one on the bicep. Yep, just like having a brother, in arms or no. "You've already got the dad jokes down. No, seriously. Back up. Jory asked you, and you said yes?" When Darius nodded, Grant blew out a breath. "Wow. No wonder you were staring off into space. Me, I'd be running for Mexico so fast I'd kick dust trails up behind me." A moment's pause. "You're almost as good as married to Jory. But still."

Darius arched an eyebrow. "Are you done, or should I wait for another salvo of snark?"

"I think that's about all I've got for now." Grant coughed once, and managed to make it sound more on the empathetic side of brotherliness. He leaned against Darius, offering comfort if he needed any. "Could get complicated, you know."

Darius leaned back. "Trust me, I know. We spent hours talking last night, working out the details. Assuming everything goes the way it should, that he does get pregnant -- we don't know if we'll be compatible that way yet --"

Grant coughed behind one hand, but when Darius frowned Grant gave him an innocent look and waved for him to go on.

Weird. Well, whatever. "*If* he gets pregnant, then we'll share custody," Darius said. "Weekends, as soon as the cub's old enough to walk, and the Omega hormones die down enough for Jory to let him out of his sight. A year or so. I'll be there as much as I can until then, taking care of them, lending a hand where I can. I'll make it work."

"Hmm," Grant said cryptically. "That wasn't quite what I asked, so let me try again. Do you *want* this? Not just the sex part. The being a dad part. That's fucking huge, friend, and as for me I'm never getting tied down to that particular stake, so let me ask again and with all the emphasis I can bring to bear. Are you *sure*?"

Zing. Straight to the heart, but that was Grant for you. Darius rubbed at his breastbone, but he'd stayed up all night, long after saying goodnight to Jory, thinking this over, and he knew his answer. "Yes."

Grant made a thoughtful noise.

"Yes," Darius said again, taking a deep breath. He dug his heels down hard against the trailer's rust-and-oil-covered steel flooring. "I want this. I'm -- excited. Wild. Buck wild. Never had this happen before, but I like it. I'm glad. Fiercely so. And a little terrified. And horny as hell."

"Alphas," he and Grant said together.

Darius drew a freer breath. "It's Jory," he said, simple and true. "I'd do anything for him. This is just part of that."

Grant nodded again, still thoughtful, but then surprised Darius by standing on tiptoe to knuckle the top of his head almost affectionately. As if that'd satisfied him, as if it'd explained everything.

But then again, Darius guessed it kind of did.

* * *

"We could go shopping," Kit said. "Not even for baby things, I know it's too early for that. You need protein. We could grab some *tapas*, go for a run along the shore, maybe see what's playing at the theatre. Something to distract you."

"I can't. Darius will be here any time. You know that," Jory said. He technically had almost an hour and a half before Darius showed up, but Darius had never been late in his life if he could be deeply, unfashionably early. That cut it down to forty-five minutes at best.

Kit, Jory's closest Omega friend and neighbor -- as Darius had that dickhead Grant, Jory had Kit -- sat curled up in a chair, chin in hand, watching Jory with a frown. "It's just that you've never made a nest before, and you're already wound tighter than a cheap watch spring," he said frankly. Sweet as sugar and romantic to the bone, he was also paradoxically practical and had a stubborn streak fit to match Jory's. "You're going to spiral out and go *sproing* when you should be going *oh God, harder, harder.*"

Jory gave Kit a long, level look.

Kit laughed, his cheeks pink. "I know, I know. Deacon was in town last night. I've got sex on my mind."

"Deacon, hmm?" Kit's long-term honey was an ex-Marine who'd turned trucker. He spent more time out of town than otherwise, but whenever he came around he and Kit kept each other plenty busy. "How long's he staying this time?"

"He's not." Kit turned glum. "It was just a one-night thing, a detour on his way south. He's headed for Texarkana next, and he'll be gone for ages doing runs through there."

"Sucks," Jory said, sympathetic. Deacon and Kit didn't have the most conventional relationship, but it sure as hell worked for them. Kit liked his independence, and Deacon loved his work. They made up for the interim loneliness with sex. Simple.

"Ah well, he'll be back." Kit stood up and stretched. "Are you sure you don't want to get out of here before taking another crack at building a nest? Breeding nests aren't even that much of a thing anymore."

"But they help fertility," Jory insisted. "They do. You've heard the stories."

Kit looked doubtful. "Mm-hmm. I've also heard the stories about Omegas getting pregnant on the first time, or up against a wall in a bathhouse backroom, so I don't think it matters *that* much."

"I know, I just -- I still want to do it, and I want to do it right," Jory insisted. He gave Kit a helpless shrug. "I feel driven. I can't explain it. All I can do is try and satisfy the urge."

"Then do your best, and your worst, and try to chill out just a little, okay?" Kit kissed Jory on the cheek. "And keep the noise to a rock concert level. Some of us are sleeping alone tonight."

Jory kissed his cheek in turn. "Bitch much?"

Kit laughed, tousled Jory's hair, and was out the door in a twinkling, leaving him behind with forty-odd minutes to go and... one hell of a mess to deal with.

When he'd rented this apartment, one of the deciding factors had been its big bay window with a seat broad enough to curl up in. He sat down now with a heavy thump. The armload of soft bedding he'd been carrying around with him for half an hour overflowed his arms and slithered down to pool uselessly at his feet. Omegas were supposed to know how to nest properly, weren't they? So why wasn't it coming naturally to him? The best he'd managed was a tangle in the middle of his living room floor that looked like a collapsed pillow fort after an entire slumber party's worth of preteens had kicked it over like Godzilla on a rampage.

"This is not how it's supposed to work," Jory muttered, covering his eyes again. "When I look up, all those pillows and blankets are going to have organized themselves into a neat, cozy, comfy breeding nest. I love romantic comedies. I've watched greeting card company home-for-the-holidays movies by the dozen. *I have seen how* this *part of it works*. Okay? So no more nonsense. On the count of three, you're going to get yourself in shape. Got it? Good. One -- two -- three."

He took a peek.

Nope.

Damn. Well, it'd been worth a shot. Jory scowled

at the tangled blankets, then bent from the waist to pick one up and fold it preparatory to trying again. He'd get it right, before Darius showed up, or die trying.

Though that wasn't the only thing not going quite to plan tonight. His suppressants, for one. The insert in every box of pills he'd been prescribed since he'd enlisted warned that failing to take them even one day could result in an unplanned pregnancy. Missing three days should have meant he'd have to go back and start a new month's pack. Miss a week, and he should have gone into heat harder and deeper than a professional breeder.

Maybe. But in Jory's opinion? Whoever wrote those inserts needed some reeducation in reality. He'd resorted to searching Reddit in the end, and discovered that a heck of a lot of omegas who'd been on suppressants for years might take *weeks* to clear their systems. It wasn't supposed to work that way, but for some it did. Some never got back on track.

If this didn't work -- if he couldn't have the baby his heart yearned for, *Darius's* baby...

Jory bit his lip, hard. It had to work. He wouldn't not let it work. They'd see. He kept fantasizing about how it could be. Dreams. Snatches of fancies that seemed so real he almost lost track of the difference between imagination and reality. They teased at him, tickling his senses, tempting him back and back again. If he closed his eyes he could almost see, feel, hear, smell, taste Darius pressed close to him.

* * *

Naked, they stood chest to chest, their legs tangled the way they'd always done in booths and under tables, but so much better now. The rough hair on Darius's chest scraped at Jory's softer skin, giving him chills that contrasted so wonderfully with the fever heat of his body that it made him moan.

"So beautiful," Darius murmured, slowly going to his knees. Tall as he was, he could rest on one knee and press his mouth to Jory's still-smooth, still-flat belly. He pressed his tongue into Jory's navel, then blew a stream of cool air over the wet skin. "Can't wait for this to be round and full. You're going to look so hot with my baby in you. I'll measure you every day and I'll fuck you for every inch you grow, fuck you so hard you'll feel me for hours. And when you're in labor I'll sit in the bed behind you and hold your legs open, and you'll remember how I got you there, and you'll beg me for another."

Jory's cock jerked and spurted, not fully orgasming yet, but close enough that spunk trickled down their entwined legs.

"Oh, you like that," Darius said with dark satisfaction. "You like that idea." He slipped his hand between Jory's legs and slid two fingers into the small slit between balls and ass where an Alpha would have only a blind dimple. Normally barely noticeable, it dripped with honey-sweet slickness and it was swollen, open, eager for penetration.

Jory cried out and bucked forward, trying to take Darius deeper. "More," he panted. "More…"

A cough started Jory out of his fantasy. His eyes snapped open, and he promptly realized three things. One, his apartment looked like an explosion in a textile mill. Two, at some point he'd worked his hand between his legs and started finger-fucking himself like a whore. Three, Darius was standing in the open door of Jory's apartment, the key he'd long had dangling idly from one finger, and that his gaze was fixed on Jory as if he was the biggest freak on planet earth.

Or… Wait.

No.

No, not like he was a freak.

Like he was a piece of chocolate fucking cake, and like Darius hadn't eaten all day.

Hot damn.

Chapter Three

Jory caught his breath. "You're here," he said, still out of breath and, he realized, achingly hard. "You came."

"You almost did too, just now," Darius said, equally quiet, equally breathless. "I almost didn't say anything to stop you."

He had to know. "Why did you?"

"Because," Darius said. He kicked the door shut, dropped the key, his jacket, and pulled his shirt over his head in one smooth motion. "Because I've been wondering all day how awkward this might be, but I know now if I don't get my mouth on you in the next ten seconds…"

Jory's heart gave a great lurch. "The nest isn't right."

"Don't give a damn." Darius prowled toward him, shedding clothes as he went. His eyes were huge, the pupils dark pools of lust. "Skin, Jory. Let me see skin."

Jory tried again, just because Darius needed to *know*. "My suppressants haven't cleared. I won't get pregnant tonight."

"Don't give a damn." Darius had reached Jory by now, and undid the fastenings on Jory's jeans with deft, brutal quickness, thrusting his hand inside. "Take these off, or I'll do it for you."

One last hindrance -- and maybe it was far, far too late to be asking this *now*, but -- Jory laid a hand on Darius's chest, over his galloping heart. "Will you still be my friend, afterward?"

"Jory." Darius lay his hand over Jory's heart. "Yes. Always, yes. But I want -- I need -- I'm going, I'm *going* to fuck you until you scream, and you don't stop, until you come and you beg for more. The way you smell, even without the suppressants gone... *God.*" His eyes were huge and dark, deep, fathomless. Hungry. "Get on the floor and open your legs for me, Jory. Now."

Well then. Jory grinned without expecting to, a blazing grin that felt bright as Times Square to him. "Put me on the floor yourself," he purred. "And keep me there, Alpha."

A glint of challenge and *challenge accepted* gleamed in Darius's eye, and that was all the warning Jory got. Strong arms, stronger than he'd imagined, wrapped around Jory and crowded him against the nearest wall in a rush of limbs and muscle. Pinned him there, body pressed to body, tight and hard -- not quite the way Jory had dreamed of but so much better.

Jory opened his mouth to pant with lust. *Yes. Oh, yes.* "Good for a start," he said on a ragged breath. "That your best move?"

"Best move?" Darius put his lips to the sweet spot on Jory's neck and scraped his teeth across it, making Jory cry out. "I haven't even started." He licked over the shell of Jory's ear, then bit it. "You'll know my best move when you feel it."

Jory's knees wobbled. Darius caught him, laughing low in his throat, and lifted him back up until he was steady on his legs.

"Before you ask, yes, I liked the sound of that." Jory did a little nipping of his own, catching the lobe of Darius's left ear briefly between his teeth.

Darius made a deep humming noise that Jory thought meant *good*. Or maybe it meant *hang on to your hat, because otherwise it's going flying across the room with the rest of your clothes.*

Discovery. When Darius undressed a man, he

did it like he meant it, like a wide-eyed wonder-filled innocent under a Christmas tree unpeeling packages full of treasure, and at the same time, like a filthy-minded monster bent on devouring each treasure whole.

How did he do it? It shouldn't have been possible.

Jory decided he didn't care. He let Darius, in full Alpha mode, manhandle him about and went ragdoll-limp with delight. Buttons popped under impatient fingers and ricocheted against the wall. Zippers were lowered carefully, then denim shoved roughly off hips, the boxers underneath given their due of appreciation and ghosted off him with the barest touch of fingertips.

When he stood naked in front of Darius, a momentary twinge of shyness almost made Jory want to cover himself again. He knew how he must look -- red with passion, his hair curling damp with sweat, his cock engorged and his thighs dripping wet with his own slick. His smell was almost too strong for him to take.

What must Darius… *Oh.*

What must Darius, indeed. Kneeling in front of Jory, where he'd landed to help get shoes and socks off, *Darius* looked as if he'd been hit between the eyes with a ten pound hammer. His lips were parted, and only the thinnest ring of iris showed around the bottomless depths of his pupils. He looked like a hunting cat ready to pounce.

Jory stood up straight, chin high, on display and proud of it. He lifted one foot to nudge Darius's knee with his bare toes. "Well?"

Darius shook his head without a word, but Jory's voice jolted him back into action. He surged to his feet and caught Jory up in some odd, sinuous, thoroughly effective twisting motion. Afterward, Jory wouldn't have been able to describe what Darius had done or how if his life had depended on it. But it didn't matter. All that *did* was that the impromptu twister landed them both deep in the tangled mess of what Jory had assumed was a badly failed nest.

Failed? Not so much. Sheets and quilts billowed around him, enveloping him, soft under his back and buoyant around the sides. The lighter scent of laundry detergent, homey and real-world as it got, grounded him as much as the firm floor underneath, and brought everything into sharp, clear focus. Darius knelt above him, watching the way a hawk would watch its dinner a thousand miles below, simultaneously far too far away and so close that Jory could taste his scent too.

Jory shook his head, awed. He'd had sex before. Some of it had even been good sex. Nothing like this. He wanted to savor every second of it. He wanted… He arched his back and stretched as he watched Darius shedding clothes above him. He wanted *Darius*, and by God, he was about to have him.

The thought made his mouth water, and not only that. There was a shallow pool between his thighs that amazed him when he dipped a finger in the sticky puddle to play with it. How could he possibly make so much when he wasn't even in proper heat yet? Good Lord, what would it be like when he *was*?

He stopped, feeling Darius's gaze zero in on him again, going from his slippery fingers to his cock and to his face, dumbstruck anew. So Darius liked that, did he? Well. He'd love this. Jory slid two fingers between his legs and into his channel, meaning only to frig himself lightly, to tease Darius and egg him on.

It didn't work out that way. The second his fingers went inside, his channel clamped down around them with the most exquisite spasm of sensation he'd ever known, and he'd masturbated so many times as a teenager it was a wonder he didn't have a full crop of hair on both palms. He *knew* what jacking off felt like, and it didn't feel like *this*, not ever.

Except it did, now, and he shouted for the shock and the bliss of it, a shout that died to a moan and a breathless cry. He managed to slide his fingers free, though the instant sense of throbbing emptiness made him want to weep. His channel contracted, open and closed like a tiny eye -- so small, for something that could open wide enough to let a baby out -- and drooled more slick onto the sheets.

Darius made a sharp, deep, shocked noise and leaned forward, reaching out... stopping...

No, that wouldn't do. No matter why he'd stopped, Jory wasn't having it. "*Darius,*" he rasped, spreading his legs. "God, Darius. Get down here and fuck me before I die from wanting your cock inside me. Fuck me, fuck me *hard.*"

"That's it," Darius said, equally ragged, equally rough and out of breath. "That's what I wanted. For you to ask me."

Jory reached up for him. "No turning back now."

"None," Darius agreed, and lowered himself on top of Jory in another great, shuddering rush. His cock bumped blindly at the mouth of Jory's channel, but there must not have been enough room. He took hold of Jory's legs, one in each hand, and spread them so wide that the ligaments made a sharp protest -- one that Jory forgot immediately, because Darius was *in* him at last, at last, hard and hot and impossibly thick, and sliding home until there was no more left to give.

It hurt. Jory thought he would split apart from the size and weight and pressure of Darius's cock, and he hadn't even started moving yet. He hovered there, breathing in noisy gasps that matched Jory's.

"Fuck," Darius whispered. "It's you. I'm in you. Holy *shit*, Jory. I'm fucking you."

"You are," Jory whispered back. He twined his arms around Darius's neck, and wrapped his aching legs around Darius's back. "Please. Please, Darius, now. Now."

Darius pressed his mouth to Jory's in a kiss that startled him, somehow, so fierce and sweet at the same time, and then -- *oh!* Jory flung his arm over his mouth and bit at his wrist. He'd imagined what being fucked by an Alpha in near-rut would be like, but he hadn't come close! Red-hot hardness and deep, aching shoves and grips that would leave bruises and the most obscene squelching sound of slick coating both of them, and the taste of his sweat, the weight of him, all of it taken together that made him want to come, need to come, he was coming, he was..."Help," he pleaded, right on the edge and not able to tip over. "Darius, help me!"

And Darius did. He put his teeth over the vein and nerve on Jory's neck and bit, properly that time, and oh, that was what he'd needed. Jory bucked up, scrabbling at Darius's back and trying to hold him closer, while his cock erupted with sticky-thick Omega spunk. Would he need to bite Darius too? He wanted to, but he didn't get the chance. Darius pressed Jory's hand to his mouth and bit him there as well, and let out a deep groan. Jory could feel Darius coming, spasms of wet heat within that matched the shaking of their thighs.

Then it was over. This part of it. Darius's head was on Jory's chest, and Jory's fingers speared through his dark hair, each breathing so hard they lifted and pressed the other down.

Jory heard an... odd sort of noise, then. He lifted his head and looked up to see a grin on Darius's face, and then he recognized the noise as laughing. Maybe it shouldn't have, but it was ticklish, that laugh, and it made Jory laugh, too.

* * *

"So that was us, huh?" Jory teased, poking Darius.

"I think it was," Darius agreed. He bent to bump his forehead with Jory, who looked worn out but so delighted it all but made him light up. "Not bad, us. We'll have to do it again. Soon."

Jory's delighted grin was a worthwhile reward. He feinted a bite at Darius's chin that missed on purpose, but followed it up with a quick kiss to the cleft there. "How soon?"

"Soon enough for both of us. And not soon enough, either." A drop of sweat rolled down Darius's forehead and dropped like rain on Jory's cheek. Hmm. Jory looked good and fucked out, and that was a fine look, but also..."Water?" Darius asked.

Jory half closed his eyes. "Mmm. Yes, please."

"You stay there. I'll go get it." Darius bent forward to feint a bite at the tip of Jory's nose, then got his knees bent and his legs somehow steady beneath him. "Same place?"

"Bottom shelf of the fridge," Jory agreed with a contented sigh.

Darius liked the sound of it. As he looked back over his shoulder, Jory rolled to his back and splayed himself out like a starfish. A happy, well-fucked starfish, and hmm, maybe that wasn't the best analogy but to be honest Darius couldn't give that much of a damn. He hadn't had sex that good in -- he couldn't remember how long. If ever. He walked to the kitchen like an animal, naked and sticky with sweat and spunk and still half-hard, and it was like walking on air. He whistled to himself as he snagged two bottles of icy cold water from Jory's fridge.

Why hadn't they done this before? More fools them for not.

Darius started to close the fridge, then checked himself and doubled back. Man couldn't live on water alone. He needed better fuel than that to fuck with, and they might be taking a breather but that breather wouldn't last forever. There were so *many* things he wanted to do to, to do with Jory, tonight.

Food, then. Darius narrowed his eyes as he made his choices. Protein, fats, carbs, sweets. Chocolate? Definitely chocolate. And now he had more than he could carry, so he snagged a fruit basket from the counter and upended it, scattering all but one mango and one Japanese pear. The empty space filled up fast, jammed with thin-sliced prosciutto, rich pâté, almonds, pistachios, ale cheddar and some reeking French cheese and whole wheat crackers, a slice of tiramisu and a handful of marzipan... *what the fuck*?

"Why do you have marzipan penises in your fridge?" Darius asked, baffled, as he reentered the living room.

Jory burst into laughter and covered his eyes. "How deep were you digging to find those?"

Darius picked one of the tiny candy dicks out of the basket and flicked it at Jory, who batted it handily aside. "Deep enough. Bachelor party?"

"Bachelor party," Jory confirmed. He sat up and gestured to the space across from him. "I don't know how much food you've got there but I think I could eat it all. Come share my sad, sorry excuse for a nest.

Two's company."

"It's not that bad."

In answer, Jory raised an eyebrow at him, and Darius had no choice but to shrug. Okay, it was bad. "Not in the way you're thinking," he insisted. Then, "Get up. Eat, and let me take a crack at it. See what I can do."

The eyebrow stayed arched, but Jory took the basket and retreated to the window seat. He dug out the pear and tossed it to Darius. "Only if you eat too."

"Fair enough." Darius took a bite -- gritty, sweet, cool -- and chewed thoughtfully.

Jory watched him idly. "I've never known an Alpha to try building a nest before," he said. "Of course, I've never known an Omega to fail quite so catastrophically, either." He grinned when Darius laughed. "I know, right? I just couldn't keep my mind on what I was doing."

Mm-hmm. Darius knew his friend. "You were trying too hard," he said. "Worried about making it perfect."

Jory made a disgruntled noise. "I can't help it. I think, therefore I am. I overthink, therefore I'm me."

In answer, Darius reached over to dig another tiny marzipan pecker out of the basket and press it between Jory's lips. Pink rose to Jory's cheeks as he ate the morsel. "Does that mean 'stop it and let me work'?"

Darius meant to say *yes*, or maybe to tell Jory it wasn't that bad, to relax and let him help. "It means I like seeing you with such-like in your mouth," he murmured instead, caressing Jory's lip with the ball of his thumb.

Well then. Darius had no idea where that had come from, but he'd be damned if he would take it back. Now that he was in this, he meant to be *in* this. Jory's blush deepened to ruby red, but his eyes glowed. He bowed his head, just for a moment the very image of a bashful Omega from the old stories, and the surge of lust that roared through Darius's groin should have put him to shame, but didn't. Not even a little.

He almost made use of it, his body wanted nothing more than to throw Jory down and ravage him until their muscles burned and their mouths were soft from kissing, but the nest wasn't done, and an Alpha provided for his Omega. Darius kept working. Thick padded quilts first, to soften the floor, then more sensual things -- a cashmere throw and a furry angora blanket, to make the nest warm and enticing. Pillows for their heads and under their backs, with anything Darius knew wouldn't be washable discreetly kicked aside.

"I was distracted," Jory said, jolting Darius's concentration. When Darius frowned at him Jory wasn't looking back, but instead stared meditatively down at the half-emptied basket of food. "My suppressants..."

"They aren't cleared yet. You said. I can smell for myself, and they're *not* gone, but they are fading."

From the way he frowned, that seemed to bother Jory more than it did Darius. "I just don't want you to think I was lying to you. Just trying to get you in bed for no reason."

Huh? "I wouldn't have thought it. You've never lied to me."

"This is different," Jory insisted.

Jory wasn't wrong. And yet, he wasn't *right* either. Trouble was, Darius didn't know how to explain that. He shook his head, pushing that aside to think about later when his hormones weren't stealing all the blood from his brain. He tucked the remains of the food and water in a nook between two pillows, threw one more soft shawl over the top, and turned back a corner of the topmost blanket. *There.* That should do it.

"Not bad," Jory murmured. When Darius glanced over at him, his eyes were still warm with desire, but with approval, too. "Not bad at all."

Darius took a step back and studied his work. It looked like an Alpha had built it, but... no. Not bad at all. But..."Was that it?"

"Was what it?"

"The suppressants," Darius said. He had to know. "Was that the only thing keeping your mind off the job before?"

Jory fidgeted in a way that made Darius's pulse jump, as if he were pressing his thighs together against an instinctive body response, an Omega's pulse of slick that eased the way whenever they were hungry for cock. Darius sniffed the air and was sure of it. Nothing else smelled quite like that, like faint honey and rainwater without the bitterness of ozone.

"That wasn't it," Jory said, licking his lips. His pupils were huge when he looked up. "I couldn't stop thinking about being with you. And I can't stop thinking about it now. Come back to bed, Darius. Later is now."

Darius could do that. Darius wanted nothing more in the world than to do just that. A warm, willing Omega lying beneath him, begging for his cock, now that was living the dream. And it was Jory. That made it...

Darius lost his train of thought. Couldn't help himself when Jory reached for him, coaxing him closer.

He pulled Jory down from the window seat, rolled them over, and draped himself over the length of Jory's body in one fluid, sinuous motion. The movement made Jory draw in a short, sharp breath. His pupils were huge, and the scent of Omega musk welling up was sweet and thick enough to drown in. He could almost taste it. He *wanted* to taste it. He licked his lips, hungry, and watched Jory swallow hard.

"All right?" Darius asked, reaching up to brush a lock of hair off Jory's forehead.

Jory didn't seem to have heard him. He reached up in an echo of Darius's movement and traced his fingertips along Darius's cheek, his jawline, his neck. Either lost in his own thoughts or lost for words, Darius couldn't tell, but a hint of a frown had started to crease his forehead.

"Are you sure?" he asked, catching his lip between his teeth. "Do you want to wait until it's the right time, the real thing?"

Did he... Darius wrinkled his nose at Jory. Talk like that, that wouldn't do. It was like he'd said before, Jory thought too much sometimes. But Darius could do something about that. He stretched out one arm and caught hold of the wine they hadn't opened. Biting the cork out and spitting it to one side, he took a mouthful and held it without swallowing. White, crisp, a little sweet, and still cold, delicious. Darius watched Jory watch him rest his weight on his arms, and tasted Jory's small, desperate sound when he brought their mouths together. He let the wine trickle from between his lips and through Jory's, drop by drop until Jory roused himself and wound an arm around Darius's neck.

Now. Now, this was something like a proper kiss. Darius fed Jory the last tastes of wine as he deepened the kiss, tasting as much of Jory as he could. His mouth had a faint flavor of Omega sweetness that went well with the sharper wine, and that could have made him drunk all on its own. Maybe it had. He didn't feel like himself... but better.

Darius broke the kiss to look at Jory from two inches, maybe less, away. Their eyelashes nearly tangled when they blinked, like their legs under so many tables over the years. "Feels real enough to me."

Jory was stubborn, Darius had to give him that. "But..."

"Then call it practice," Darius said, just as stubborn. "Practice makes everything perfect and you just watch, you'll see how well we do."

Jory gave him a wry look, but his resolve was weakening, Darius could tell. "When did you get so smooth?"

"You're saying I haven't always been?" When Jory laughed, he caught Jory's pretty mouth in another deep kiss, and didn't stop until *he* was dizzy from lack of air. "I asked you before, but I'll ask you again. All right?"

Jory drew a sharp breath through his nose. and his eyes were wide as saucers, but he nodded. He raised one leg to hook it around the back of Darius's thigh, and then the other, giving him a warm, slick cradle to rest in. Darius hissed at the raw contact of his cock and satiny-slippery Omega skin, but hushed and soothed Jory before Jory's brain could kick in and send the wrong message.

"I want to taste you," Darius said, reaching down between them. "I want to put my face between your legs and fucking *feast*, Jory. Someday I'm going to eat you out until you beg me to stop."

Jory looked dazed, but his lips parted in what

Darius thought was lust. His eyelids slammed shut when Darius reached his groin. Though Darius could have spent hours sucking the fine, firm cock Jory was packing, he slid below and pressed just the tip of his thumb into Jory's slit.

His reaction -- *electric*. At Darius's touch Jory spasmed, limbs clamping desperately tighter around him, slit seizing around his thumb. He was so wet he'd soak through all the layers of blankets if they weren't careful. Darius hoped he would. Wanted Jory to be able to smell this every time he went to bed for the rest of his life. And he'd be damned if he didn't "borrow" one to take home for his bed, too.

"More," Jory said, panting now. His body was so slick with beads of perspiration he looked as if he'd just come from swimming, and Darius knew he must be in the same state. Their bodies glided one against the other, sleek as seals. "Darius. More. *Please.*"

Darius wanted to, but he couldn't resist. He bent his wrist so he could slide two fingers inside Jory instead of his thumb, then hooked and curled them, stroking at just the spot inside he hoped would make Jory go crazy. And oh, it did, it did. It turned him wild, made him beg and rut up against Darius, and when Darius teased him by angling away, he growled and wrapped his legs tighter still to make Darius go where Jory wanted him.

"Not thinking too hard now, are you?" Darius whispered, tracing the words with the tip of his tongue against Jory's throat. "Say it. Tell me to fuck you."

Jory gave a strangled, frustrated scream. "Fuck me, Darius! Fuck me hard and don't stop, don't you dare stop. Fuck me *now*!"

No one could say no to that, and Darius didn't want to. He guided himself inside Jory, as deep as he could possibly go, and put his hand tight around Jory's cock when he'd bottomed out. "I'll fuck you," he breathed. "Hold on tight, Jory. Hold on to me."

"Say you want this," Jory said, his cheeks red hot and his lips parted, gasping for air. He rocked up as Darius ground down, taking him deep, gripping him tight.

"You have to ask?" Darius panted. "Feel this. Feel me, inside of you. Feel how much I love fucking you."

Jory's suppressants might not have fully cleared yet but his slit recognized an Alpha cock when it felt one and began to swell, tightening in a seal around Darius's dick and locking him there, a trick of the body that all but ensured fertilization. Oh, Darius could slide loose, but wasn't it fine to pretend otherwise? To imagine they could come and stay locked together for hours, knotted like wild creatures, coming again and again until they were dry.

Darius bit his lip hard, hoping the stab of pain would keep him from coming now, but it wasn't far off and he knew it. He tightened his hold around Jory's cock and jacked him without grace or mercy or gentleness, knowing it was what Jory wanted right now, as much as he wanted to be fucked so hard the floor beneath them creaked.

Something was happening, he could tell. Jory's muscles flexed and quaked around him, and he keened as if each thrust hit something so good he had to scream with each stroke. Darius had fucked before, Alphas and Betas and Omegas on suppressants, and it'd never been like this. Hell, Jory was hot for it, wasn't he?

"Darius," Jory gasped, running his name together in a chant as fast and hard as a heartbeat.

"Darius, Darius, Darius, Darius, *Darius*, oh God!" He bucked up, his cock jerking in Darius's hand, fresh spunk adding its own tang to the thick smell of sex in the room, and Darius couldn't take it. He bowed his head and put his teeth to Jory's neck.

Only at the last second did he remember not to bite there like a mate would, but it was a near thing. So near he could taste the salt on Jory's skin. His friend chanted his name over and over, the sound echoing in his ears: *Darius, Darius, Darius!* until he came hard. Then, there was nothing but blackness until his lungs seized and drew in a deep, lusty breath of cool air.

Darius opened his eyes, dazed. He'd rolled onto his back and somehow carried Jory along with him so Jory's head rested on his chest, and he couldn't have been happier about that. And yet he could sense a change in the air. The frantic urge to rut until they were both raw had passed. They could still fuck, and Darius hoped they would, but they'd have more choice about it now.

Jory looked up as Darius looked down. "It won't have worked this time. Not with the suppressants still hanging on," he said dazedly. "But *damn*, Darius. You fucked me like you were going for triplets. Who knew you had that in you?"

"You," Darius replied promptly. "Because you just had it in you." He grinned proudly when Jory groaned and covered his eyes, and dropped a loud smacking kiss on the top of Jory's head. "So it was good for you?"

"I can't feel my legs. Yes, God yes, it was good."

Darius hummed, pleased, even more so when Jory let his hands fall to gaze fondly at him. "And?"

"If you have to ask if that was good for me, you haven't been paying attention." Darius brushed the back of his hand against Jory's cheek, then relented. "Best I've ever had."

"Flatterer."

"Truth," Darius countered. "And so what if your suppressants haven't worn off yet? I'll still be here when they clear out. I'm in, Jory, still in, and you won't be getting rid of me now."

"I don't want to," Jory said. "I won't, ever."

"Good," Darius replied, pleased down to his toes and warming back up, a gentler simmer, from the inside out. He bent his head to lick Jory's mouth open, ready for more. "Good."

Chapter Four

"So what do we do now?" Jory asked the next morning, hands wrapped around a mug of steaming coffee. He took his black as night, while Darius liked his pale with cream and sweetened with a dollop of honey. "What comes next?"

Darius took his time to consider that, sipping the hot coffee, wisps of steam curling up around his face.

Jory watched him, strangely content. No urge to hurry him up, to prod at him and make him think faster, to do something else. Just... content. Glad to be there, and with him.

"We wait," Darius said at last, his smile lopsided. "Wait, and see. You don't know. It might have worked."

Jory shook his head. He could still smell the suppressants working their way out, and nothing of fertility, and though he'd expected nothing less, he hadn't realized what a disappointment it would feel like. "I'm an Omega. I'm pretty sure I do know, and it didn't work."

"Then we try again."

"It'll be a busy week," Jory warned him. "I know I'm tied up, and from what I remember you are too."

Darius only shrugged. "We wait for next weekend, and we try again then."

"You make it sound simple," Jory said, marveling at how Darius was taking it all in his stride. "You'd be willing?"

Darius laughed, then bent to brush a kiss over Jory's lips. He left behind a hint of honey taste. "Three guesses. It's just us, Jory. It's just life as usual, with a little something extra."

And that was true, wasn't it? So he needed to

shape up. They'd wait. And they'd see. And either way, they'd each still have their best friend. Could anyone really ask for more than that? Even if they wanted to?

* * *

They had breakfast together Sunday morning rather than fill up on coffee and marzipan dicks, their legs tangled comfortably under the table just like always, but Jory could still feel Darius deep inside. From the way Darius blushed when Jory glanced up and caught him watching, he thought maybe Darius could still feel what it was like to *be* inside.

And he wanted more. Jory could smell that. And he knew Darius could smell how much he wanted it too. They might have to wait a week, but exactly how were they going to make it? Jory would be damned if he knew.

* * *

"You made love all weekend long? Are you serious?"

Jory gave Kit the very lightest of pushes. Not enough to knock him off the sidewalk they were headed down, two abreast and headed for lunch during their mutual breaks, but not exactly gently either. "All weekend long."

"How many times?"

"Honestly? I lost count."

"And you're walking?" Kit sounded awed. "Upright and functional and not requiring ice packs? You *trollop*."

It'd been a close thing Monday morning…"Let's just say I have very fond and vivid memories with every step," Jory said instead, with a wicked grin. "And trollop yourself, Omega! Don't tell me it wasn't like that when you and Deacon first got together."

Kit's gaze went distant and soft, and he giggled like a teenager with his first crush. Laughing, Jory gave him another nudge.

This time, Kit pushed back, nearly knocking Jory into a boutique's sidewalk display. They winced guiltily and stopped moving, pretending to study the scarves and bangles they'd nearly upset. There was a baby hat near the back that looked hand-knitted that caught Jory's eye, so soft-looking it begged to be touched. He bit his lip and held back.

"And after all that, you're so sure it didn't work?" Kit asked. "Usually a weekender like that's a guarantee."

Jory shook his head. He offered Kit his wrist to sniff, an intimate gesture, but he'd be able to tell straight and clear from the scent there. Suppressants, still hanging on, the stubborn little assholes.

Kit looked disappointed when he pulled back, but patted him on both shoulders in sympathy. "It'll happen," he soothed. "Soon. You'll see. I bet you it'll happen this weekend. Or! Maybe your scent receptors are off. Maybe you should take a test just to see."

"No point," Jory said. He turned away from the display, particularly the tiny hat that he itched to buy and take home *right now*. "I know my body, and I know how it feels on suppressants. They're still active. I don't want to build up my hopes just to get disappointed."

"Fair enough," Kit replied. "But what if you aren't? Disappointed, that is?"

* * *

On Tuesday, Jory's phone chimed during his lunch break. *Saw a billboard that made me think about your nest.*

Jory gave a startled laugh and fired back, *Say*

what now? Was the billboard falling down in strips?

A pause, then the reply. *Colorful. Nice.*

Jory started to respond, then stopped. Darius really hadn't minded the mess he'd made of his first try at an Omega nest, and that wasn't just him being nice. He'd meant it. This was why he'd chosen Darius.

God, he wished he was pregnant. And fuck, he wished he wasn't -- and that it was Friday already so they could get busy trying again!

* * *

Jory lasted almost through Wednesday before he took a pregnancy test. He couldn't help it, he told himself. Honest. He'd used the last of his laundry detergent washing half a dozen loads of linens, run down to the bodega on the corner to get more, and they'd been on display right by the register next to the lottery cards and cigarettes. All charm, but he couldn't have resisted the temptation any more than a smoker or a gambler might. He'd had the test in his hand before he'd known what he was doing, and then was back home and waiting for it to develop almost before he could blink.

He waited, his heart in his throat. It would be negative. He knew that. It was just... if it wasn't...

A baby. One with his hair and Darius's eyes, or the other way around. He didn't care. Healthy, happy, safe. His body ached and he felt tender inside, as if his organs were already shifting to give an infant room to grow.

Darius would make such a good father. He'd love their child more than anyone else except Jory, and he'd burn the world down to keep them safe. Jory wanted that. He wanted it *so* much. He swallowed hard, and turned the pregnancy test stick over.

Negative.

Damn. Next time, he told himself. Like Darius said. Just wait. *Next time. There's still plenty of hope and no reason to doubt your chances yet.*

* * *

And for all that, Jory woke up Thursday morning in the blackest possible of moods. A real stinker of a mood, the kind that kicked cans and cursed anyone who dared stumbled across his path. The itchiness of the wool in his favorite sweater made him want to scratch himself raw, and the radiator in his kitchen stank of boiled cabbage for some ungodly unknown reason. If glares could kill then the poor bastard who'd dared to chew gum while standing next to Jory in line at the bodega would have been reduced to a greasy spot on the linoleum. And the last stubborn edge of his suppressants *still* hadn't cleared. Were the manufacturers sadists? Did they enjoy tormenting Omegas for daring to try and control their fertility when the time wasn't right?

He fumed and fretted until his student teacher kicked him out of their classroom to go and, "Do whatever it takes, just don't come back until you're acting human again. This is kindergarten, not Grimm's!"

At least he hadn't scared any of the kids. He hoped.

All things taken into consideration, it probably would have been a bad time for Mother Theresa to drop a dime on him, let alone the object of his frustrations. Obsessions. Fantasies. Six of one, half a dozen of the other.

Darius.

Being busily occupied with lying on his bed, palms pressed hard over his eyes -- hormones were a bitch, were a royal bitch, were the queen of all evil

bitches, and adjusting to changes in them doubly so --
Jory didn't answer his phone when it rang. He had no
idea who it was. He'd stopped customizing ringtones
about the time he switched from a flip model to a
smartphone, and after too long lying in one spot his
joints throbbed sullenly at the thought of rolling out of
bed.

When the ringing stopped, he subsided back into
his pillows with a grumble. What was wrong with him,
seriously? *Was* it all the hormones? Did they do this to
everyone when they came off the pills?

Or was it just him? Was he broken somehow?
He'd known better, he had, but just in case the first one
had been wrong he'd taken a second pregnancy test.
Name brand, physician approved, guaranteed
accurate.

And negative.

His phone chimed with an incoming text. Jory
growled between gritted teeth, flipped to his stomach
to hang over the side of the bed, and dug through his
discarded work clothes until he found his phone.
Sharp stabs brought it to life.

One text. From Darius.

Heard you were having a bad day.

And that was it. No more.

Now, if he had followed that up with *sorry to hear
about it* or *need anything?* or even *how 'bout them Bears?*
then his reaction would have been a different thing.
Jory hoped. Not what *did* happen, which was his
throwing his phone against the wall with a crack! Like
a gunshot.

The damned thing didn't even break. It *bounced.*
Jory expected he would be all kinds of grateful to the
resilient design of his phone case when he had his wits
about him, but for right now, since it'd failed to shatter

into a million pieces, he would have settled for biting the fucking thing in half. Which might have been wiser than stalking over, snatching it up, and stab-typing a reply.

Who are you talking to about me?

Silence for five minutes. Then, finally, an answer.

OK, so they weren't wrong. What the fuck?

A sane, sober Jory would have admitted he deserved that, and explained himself. Sane, sober Jory had left the building.

Are you with them right now? Jory demanded, suddenly aware of what was wrong with him. He ached with loneliness, as bitter with it as if he'd been tossed out naked into the cold, and he burned to have his Alp -- to have Darius -- to not be alone. Hot tears, humiliating in their suddenness, made his eyes burn as he typed. *Are they better than me? Do you want to breed them instead?*

Silence.

More silence.

Nothing.

He'd really pissed Darius off, then. Or hurt him. Or both. *Damn it!* Jory started to throw his phone across the room again, stopping himself only a split second before it left his hand. He shoved it under his pillow instead and threw himself onto his stomach, fisting double handfuls of the tousled comforter.

The one he and Darius had fucked on first, as it happened. Slowly, Jory's fists opened and he stroked the material instead of wanting to shred it. Slowly, the tension in his shoulders eased and he managed to let go of a shuddering breath.

Carefully, he picked up his phone and sent a text. *I'm sorry. That was uncalled for. My head's in a dark place this week but I shouldn't take it out on you. Please forgive me. I promise I won't bite your head off again.*

The silence went on for another minute, long enough to make him nervous, before the incoming message chime sounded. *Talk to me.*

Not much, but enough. *It's been a bad day. I didn't have any right to accuse you.*

Darius's reply was simple, and sliced cleanly through the dark tatters wrapped around Jory's heart. *You trusted me with everything this weekend, and you haven't seen me since. I'd be pissed too.*

Even so.

Even so, Jory.

Jory let out another long breath. He didn't feel *better* yet, but he might be in about the same ZIP code.

I'll see you tomorrow Darius texted. *And don't worry. It'll turn out all right in the end. You'll see.*

"You're that sure it'll turn out all right?" Jory murmured at his phone. He pressed it to his forehead as he lay back down. "Even if I love you, and I can't say it? And even if I can't ever have your baby? What then, Darius? What happens then?"

* * *

And maybe that was what had needed to happen. Something to clear the air. Jory woke up feeling... different. He studied himself in the mirror, in the early twilight of Friday night, cataloguing the changes. Some were bold and easy to read. His temper had faded and taken with it the tight lines around his eyes and mouth, the tension from the tendons in his neck, the flex and curl of hands that wanted to fist and the stalk-stomp of his walk. His skin had faded from irritable red to its normal pale with a faint sprinkling of freckles.

Some changes were more subtle, deep under the skin. The sullen ache that'd plagued his joints had eased, leaving him loose-limbed with relief. Itches in places impossible to reach were gone. His hips felt looser, too, strung less tightly than usual, and in the very center of him he felt warm and soft and fluid, not dry and hard and cold. It was the strangest sensation, the hardest to describe, but it made him want to reach between his legs and finger himself wide open enough to admit a fist. Two fists, maybe. A sharp emptiness that begged to be filled.

Best of all, the scent of suppressants was almost, almost, *almost* gone. Jory had to close his eyes and sniff hard to catch the faintest edge of their chemical scent.

Jory's breath came quick and light with anticipation as he washed and dressed himself, though when he remembered, he tried to take slower sips of air to keep himself calm. He could do a lot when he put his mind to it, and managed not to fist-fuck himself in the shower though he almost bit his cheek bloody in the struggle.

He smelled like a ripening Omega, and he wanted Darius to get that full force. He could wait. It showed in his step, he thought, as he walked the few blocks between his apartment and MacInnes's. Familiar strangers, faces he knew by sight but whose owners he'd never spoken to, stopped and turned their heads to give him a second glance. Omegas, Alphas, Betas too. Maybe they didn't know why, but the pheromones on the air made them all prick up their ears. Jory walked faster, feeling himself already starting to get wet, even the wind that tugged at his clothes an erotic inflammation.

Which, in itself, was starting to make his mood simmer again. Felt like having his collar one button too tight, or his jeans half an inch too short. Something wrong that needed fixing, something that needed correction.

Jory walked faster, cutting through the early night, darker than usual with what looked like storm clouds gathering overhead, and then faster still, until he was nearly running. He didn't stop until he'd clattered down the half-stairwell to MacInnes's door, and only paused for a moment then because he caught sight of his reflection in the door.

He looked… Jory licked his lips. He looked like he wanted to be fucked. His eyes were huge, pupils belladonna-wide and dark, and his lips red from being bitten, his cheeks boldly marked with a pink flush. He exhaled, his breath making a warm patch of fog on the glass, and almost couldn't smell even that final shred of suppressants there.

A hot flush suffused him, triumphant. He'd done it. Or he'd almost done it. The irritation eased a little, and when he opened the door to a roar of song and an overwhelming gust of hops and barley, and saw Darius in their usual spot, it dissipated entirely.

Darius must have felt Jory's gaze land on him. He turned his head, eyes bright with beer and Friday night freedom, and raised his pint glass. He tilted his head, beckoning Jory to the table.

A pulse of… something… grabbed Jory's heart and *squeezed*, and he knew one thing then for damn surer than ever before. They *would* be all right. Come hell or high water, Jory would make it so. He raised his hand in greeting and flowed down the stairs, headed straight for Darius's side.

Chapter Five

It felt like coming home, sitting next to Jory. It felt right, and it made things in Darius relax that he hadn't even realized were tense and tight. His shoulders twanged with exquisite pleasure-pain when he raised his arm and waved to ask for another round.

Jory grinned at him, points of mischief dancing in his eyes. "Need a massage?"

"Too much jerking off," Darius told him, straight-faced, only laughing when Jory threw a handful of popcorn at him. "*You* get your kinks worked out already?"

"I might have. And even if I hadn't, I exorcised my -- everything -- being a hormonal asshole yesterday," Jory said as he stood. He offered Darius a hand up. "C'mon. The beer can wait. We need to get you limbered up."

Ideas danced in Darius's head, none of them particularly PG-rated.

Jory hooted at him. "Mind out of the gutter, Alpha!" He pointed at the dart board, empty of players. "Two out of three, and the loser buys tonight's rounds?"

Any other night, Darius would have said *yes* and been on his feet already. Tonight… He shook his head. "Maybe later."

"How come? You love darts."

"I'd rather be here with you," Darius said simply, because it was true. He kicked Jory's shin lightly. "And I've got plans for getting us both warmed up and worn out later that don't involve bar games."

Jory's cheeks bloomed a beautiful red. Darius watched him duck his head, enjoying the view, content to be lazy and indulge in watching him color with pleasure. He'd missed that, this week. He'd only had it for one weekend, granted, but it'd already become something of an addiction.

And that could be a problem if he let it. Jory wasn't in love with him, for Pete's sake. He'd asked Darius because Darius was his best friend. He imagined Jory had thought just as much about him as he had about Jory this past week, but it wasn't vanity. It was only natural. It was chemistry.

Speaking of which… Darius scented the air as subtly as he could. Still just a tang of suppressants clung to Jory.

"I know," Jory said, downing a gulp of his fresh beer. He looked dejected now. "I can't figure why it's taking so long for them to clear."

Darius caught Jory's wrist and gave it a gentle squeeze before he could get any farther with that train of thought. "It wasn't a criticism."

"Not from you. From me?" Jory made a face. "I can't shake the feeling that I'm doing something wrong. Like I've missed a step somehow and I won't get where I want to go until I sort it out."

Darius clicked his tongue to get Jory's attention, then batted him lightly on the head. "And that's because you think too much. Come on. I changed my mind. Let's play darts after all."

Jory could have said no. Darius didn't think he would have. But just in case, he put a touch of the Alpha in his voice, when he asked, and had the pleasure of seeing Jory's eyes dilate. It was almost as good as the feel of Jory's hand in his, warm and dry, and only the first touch they'd enjoy that night.

A good start.

A better one, in a few minutes, when they had a box of darts in hand and Darius stood just a little behind Jory, watching him line up his throw. Well, mostly just watching him -- the curve of his hip, the flow of muscles in his arms and back. From the way Jory glanced over his shoulder, Darius could tell he knew he was being watched and he didn't mind it. Mercurial, now that he had the darts in his hands he'd turned away and to his second favorite game of people-watching.

Darius decided he didn't mind. He closed the small gap between them with two and a half steps and spoke quietly, so that only Jory could hear him. "Some newcomers tonight. Did you see the blind date in the corner?"

Jory's eyes sparkled as he nodded. They were hard to miss -- a threesome instead of a pair. That happened sometimes, when an alpha and an omega needed a beta to really work. It could be tricky, but this threesome had the hallmarks of clicking like old lovers in young bodies. Nice. "And the golden newlyweds?" he asked Darius in return.

Darius raised an eyebrow. He hadn't noticed, but when Jory pointed toward the bar he wondered how it'd escaped him. Alpha and Omega, but neither could have been younger than seventy at the least. Probably closer to eighty, with smile lines and frown lines and all other kinds of lines, age spots and crepe paper skin and awkward joints as they toasted each other, but the love in the way they looked at each other would knock a man down. Let alone a drunken sailor.

His turn, and he cast about for someone worth commenting on. He took his time, but settled on an Omega alone by the bar, phone in hand. He hadn't looked away from it, but hadn't moved a finger to text. Not talking, just waiting. They looked three, maybe four months pregnant, only just enough to notice, and normally a pregnant Omega sitting alone at a bar was the start to a sad, sad story. But not this one.

"He's happy," Jory said, almost in time with what Darius was thinking. "I can't tell if he's waiting on someone or he's glad no one's coming, but he is glad. Glad right down to his toes. Am I wrong?"

Darius shook his head slowly, fascinated. "His life's just the way he wants it."

"I think he *is* waiting for someone," Jory said after a moment. "He just doesn't know when they're going to show up."

"No?"

"No. But he's positive they will. That's the thing. That's what's behind that smile. Belief. Faith. He's sure his Alpha's going to be there when the baby's born. Not a drop of doubt. Now, am *I* wrong?"

Darius looked, and sure, it was all imagination, but he couldn't say that Jory was wrong when he didn't know. "We should drink to it. His luck. Their luck." He raised a hand to signal a passing waitress for another round, and while they waited he edged a few inches closer to Jory. Their bodies touched down, his chest to Jory's back, and as he moved forward Jory moved back, increasing the pressure from gentle to firm. He drew in a sharp breath when Jory shivered and made a low noise.

But that was where their flights of fancy diverged. Jory cocked his head right before Darius meant to make a move and asked, "Have you ever seen a live birth?"

Now that right there would have shriveled many an Alpha's erection before it even got started, but not Darius. It didn't exactly jump up and shout hooray, but it didn't tuck tail and run, either. So to speak. "A few times, actually." He tucked his chin over Jory's shoulder, not sure where they were headed with this but okay to go along for the ride, for now. "Basic training, sex ed class in school, one truly memorable weekend hunting trip in the country."

Jory turned his head in keen interest. "That's a story I have to hear."

Darius started to say, *not much to tell*, but stopped. Had he noticed... yes, he had. Jory shivered deeply again, and the sweet smell of an eager Omega grew stronger, richer, earthier. *So.* Jory liked the idea of giving birth, did he? There were stranger kinks, and Darius had heard a few things about orgasmic labor before. Which could get you some strange looks for mentioning, especially if you were an Alpha, but it was a thing.

Might be Jory's thing. *Hmm.* Darius thought he'd like to find out. And if it was asking for trouble, then what was life without a little risk?

"Did I never tell you this story before?" he murmured in Jory's ear. His lips touched the shell, brushing cartilage, with every syllable. "Do you want to hear it from the beginning?"

Jory barely breathed as he nodded, but nod he did.

Darius hummed as he settled in, his chin hooked over Jory's shoulder. They weren't even pretending to play darts now, but the worst they got were some tolerantly rolled eyes. He wrapped his arms around Jory's waist and enjoyed the quick, hot thrill of something like possessiveness, present and future tense. He *liked* it.

"It was about two years ago," Darius started. "Almost three. Do you remember that couple who lived upstairs from me at the time? The potter and the painter."

"I remember how your apartment smelled. Linseed oil and clay. I didn't know they were pregnant. The smells from the one covered the other, then?"

Darius nodded. "I only knew because I saw them walking together, and I watched the potter -- the Omega -- grow." He laid his hand a little more firmly on Jory's waist, kneading lightly over the soft skin beneath his warm sweater. "I don't know if you can track it day by day, but I only saw them every other week or so at first, and it almost knocked me off my feet every time how different they were. They were... *ripe*. Ripe as a pear bursting with juice."

Jory shivered -- no, vibrated -- and his lips parted as he breathed, "Go on. How did you..."

"The Omega needed to be on bed rest after a while. I'm told that happens?"

Jory frowned, but nodded.

"It wasn't anything terrible. Just precautions."

Jory's frown didn't disappear, but a minute amount of tension dissipated.

"The Alpha asked me for help," Darius said with a slightly embarrassed shrug. He hadn't known the guy that well, and it'd been stiff and awkward for both of them, at first. The way Jory chuckled and shook his head slightly, Darius figured he'd intuited as much. No need to spell it out. "I started picking up groceries, mail, taking them up the stairs. They laughed when they saw I was wary at first, called me a 'typical Alpha' and when I called 'em on it, they called me on it. Said to get over there and feel the cub move if I was so big and bad."

Jory's eyes drifted half closed, and he was warm and pliant in Darius's arms as a teddy bear. "Did you?"

"I did."

"And? Scary?"

"Fucking terrifying," Darius said on a laugh, pleased when Jory joined in. "So I did it again, and before I knew it I was being called a friend and asked if I'd like to be present at the birth. A home birth."

Jory twisted his neck to look up at Darius seriously. "That's an honor."

And didn't he know it. "It wasn't just me, though. They had half a dozen other people there. Some parents, some not, but everyone had a decent idea of what to expect, except me. The Omega still thought I was hilarious. Put me on back rubbing duty during contractions so I didn't have a chance to bolt."

"I *like* this Omega," Jory said with conviction. "They don't still live upstairs?"

"I hear from them from time to time, but they moved across town. Sorry." Darius laid a finger across Jory's lips, both surprised and aroused when Jory bit down just lightly enough to prickle. "Feisty. Save that for later. We're getting to the good part."

A deeper shiver rolled through Jory. The scent of Omega, which had faded during the warm and fuzzy part of the story, thickened. Darius readjusted his hold on Jory, snugging his groin to the curve of Jory's ass. A good fit, nice and tight, and he knew Jory could feel his hard-on.

"There almost aren't words," he said, for Jory's ears alone, soft and low. "No doctor. No hospital. Just the apartment they'd made a home, and a midwife standing by. No one helping them, at their request. Just them on their hands and knees. Fucking feral, Jory, fucking primal and raw and... like nothing I've ever seen. For hours and hours. I didn't know how they could go on, but they had the strength. They kept going."

Jory breathed in quick, short gasps. His eyes were dilated, deep and dark. "And?"

"And when it'd been almost twelve hours, they put their hands between their legs and brought that baby into the world themselves."

A small moan escaped Jory. He canted his hips, bringing them back hard against Darius's groin. Darius bit his lip hard, the sting of pain the only thing that stopped him from coming then and there.

"And that'll be you," he said, punctuated with a small bite to Jory's earlobe, because fair was fair. "Soon. Soon as can be. And I'll be there with you."

Jory stiffened, panting quietly. He reached behind himself and took hold of Darius's hip, digging in with his fingers, his muscles flexing. If he hadn't been able to smell that it wasn't so, Darius would have thought he'd come.

But not yet. By the skin of his teeth, perhaps, but not yet.

"Darius," Jory said. "Take me back to my place. Take me back there now, and fuck me hard. Or so help me God, I'll knock you down and fuck myself raw on your cock here and now." And a request like that, well. That deserved only one response.

* * *

Together, they ran.

It'd started raining while they were in MacInnes's, and though it'd slowed to a shower for now, it must have been pouring like God had upended a fire brigade's worth of buckets over the city. Everything not gleaming wet was crisp with frost, and the strong smell of ozone said the storm wasn't done yet. He and Jory had maybe five minutes to get inside before those buckets got refilled and drenched the world a second time.

They made it in three and a half.

Darius stole one kiss before they got inside the apartment, just one, but one he'd had to have. Jory looked too good with fat raindrops caught in his lashes and on the tips of his hair, running over his collarbones and down the back of his neck. He set his mouth over the bend between Jory's neck and shoulder and gnawed just a little, just lightly, but enough to make him moan. He caught that moan in his mouth, swallowing it down and coaxing another wild, desperate noise out of Jory.

Jory undulated against him, his Omega smell so strong it was dizzying. "Inside," he said hoarsely and against Darius's mouth. He shoved his keys into Darius's hand. "Inside, fucking now."

Darius thrust the key into the lock with more luck than skill, and a good thing too. He'd have broken the door down if it'd taken any longer. He pushed Jory inside ahead of him and tumbled afterward, already reaching out for him with hungry arms. The door slammed shut with Jory's back pressed hard against it, Darius pressing into him, and nothing but writhing heat between them. It almost made the air ripple, it was that strong.

He didn't have to steal the second kiss -- Jory gave it freely, willingly, and took just as much, as hungry for it as Darius was himself. Jory let Darius take both his wrists and raise them over his head, pinning them there out of the way.

Darius liked the look of that. "Hold those there for me," he said roughly, licking his lips and tasting pure Jory. Jory's eyes were wide, dazed, so Darius gave his wrists a little shake to get his attention. "Keep your wrists there."

A wild gleam in his eye made Jory look almost

feral. He rolled his hips as if to say *I dare you, make me*, but he threw his shoulders back.

"Contradiction," Darius said, hands busy getting Jory's shirt worked open. "Up is down, left is right, and my God I want you, I want you so much I can't think. You make me crazy, wanting you. Why didn't we do this years ago?"

Jory leaned forward to bite at Darius, his sharp teeth only just missing contact.

Now what was that for? Darius brushed it aside. He'd figure that out later. He had Jory's shirt open and peeled the wet fabric off his shoulders to display so much firm, supple skin dusted with dark auburn curls that it made his mouth water all over again. Were his nipples larger than usual? Yes, yes, they were, swollen plump, and sweet tasting when Darius took one into his mouth and sucked hard.

Jory cried out and dropped his head back. It landed with a thump that made the door rattle in its frame, but he barely seemed to notice. He let one arm fall to thrust his fingers through Darius's hair and tug, urging him closer.

Darius pinched the other nipple good and hard, and when Jory yelped he took that fallen wrist and brought it right back up. He laid the pad of his thumb on Jory's kiss-swollen lower lip and looked him square in his dilated eyes. "I said keep them there."

Jory shuddered, a full-body writhe, and let his legs fall a little apart. On purpose, or not? Darius couldn't tell. Didn't matter. He thrust one knee between them, both to give Jory something to grind against *and* for the bliss of feeling that warm, wet hardness riding his leg.

God. *Damn.* "You're soaked," he said between harsh drags of breath and deep, open-mouthed kisses.

"Mmm," Jory vocalized, riding his leg. He started to lower one arm, stopped, and rubbed harder, shameless as a cat in heat. "Feel me. Put your hand on me, your fingers in me. Put your whole fucking fist in me Darius! I'm so wet, so open, I need, I *need*."

Darius shushed him. "I'll take care of you. Always."

"Then do it. God, do it, before I die."

Drama queen -- maybe. From the way he shivered and shook, maybe it felt like that to him, and coming to his rescue made Darius feel like God. He wrestled the fastening of Jory's jeans open just far enough to tug them down his hips -- not easy, they were wet from rain and slick and clung to his skin -- to thrust his hand inside. He curled his fingers, searching for Jory's Omega slit, and found it as swollen as his mouth. Two fingers circled, just to make him cry out and buck forward, and then three went inside, no warning, no gentleness, no finesse. Just... hard. Fast. Fucking.

Jory arched forward, beautiful as a drawn bow, and came without a hand on his cock. He groaned from deep in his center, and it reminded Darius of the noises that Omega giving birth had made. Primal, ancient, noises Omegas had been making since they started getting pregnant and bearing fruit. He used his other hand to rub Jory's stomach hard, so damn turned on by the thought of Jory being filled with his baby that he fucking near came himself.

He could barely breathe, but he used his air in kissing, and what little focus he had left in rubbing the inner walls of Jory's slit. First soft and slow, then harder, faster, deeper.

"Stop! I can't..." Jory moaned, but he rubbed up against Darius as he said it.

Darius dragged his thumb around the outside of Jory's slit. He was swollen with the fingers inside him, and it almost looked and felt as if he were giving birth. A jolt, almost electric, made Darius's dick jerk and let loose a thick pearl of precum. He let go only long enough to free himself from his jeans.

His cock surged forward, intent on reaching Jory.

Jory noticed. His mouth, drawn tight with agony and ecstasy, curved into the wickedest of smiles, and he hooked one ankle around Darius's to keep him there, to pull him closer. "Fuck me," he breathed. "Fuck me right here, right now."

"Thought you couldn't," Darius teased, deliberately taunting.

Jory bit at him again, and this time his teeth closed just hard enough to pinch the cleft of Darius's chin. "Watch me and see. And *fuck* me, Darius. I think - - I think maybe--" He shuddered. "I don't smell the suppressants. Do you? I don't. I don't... I don't *care*. Oh God. Fuck me or I'll turn inside out. Darius, *fuck me*."

Darius couldn't last through half of that. Who could? He freed his hand and pressed it, slick-wet, against Jory's mouth, then angled forward and sank home, balls-deep in Jory, devoured by his hungry slit and plundering with the hardest, fastest strokes his body could manage -- and he could manage a fucking hell of a lot. He was wild, on fire, crazy for it and for Jory. He stopped seeing shapes and colors, so focused on fucking deeper and harder.

Somehow, he kept Jory's wrists pinned against the door above them, the door that rattled and banged and let every-fucking-body in the building know what they were up to.

Good!

Jory clung to him, the ankle he'd used to hook

Darius with becoming a leg wrapped around his, and then somehow both legs around Darius's waist. He kept his own wrists up when Darius dropped his arms to support Jory's weight. "Close," he keened between thrusts. His nails raked at Darius's back. "So close. Deeper, deeper, *please*, deeper."

Darius set his head against Jory's shoulder and bottomed out with every stroke. He'd be bruised -- they'd both be bruised -- and he didn't care. He was close, so close, he was -- he was coming... nothing else existed except Jory, hot and fluid and solid in his arms... And a thought, just one thought, so crystal clear that it echoed in his head like a bell gone mad. *Oh. That's what this is. I'm in love with him.*

Darius lost track of himself, of space, of time, coming and coming until he could come no more. He found himself on his back gasping for air, his groin burning and aching as if he'd wrenched the muscles, with his hands over his eyes and his lips parted in shock and aftershock.

He was in love with Jory. It made sense. No one could ever have been for him what Jory was, and had been, would be. No one could be. They'd been damned near made for each other, a key and a lock shaped to fit. But all Jory wanted from him was friendship.

And a baby.

He couldn't keep doing this. Not if he loved Jory and Jory didn't love him. He couldn't. He wouldn't father a child on the man and then watch him wander off, fall in love with someone else, never fully be a part of his life. It'd break Darius.

So he'd have to break it to Jory. Now. Tonight. And kick his own ass for the timing, which couldn't have been worse, but how could he string it out any longer, something this... true?

He'd just make sure of how Jory felt first, though. Surely he could do that without giving the whole game away. *Right?*

* * *

Jory's knees weren't working. They wobbled and nearly gave way beneath him, and if he hadn't had a good sturdy door behind his back he might have tumbled to the floor in a messy heap of boneless satiation. His slit ached, still clenching around Darius's fingers as Darius slid them out -- thick, gorgeous fingers -- and his ass burned from being rubbed half raw against that selfsame door. He dragged in greedy lungfuls of breath that made his chest clench up, and he could taste the sweat that'd beaded on his skin when he licked his lips.

He'd never been fucked like that, not ever. And it was Darius who'd done it! *If only.. If only…*

Jory lost the train of his thought. He licked his lips again and tried to swallow, clumsily pushing at Darius as he did. Better to get some distance between them before he got too tangled up in the kinds of feelings that *happened* after really good sex. "Couch," he muttered, then changed his mind and said, "No, wait. Floor."

Darius snorted quietly. "Floor?"

"Don't care." Jory waved one hand vaguely between them. "Just don't let me fall."

Darius muttered something Jory didn't catch, pressed a messy kiss against Jory's temple, and slung his arm around Jory's waist. A heave, a ho, and they were shambling forward on two sets of rubbery knees. Half a dozen steps brought them to Jory's couch where they collapsed in a boneless heap, as tangled up together as two skeins of yarn.

And just like always, they *fit* together.

Jory let out a long breath and leaned hard against Darius's chest. Hard, sturdy, comfortable, smelling so finely of sweat and sex and Alpha musk. *Mmm.* Ripe, after all that exertion, but Jory liked it. He nuzzled the smooth skin stretched tight over Darius's stomach muscles and purred with pleasure. Darius laughed, batted at him as if it tickled, and tucked him into a careless arm lock. He tucked his head against Jory's shoulder, face hidden, and -- shivered? Shuddered? His muscles vibrated in a way Jory couldn't easily put a name to, as if whatever he was feeling was too much.

He could identify with that, at least. If only Darius loved him the way he loved Darius... Jory dropped his head back against the couch cushions and raised one arm to cover his eyes. He still hadn't caught his breath and it'd begun to make him dizzy. He tried going slowly, and that worked better, introducing some calm to blood gone fizzy as champagne.

In... The scent of Darius, of sex, of himself.

Out... The soft welcoming embrace of the couch, the supple hardness of Darius's limbs.

In... A more nuanced sense of the way he and Darius smelled together, Alpha and Omega, and... Jory caught his breath. He hadn't been thinking about trying to get pregnant this time around, it hadn't entered his mind, but what if... what if... He exhaled, blowing all his air out, and sniffed.

There. Subtle, barely present, but still identifiable. The suppressants. They were still hanging on by the barest thread, and that meant he couldn't be pregnant. His body howled in protest and his insides spasmed, a cramp rather than an orgasm, a complaint against being empty. His arms ached in sympathy, and his nipples too. His body demanded to be bred, craved like air and water and salt to be swelled out with

Darius's baby, and wailed in disappointment that it hadn't been. Jory didn't mean to, but he groaned and curled a little away from Darius. *Damn it*!

He hadn't realized Darius was paying attention, or imagined that he'd be keen enough right now to intuit all the nuances, but if Jory'd laid a bet on that he would have lost. Darius stiffened and pulled away from him, his warmth immediately missed as he drew toward the corner of the couch.

Jory frowned at him. "What?"

"Was that the only reason?" Darius asked baldly, meeting his gaze. "Did you even want *me* at all, Jory? Or am I just a cock that comes attached to a friendly face?"

"Whoa!" Jory sat up straight himself. His face burned with surprise and indignation. It wasn't true, not even a crumb. It wasn't! But Darius…"Back up. You *are* my friend, Darius, and --"

Either Darius didn't hear him or wasn't listening, and it was anybody's guess which of the two was true. He rolled off the couch, irritation crackling off him in waves, and when he turned to face Jory he wasn't smiling, wasn't sad, but his mouth was twisted at the corners in a darker expression. "Got it. Just friends. Sorry to disappoint."

"I'm sorry, were you in the same room as me just now? In what universe was sex like that disappointing? Since when has being friends ever been any kind of disappointment for either of us?"

Darius really *wasn't* listening. The twist to his lips deepened, wounded and angry, and he stalked toward the door without another word. Jory gathered his wobbly jelly legs under him somehow and beat Darius there. He put his back against the wood, not enjoying it nearly as much this time. "Stop. Talk to me.

What's going on? Why are you pissed off? What did I do?"

"Don't play dumb, Jory." Darius took him by the upper arms and moved him bodily aside. "Even if it wasn't for -- never mind that. All on its own, I can't sit here after something like that and feel you being disappointed. In me, in the sex, whatever it is we're doing wrong, I can't. It's too much."

Jory shook his head, still not understanding. "But --"

"Let me go, Jory." Darius had his hand on the knob, and he wouldn't meet Jory's eyes. He did pause, though, and his shoulders went stiff. "Look, I -- I'm sorry. I am. But I shouldn't have started this."

Jory had good ears, and knew he'd heard Darius right, but he couldn't quite believe it all the same. "Excuse me?"

Darius's chin jutted out. Stubborn ass! "I think you need to find someone else to help you with this."

"What?" Jory spluttered, but Darius moved too quickly for Jory to grab. Before Jory could make a swipe at him he was out the door and gone, the lock clicking shut behind him, leaving Jory to stare at the door in baffled anger.

What the *fuck*?

Chapter Six

"War council," Jory said.

Kit blinked at him. He'd come over in the middle of the night when Jory called, still dressed in his pajamas under a robe that looked more or less like a trench coat. He sat in his usual place on Jory's couch like a sleep-drunk toddler still confused about what was going on. "Say again? War what?"

"Hang on." Sleep-drunk was one thing, but Jory needed a proper wine-drunk for this. He stalked into his kitchen and rummaged in the back of his fridge for a bottle of -- anything -- and, savagely pleased, came up with an unopened Chardonnay from the other week. He'd have settled for wine coolers if those had been all he had on hand, but a quality Chardonnay could go a long way toward soothing sharply wounded feelings. At least in the short term.

And he'd take the short term, if it was what he could get, because out of short terms, long terms could be built. He grabbed two glasses and carried the lot back into his living room, where he saw Kit had tilted over to doze off on the arm of his couch. He startled awake at the sound of his footsteps. "War council what?" he repeated.

"War. Fucking. Council." Jory poured half a glass for both of them and pressed one on him. "Drink up, and get ready for a refill."

"Ah. That kind of war council." Visibly, if slowly, waking, Kit peered at his glass, then back up at Jory. He sniffed the air delicately, though he wouldn't have had to. "You smell like sex and chemicals and a whole lot of Alpha aggression. Date didn't go well, huh?"

"No, which is why we're having this conversation in the wee smalls of Saturday morning instead of Monday ten minutes before work."

Kit considered that, then sighed and tucked his feet underneath him. "Tell me what happened?"

Jory filled him in between slugs of wine and not one but two refills, the crisp white dry and delicious, its acid bitterness just what he craved. He kneaded his stomach absently, glad for just this moment that he wasn't pregnant. He could have a fourth glass if he wanted, and he damned well might. "So, you tell me," he finished. "What happened? I'll be fucked if I can figure it out, and I've already been fucked twice tonight. Once properly in bed, once fucked-over, and I'm done."

Gratifyingly, Kit took the question seriously. He leaned back into the corner of the couch and swirled his wine while he thought. "The suppressants, maybe? Seems like everything tripped off for both of you when you caught their scent."

"But that doesn't make sense. I keep asking if Darius would blame me for my body not cooperating, not behaving the way it ought to. He kept saying no, and I know him. He meant it." Jory sat on the opposite end of the couch. His glass was empty, but he'd have to gather the energy to get up and fill it again and just at the moment he was running low.

"And?"

Jory bit at his lip. "Is he maybe blaming himself for… not alpha-ing the drugs out of me?"

Kit wrinkled his nose "No. He's got too much sense to blame himself for a Big Pharma fuckup. And he's got a good nose. He probably smelled the suppressants on you before you even got started. You did, didn't you?"

"And he went with me just the same," Jory realized. "Knowing it all, he went with me."

They fell silent for a moment, Jory digesting that, pretty sure Kit was doing the same.

"Scents can be pretty misleading," Kit said after another sip at his Chardonnay. "We've all heard the stories about Betas who fool people into thinking they're Alphas, or Omegas who don't know they're pregnant until they give birth. So Darius knew the score."

"That makes it something else. But what?" Jory threw his hands up in the air. "I don't get it. I have no fucking clue what's wrong with him, and I know him like I know myself."

Kit watched Jory while he spoke, chin in his hand, and took a deep breath when he was finished. "Okay, say that's true. Then you do know what's bothering him. You must know, even if it's deep down where you can't see. Think about it, Jory. *Think.*"

Jory shook his head in frustration, but he gave it a try just to show willing. He searched through everything they'd been through that night, everything they'd done and said and…

Oh.

Oh hell. Jory clapped his hands to his mouth.

"And there we have it," Kit said quietly. "Say it out loud, Jory. It'll help."

Jory couldn't keep it inside any longer. "I… love him," he said, the first word slow, the second two bursting out. "Kit. Kit. What if he loves me?"

Kit kept silent, watching and waiting.

Jory couldn't match that. He jumped to his feet and started to pace despite the smallness of his living room, tracing fast circles around the room. He raked a hand through his curls as he raced through his thoughts out loud. "I've loved him for I don't know how long. Years. Maybe since we met. He's always been half of my heart. But he doesn't know. I never told him because I was sure he didn't love me. And now... Kit, what if I left it too late? What if I lose him over this?"

"You won't. Not Darius."

"But it's all coming apart." Jory shook his head, feeling the pieces come together in his head. "If he loves me, I have to do right by him. And if this doesn't work, it's going to grind at him. It'll eat at us like a cancer, Kit, and I could stand anything in the world except Darius looking at me like he did tonight."

"Jory. *Jory.* " Kit was out of his chair and stopped Jory mid-pace by cupping his palms to Jory's cheeks. "That is so not the direction I was wanting you to go with this! But okay, say all that steaming pile of B.S. is true. What are you going to do about it?"

"What I have to. I can't let things go on the way they have been."

Kit narrowed his eyes. "I don't like the sound of that."

"You think I do? But I have to fix this." Jory set his wine glass down, somehow unbroken even in his agitation, but it vibrated against the table when it landed. He knew he was pale to the lips but seeing every bit of it clearly, and feeling a bone-deep stubbornness setting in. The kind that got things done come hell or high water. "I know what I have to do. And I will, the first chance I get."

"When is that?"

"Today. As soon as I see him again."

* * *

So, what *did* you do with a former sailor in dire need of a strong drink?

If he called on a night owl of a friend before noon, even if only just, he gritted his teeth and asked to be brought a coffee when that friend bought one, for one thing. And for another, he didn't dick around with taking steps and making choices. Lack of caffeine would do that. So would a sleepless night spent trying to wrap his head around the ins and outs of an Omega's mind -- even an Omega as normally sane and sensible as Jory.

Arms folded over his chest, shoulders back and stiff, Darius waited impatiently at the corner where turning right would take him to Jory's place, and turning left would take him to MacInnes's. Though the morning was cold, his blood ran hot enough that waiting wouldn't hurt him.

Even so, he didn't wait long. Grant ambled around the corner fifteen minutes after Darius had called him. He carried a sturdy paper cup in each hand, both sloshing full with coffee so strong, rich and hot it should have come with pre-nuptial agreements and an *Adult Advisory* sticker on the side.

As the fumes rolled down the sidewalk ahead of Grant, Darius caught a generous whiff of Irish whiskey well mixed in. He bared his teeth in a grin. Best of both worlds. *Perfect.*

"Calm down, Cujo, you don't have to fight me for it." Grant passed one of the cups over with a supreme lack of concern for his fingers, but with a kick to Darius's boot, which was as good as a hug from the tough little Alpha. "War council?"

"War council," Darius confirmed. He swigged the coffee, savoring the heat of it -- just barely escaped scalding his tongue -- and the bitter strength. "About me. And Jory."

"I didn't figure we were going to go to battle against the local weatherman," Grant said with a shrug. "What happened?"

Darius told him.

When he'd finished, Grant stood for a moment sipping his coffee and frowning down at its plastic cap. He pressed his thumbnail into the cardboard sign a few times, then said, "Huh."

Darius raised his arms. "Tell me about it. And while you're at it, follow me." He took off at a brisk stride, beckoning for Grant to come with him down the sidewalk. Not toward Jory's, and not toward the pub, but in an entirely different direction. Forward. "This way. And talk while you walk."

"I don't know how you think I can help," Grant said dubiously as he kept pace with Darius. "Even with as many as I've dated, my friend, I still have no idea how Omega minds work."

"That's not what I'm asking for help with."

"Well, thank fuck," Grant said emphatically. "Because I've got a meeting at noon with the realtor."

That drew Darius up momentarily short. "The realtor? What... the old tattoo shop." Grant's grandfather's legacy, before it'd been sold out of the family to pay off medical bills. Grant had been working for years to get it back. "You're buying the tattoo shop?"

Now it was Grant's turn to show his teeth. "I've got every penny of the asking price in my bank account and I'm ready to lay down a fat check. Granddad would be fucking proud, and you'd better be too."

"I am." Darius took Grant by the forearm, giving him a good firm shake that made Grant's grin go brighter and fiercer. "Hell yes, and about time. Do you need to go now?"

"No, I've got until noon and I'm better off distracting myself. Besides, I'm swearing off Omegas until after the shop is up and running. This'll be good motivation."

Darius scowled at Grant and bounced his hand off the back of Grant's head. Grant cackled and kicked at his shin.

"Oh yeah. We're grown, mature, responsible men," Darius said with a sigh. "Let me tell you a thing, and you tell me if you think I'm right or wrong."

Grant raised an eyebrow, but nodded gamely and made a *go ahead* gesture.

Darius drew in a deep breath. "I'm in love with Jory." When Grant didn't respond, Darius looked back and found his fellow Alpha rolling his eyes. "What?"

"Darius, a dead dog could have told you that years ago. Tell me something I don't know."

Huh. Darius would come back, sooner than Grant would probably like, to his having known that and never having said anything about it. But he put a pin in it for the moment.

This one took more balls, but Darius didn't feel lacking in them. "I think Jory might be in love with me, too," he said, softer but able to taste the truth in the words. "He hasn't said so. He's got a surprising lot of pride under all that heart, but when I look back at what he's said and done -- him asking me to father his baby! -- then it comes together. It must be true."

This time Grant spared him the color commentary, but the look he gave Darius spoke volumes. He'd seen it for himself, and it *was* true.

"So," Darius said.

"So," Grant agreed. Their coffees were empty. He took Darius's and tossed both into a trash can set next to a crosswalk's light. "What are you going to do about it?"

"The only thing I can do, if I don't want to toss a lifelong friendship down the drain. The only thing anyone could do. Hell, something I should have been smart enough to see and take care of years ago, according to you." He considered that. "And to me. I should have seen it myself. I didn't, and that's on me, but now that means it's my job to take care of. To fix."

Grant eyed him warily. "And that means you're going to…"

In answer, Darius gestured at the window of the storefront they'd come to a stop in front of. "Do this."

"Shit." Grant took a step back and a glance up at Darius. "That's a hell of a step. Are you sure?"

"It has to be done." Darius faced down the shop window and knew he wouldn't back down. "And today."

Chapter Seven

Jory had been half expecting it, but the knock at his door not long after noon still made him jump half out of his seat on the couch. "Whoa!"

Kit put his wineglass aside, out of the spill danger zone. "Do you think that's him?"

No need to ask which *him* Kit meant. Jory sniffed the air, catching the scent, and nodded immediately. "Darius. I'd know him anywhere."

"Are you picking up anything emotional?"

Jory took a couple sips of air then shook his head, frustrated. Sometimes high emotion did have a particular tang to it, but ninety-nine times out of a hundred Darius kept things locked down. "No. Just when it'd be handiest, too."

Kit exchanged a grimacing glance of agreement with him. "Either way, I suspect I'd better see myself out. Unless you need help?"

Jory shook his head. He might piss Darius off from time to time, but he knew the last thing he ever had to do for any reason was fear his Alpha.

Kit knew Darius well enough to be sure of that too, but it'd been kind of him to offer. He nodded as he stashed his wine on an end table and uncoiled from his seat, then padded toward the window, the one with a fire escape, slipping his bare feet into shoes along the way.

"Headed up or down?" Jory asked, curious.

"Up." Kit flashed him that particularly bright, sweet, puckish grin that'd had all the Alphas panting after him since he was old enough to chase and to *be* chased. "Word on the street is Deacon might be in town this afternoon if he can sneak away from a bullshit conference long enough."

"And you're here instead of somewhere he can find you? Why? Go! Go go go."

Laughing, Kit slid open the window and slipped out onto the fire escape, from thence to disappear into the night. Hopefully to get happily, and righteously, laid. Jory sighed and lifted his wineglass in a salute as Darius knocked a second time, then searched for his spine, found it, and called out, "Be right there."

As Jory made his way toward the door, this time his nose did pick up something. Hot, salty, melty cheese, sweetly spicy marinara with red pepper, the earthiness of mushrooms, the tingle of fennel in sausage and the smokiness of pepperoni. Under that, the scent of cold glass. They'd be sealed too tightly for any other smells to escape, but taken together they could only mean one thing. Pizza and a six-pack, probably something good and dense and nutty.

And Darius had brought them. He wasn't mad enough not to care. Jory's mouth watered and his stomach rumbled, but neither of those was why he hurried the last few steps to the door and threw it open.

Darius waited for him on his doorstep, pizza and beer in hand. He gave Jory a lopsided grin, just as devastating as Kit's in its way. "Mind if I come in?"

Jory didn't answer right away, drinking Darius in for a moment first. He looked rumpled -- Was it raining again? Had he run through the start of a storm? -- had a red nose and cheeks from the chilly air, and his jacket sat slightly askew on his shoulders.

Jory had never seen anything he liked the looks of better than the man he loved. He had intended to start talking right away -- to explain what he'd been thinking last night, to ask what Darius had been thinking, to wonder exactly what was wrong with both of them, and maybe even come right out with an *I love you* or two just to get the pulse pounding nerves over leaping that hurdle out of the way. To see if Darius would say it back. He thought -- he hoped -- but... he changed his mind.

Instead of answering Darius's question, Jory took the six-pack from Darius's hand and set it aside, barely bothering to notice where it ended up. The pizza went next as Darius watched him, bemused, that one finding a home on his coffee table where it wouldn't leave grease stains.

There. Now both of Darius's hands were free, Jory caught them in his and drew his Alpha -- *his*, no one else's, now or ever again, he hoped -- into the apartment and pushed the door shut behind him. He went up on his toes then, with one hand at the back of Darius's neck and one arm around his waist to keep steady. Then, finally, he brought his mouth up to Darius's and asked without speaking, *let me in*.

Darius brought his arms around Jory so quickly and eagerly Jory knew he'd been forgiven without even having to ask. Not that he *wouldn't*, but still. In a minute, though. Just then Darius's hands were settling on the curves of his ass and drawing him closer, pressing them full body to full body. All the Alpha-smell he'd kept tamped down enveloped both of them, dizzying, intoxicating, making Jory moan and lean hungrily into the kiss in search of more.

It would have been perfect if Darius had been quite as with the current program as Jory. He broke the kiss far enough to mutter, "Things I need to say."

Jory put his finger to Darius's kiss-swollen lips. "Later."

Darius bit lightly at Jory's finger. "I..." He shook his head, and then they were kissing again -- bliss! --

but half a second later he'd stopped again, damn his stubborn willpower, and put his hands on Jory's shoulders to push him a few inches back. "Jory, let me speak."

The note of Alpha authority in his voice made Jory shiver pleasantly, and it won Darius the space he wanted. Jory settled back on his heels, gazing up at Darius with eyes he knew were dark and wide as if he'd been drugged, enjoying the effect that visibly had on Darius.

Obedience could be plenty fun, if you only knew how.

"Such a brat," Darius said, lifting Jory's chin with two fingers, but so gently that Jory didn't feel a bit of sting from the teasing insult. Darius's smile went from lopsided to bright. "God, you are beautiful. The finest looking Omega around. And the one with the best ass, too."

Jory burst into laughter, which made Darius chuckle too. Underneath the mirth, Jory's heart jumped and almost seemed to fizz with excitement. This definitely wasn't another *let's just be friends* speech. But was it...

Darius laid his finger over Jory's lips once again, and this time Jory let it happen. "My Jory," Darius murmured. "I said before that we couldn't go on like this. Do you remember?"

A dart of fear made Jory's crazy heart thump a little too hard, but he trusted Darius. He nodded.

"And I was right," Darius went on. "We can't. But that doesn't mean we have to go our separate ways. *Or* that we have to stop being friends. *Or* that we have to stop doing -- this." He reached between them and tucked his fingers in the waist of Jory's fortunately low-rise jeans, stroking him idly. "*Or* that we can't have a baby together, Jory. There's a way to have it all. Jory, your eyes. You can't see them, but they're like stars. The way you're looking at me makes me want to take you on the floor here and now."

Jory swallowed on a suddenly dry throat. "Then do."

Darius moved his head from side to side. *No.* "Reach into my right front pocket," he said instead. "Take a look at what you find there, and then tell me what you think."

"Darius…"

"Do it, Jory. That's my condition." Darius kissed his temple. "Go on." He watched Jory fumble, his hands clumsy with renewed nerves, and kept up his gentle stroking all the while.

A box. A small velvet box. Jory let out a shuddering breath.

"Doesn't have to be much," Darius said as Jory opened the box. "Just a yes. Or a no."

A *no*? Jory snapped his head up. "Like hell I'll say no," he blurted. "When you're giving me everything I ever wanted?"

"Then…" Darius's smile widened, brightened. "Then you do love me. Don't you?"

"Love you? Don't I just? Haven't I always? You really couldn't tell?"

"Sometimes I'm slow," Darius said. "Took me too long to figure out I loved you too, didn't it?" He put his arms around Jory and wound him back in, pausing only long enough to slip the ring, a simple platinum band, around his finger and admire it for a second. "But I'm only slow sometimes. We might have forever ahead of us, but right now I'm feeling impatient. I'm taking you to bed, Omega, and it's going to be fast."

"No you don't," Jory replied in an instant. "You're taking me right here. I was promised the floor, and I mean to have it!"

* * *

Darius hesitated for half a second, sizing up whether or not Jory really meant that. And oh, he did. Like he'd said moments ago, *didn't he just*. His eyes were fathomless dark pools of adrenaline and lust and something deeper, something purely Omega that Darius knew he wouldn't ever understand in a thousand years. He could only appreciate it.

And in the meantime, he could give Jory what he wanted.

He bared his teeth at his Omega, who fairly lit up with excitement. Jory bounced on the balls of his feet, ready for the takedown, and who was Darius to disappoint him. He pounced forward, all in a great rush that brought them tumbling down sure enough, but he managed to keep a guarding hand under Jory's head. Concussions: not sexy. Jory laughed up at him as if he'd read Darius's mind, and lifted that head of his to take Darius's mouth in a kiss so deep, wet and dirty that if Darius hadn't been half-hard already it would have gotten him there in a flash.

Darius rolled his hips down, letting Jory feel it, and gave his own, darker laugh when Jory gasped and writhed up against him. Liked that, did he? He guided Jory's legs up around him, fiercely pleased when Jory locked them around his waist without prompting, and thrust again, grinding their cocks together. He could feel the wet slick dripping from Jory's slit, soaking his jeans, threatening to pool on the floor beneath them. He wanted his fingers in there. He wanted his mouth in there. He wanted to taste, to lick, to eat Jory whole.

Jory threw his head back, already making

keening noises. He caught Darius's hand and tried to force it between his legs. "Please," he begged. "Oh, please."

But -- no. Not quite yet. Darius had a better idea. He shifted his hips until Jory made a complaining noise and unlocked his legs.

"Shh," Darius soothed him. "You'll like this."

Jory grumbled, but then made a happier noise when Darius wriggled down between his spread thighs. He shoved them as wide apart as they could go, and pushed his face briefly between them. The crown of his head fit against the cradle of Jory's Omega pelvis, only the crown, but he butted it hard against the swollen flesh there.

Yes. Jory came with a rush and a shout. He seized Darius by the hair and tugged hard enough to take out some strands, grinding his head deeper in his lust to be filled with a baby he'd bring out through that channel. It hurt, but Darius bit at the inseam of Jory's jeans and worried him playfully until he caught his breath and let his hair go.

"Where," Jory panted. "Where did you learn --"

Darius licked a stripe up the soaked crotch of Jory's jeans and looked up at him, wicked as he could be. "Good imagination."

"You're doing that again," Jory said, sounding dazed and drunk.

Satisfying words indeed, from a lover. "It's a promise," Darius swore. He caught the hand that wore his ring and gave it a squeeze. "But later. I'm not nearly done with you yet, Omega."

"Oh, God. I'm not sure I'll survive."

"I think you will."

"Promise?"

Darius grinned again. "Nope." He found the

fastenings to Jory's jeans and made quick work of opening them, though it took longer to peel them off his hips and down. He rolled onto his back then and brought Jory with him, guiding him into a good wide open straddle.

Jory's face lit up. "Oh yeah?"

Darius hummed his reply as he reached for Jory's beautiful cock. He'd only just barely gone soft after that first orgasm, unusual but not something he planned to complain about. His slick dripped on Darius's thighs with a soft *pat, pat, pat* so redolent of Omega pheromones that it made Darius's cock jump in response, straining toward Jory.

Not yet though. Not *yet*.

There was too much to savor first. Jory responded so beautifully when Darius got his fist around that cock and pumped, but even better than that when Darius let go and pushed three fingers inside him. Jory's greedy channel clenched at him, milking his fingers as if they were the real thing. Jory, knowing better, ground down hard and moaned in desperate yearning. He soaked Darius's hand.

"What do you want?" Darius murmured, even though he knew damn well. "Tell me. Show me. I want to see."

Dazed still, Jory somehow knelt up as straight as he could. His cock bobbed fat and fully hard and wet against his belly, and the opening to his channel was swollen as a rose in full bloom beneath it. Dark with engorged blood, gleaming wet. He rubbed both hands over his belly, clutching at the smooth skin there, letting go to finger himself, smearing slick over his skin. Darius had to close his eyes lest he come right then, right there. God, if he'd known how hot…

But it got better, oh yes it did. Jory had control of

himself now, at least a little, and he knew what he wanted. He reached between them to take hold of Darius's aching cock -- Darius opened his eyes for *that* -- and guide it inside him. He slid home smooth and sweet, tight enough to squeeze, hot as the fires of hell and wet as the water devils all yearned for.

Jory tilted his head back, mouth open in ecstasy. Darius could only clasp his hips at first to keep him balanced, but then he rolled his hips up once, driving deeper.

"Oh, fuck!" Jory gasped. He rolled down to meet Darius's next thrust up. "More. More, more, more. Harder."

Darius gave him what he wanted. He couldn't have not. He needed it as much as Jory did. His world narrowed to *hot* and *wet* and *tight* and nothing else until his balls drew up, full and heavy and ready to explode.

But just -- just -- as he would have come, Jory froze. He whimpered and bit his lip, shaking like an aspen in the breeze. "I can't," he panted. "It's too much. I'll come apart."

"You can," Darius said, hoarse through his lust. He caught Jory's hand again and drew it between them, touching where their bodies were joined. "You can come -- for me -- you can…"

Jory quaked, the struggle to hold himself together visible and painful. "Darius," he begged. "Darius, help me."

Darius didn't think, didn't guess, only acted on instinct. Cock still buried inside Jory, their groins flush together, he barely had room, but he slid his fingers back into Jory's channel. One. At. A. Time. Relishing Jory's desperate keens, until he had no room for a fourth but made it happen anyway, cradling his cock inside Jory, round as an infant's head.

Jory bellowed as he came, a full-throated battle roar, and came harder than Darius had ever seen before. He clenched so tight Darius didn't have a choice or a second to think about coming too before it was happening, happening like an explosion, his come flooding Jory to saturation.

When it dripped down his fingers he thrust it back up inside and drove a third, aftershock orgasm out of Jory that made his eyes roll to white and dropped him like a discarded puppet when it let him go. He collapsed in a heap on Darius's chest, heart going fast as a hummingbird's and his entire body aquiver with ecstasy.

He wasn't alone. Darius couldn't stop shaking either, at least not until he wrapped his arms around Jory and held him close, tight as he could squeeze them together. "Mine," he rasped, though he would have thought himself incapable of speech for a few hours yet.

He rolled them onto their sides, careful of the hard floor and over-sensitive muscles, then rolled once more to put Jory mostly beneath him. He wanted to look down and study Jory's face, to marvel at what a lucky son of a bitch he was to have this Omega. "You're *mine*, Jory. Now and always."

Jory raised himself a little, only far enough to kiss him, a haphazard brush of mouth against mouth with a flick of tongue for spice. Irrepressible Jory. "Yours," he agreed. "And you're mine. Now and always. Now, here." He wriggled forward on his belly until he could reach the pizza Darius had brought, somehow pulled the box onto the floor without spilling, and brought it back to them. "Eat. This is too good to waste. Then sleep."

"As long as you don't go anywhere. Deal?"

"Deal."

Darius believed him, but still made sure Jory was cuddled against him while they ate. They were a mess, and they'd be glued together with sweat and come and pizza sauce as soon as their bodies cooled, but he didn't care. This was his mate. This was his heart.

And he wasn't letting go. He didn't even loosen his hold when he fell asleep halfway through a piece of pizza, and neither did Jory.

* * *

Eventually they summoned the energy to crawl into bed. Hours passed, or they must have, though it seemed like less than a handful of seconds between the moment Darius closed his eyes and when he blinked them open again. The digital clock on Jory's nightstand blared a bright red 2:15 am into the darkness, and though after a fuck like that they *might* have slept the clock around, it wasn't likely.

Still barely half awake, Darius rolled onto his back. He and Jory had slid apart while they slept, and though he was as sticky as he'd imagined with dried fluids he didn't really mind. What else were showers for?

Besides, he liked the smell. Raw, filthy-nasty-hot, fecund as fresh turned earth. What'd woken him, though?

Darius turned his head to peer at Jory and uncovered the answer. Jory lay on one side, but not comfortably, more like he'd curled shrimp-like into himself. He had one arm tucked under his pillow and one fist clenched in the comforter they'd half tossed off the bed between them. Darius didn't think he was awake, but his face was pinched in a look somewhere between discomfort and outright pain.

A twinge of guilt stabbed at Darius. Hell, had he been too rough? They'd fallen asleep before he could check and make sure, let alone do any aftercare. But even as he watched, Jory flinched and his eyes moved fast enough to take note of behind his closed eyelids, and that likely meant one thing.

That, Darius could help with.

He nudged Jory gently, then shook him lightly by the shoulder. "Jory," he whispered. "Hey, gorgeous." And didn't it feel good to be able to say that, now? "Wake up. You're having a bad dream."

Jory came awake with a flinch, but then slowly, eyes opening and closing several times as he frowned with confusion. "Darius?"

"No, it's RuPaul." Darius stroked Jory's chest, over his pounding heart. Damn, that must have been one hell of a dream. "It's your pick of the Hemsworth brothers. It's a drunken sailor."

Jory snorted, but he smiled, and lifted one hand to rub at his eyes. "God, you're still such a dork. What is your obsession with that song?"

"Everyone's got to have a theme. And -- dork? You thought that would change? C'mere." Darius rolled and gathered the both of them, arranging Jory's sleep-lax limbs and his own until they were both of their sides, Jory's back pressed to his chest, comfortably spooned together. Just like all the years they'd tangled their legs together under pub tables, they fit exactly right now, as if they'd been made for one another.

Who knew? Maybe they had.

Jory sighed, but contentedly, and snuggled into Darius's embrace. "How'd you know I needed that?"

"I know you."

"Hmm," Jory said, a sound of agreement. He

rubbed absently at his chest, his abdomen. "The strangest thing."

Darius tucked his chin over Jory's shoulder. "Was it a bad dream?" he asked, curious.

"I don't know. I don't think so. Maybe? It was all just bits and pieces, the way most dreams are. Thinking I could fly, but I kept falling." He nudged his elbow backward. "I was just starting to get some altitude when you woke me."

Darius bit lightly over the pulse in Jory's neck. "I'll make you fly again later." He laughed when Jory groaned and drove his elbow back harder. "What? I will. It's a promise."

"I have no doubt." Jory's hand drifted lower, massaging his stomach -- still absently, as if he didn't quite realize what he was doing. "And I think I was... sword fighting? With rapiers, the narrow little swords about as big as hat pins. I kept getting poked in the gut. Like -- *ow,* ow!" He drew in a sharp breath and pressed his hand flat over his lower groin. "Ow. Like that. Like something's..." He stopped.

Darius stopped.

Darius was fairly certain they both stopped breathing.

He made himself start again while Jory was still frozen, covering Jory's outstretched fingers with his own and burying his nose deep in the crook of Jory's neck. He drew in the deepest, lustiest breath he possibly could, and...

Smelled it. The change.

"Darius," Jory whispered, twisting his hand to take Darius's and to squeeze it tightly. "Oh, Darius. I've got the scent too. Oh, *Darius.*"

Darius took another breath, savoring every nuance, and knew they were both right. *Fecund,* like he'd thought before. *Fertile.* A pregnant Omega, even if only the tiniest bit pregnant, only just beginning to be with child.

But pregnant.

Jory twisted in his arms, frantic, pressing his belly to Darius's, trapping their hands between them. Darius could taste salt in his wild kisses, and didn't know who it'd come from. Maybe both of them. Did it matter? Hell no.

Because they'd done it. They'd *done* it. They were going to have a baby.

They were going to have it all.

Epilogue

What did you do with a -- well, no, not a drunken sailor, though once this was over Darius had a bottle of the best whiskey he'd been able to buy, set aside for forty weeks, all ready to uncork as soon as Jory could share it again.

But that wouldn't be for a little while yet.

He sat behind Jory, cradling his Omega between his spread legs so Jory could brace his own on them. He needed the assist. Twenty hours this had been going on! Twenty hours and counting and yes, it'd been easy at first, lots of walking and joking about it being more of a waddle than a walk and getting knuckled in his own stomach for that kind of remark. Twenty hours of holding Jory's hand with every contraction, a little harder every hour, until his hands were stiff and purple and sore and he could barely bend them.

Twenty hours, by God. And not done yet. "I am never doing this to you again," Darius swore in Jory's ear between spasms, while Jory's sweat-soaked head lolled against his chest. "Not in a hundred years. I'm going out and getting snipped tomorrow, you watch me."

Jory, that impossible Omega, *laughed*. Not loudly or with a lot of air, but he laughed. "Oh, no, you won't," he said, confident as if he wasn't currently engaged in turning his body inside out. "And oh, yes, you will."

Darius wondered if his brain had finally started to jellify under the stress. "Which?"

"You won't get snipped. I won't let you. I --" Jory broke off in the middle of the sentence to squeeze Darius's hand again. He bore down so hard Darius had to grit his teeth to keep from yelping, and longer than before. When he could pant again, he said, "And we'll both do this again. I'll make sure of it."

For fuck's sake. Darius picked up a cool, wet cloth from a stack he'd kept handy and toweled off Jory's forehead. "Want to bet?"

Jory laughed again. "I'll take those odds."

"You're insane," Darius said, pressing his lips to Jory's cheek and to his mouth. "Don't die, all right? Don't be stupid."

The midwife, who'd been keeping his own counsel down at the business end of things, picked that moment to pipe up, and he had the audacity to look amused as he did it. "He's not dying. He doesn't even think he is, and most Omegas do around this point. He's tough and he's in excellent health. Odds are he'll be fine."

"*Odds* are?" Darius demanded, sitting straighter upright. "Since when is *odds are* on the table? If I'd known that, I wouldn't have --" He couldn't lose his best friend. He couldn't.

"Darius." Jory looked up at him, worn to a frazzle, but with such fondness and friendliness in his face that it knocked Darius utterly silent. He even, somehow, knew what Darius was thinking. "You'll never lose me."

And if Darius hadn't had his mouth firmly shut just before, that would have done the trick right there.

A brief silence fell while Jory panted. Darius recognized the signs and took hold of his hands again, ready for what looked to be a real whopper. But instead of what he'd gotten accustomed to, Jory drew in a sharp breath and shuddered. "I --" He looked confused. "I need --"

He shoved Darius with such force that Darius

tumbled back onto his elbows and then he hunched forward, gripping his knees. His face turned red as a brick and he made a noise somewhere between a grunt and a roar that would have put the fear of God into any Alpha.

"Now we're in business," the midwife said, absolutely satisfied. "Not long now at all. He's a good pusher."

"Glad to hear it," Darius growled, mostly to himself. The midwife? Busy. Jory? Utterly lost in a world that contained only himself and their child, and the final end of this struggle. But that wouldn't do. Darius reached out and shook the midwife's shoulder, not giving a damn for the warning look the man shot him.

"How do I help?" he demanded. "Tell me what to do."

"You did your part forty weeks ago," the midwife informed him tartly, but then relented. "First time fathers, I swear." He took the hand Darius had laid on his shoulder and guided it down between Jory's legs. "Here. This is what you can do. Do you feel that? That's your son's head, and it's almost born. One more little push, Jory, just one... *there*, there we go. Now what do you think about that, Alpha?"

Darius didn't think anything. His brain had temporarily frozen. He held his son's head in his hand, warm and hard and pulsing with life, and he held his mate in his arms, panting and shaking with the effort of labor.

The pause only lasted moments. Then more directions, sharp and firm. The feel of the infant moving somehow, Jory's snarl of agony and ecstasy, and a *pop*, something indefinably final, and the entirety of the baby slithered out all in a rush to land between

Jory's legs. Jory's and Darius's. Without being told what to do, Jory bent to gather him up and crush him to his chest. Jory's arms shook so that Darius had to support them, and hello, there was the mind numbing awe again.

The midwife watched them, amusement written across his face. "Well done, you two," he said. "Everyone should be so lucky."

Shouldn't they just? Darius couldn't stop staring at his son's face, except for when he turned to look at Jory and found Jory equally torn. Slowly, as if all the strain was finally catching up with him, Jory stretched up to kiss Darius. Their son wriggled and mewed between them, working up to a really good and proper roar of hunger, and they were both sticky with a mess of blood and amniotic fluid and things Darius didn't know the names of.

It wasn't possible to be happier. The human body could only hold so much, he thought.

"Thank you," Jory whispered, and Darius discovered he could hold a little more yet. He'd thought before that they had it all? Oh, he'd almost been right. Almost. But now he *did*. A husband, a mate, a partner. A son.

All the future they could seize, together. And a bottle of Glenlivet, too.

Inexplicable (Roanoke River Omegas 2)
Will Okati

Deacon's everything Kit wants. Kit's everything Deacon needs -- three days a month. Alpha and ex-jarhead Deacon's an over-the-road trucker, always on the move, and he likes it that way. And Omega Kit's... good with that. He's not going anywhere. Not seeing anyone else. He's promised himself he'll never be like his parents -- he won't tie a man down when he doesn't want to be tied.

What Kit doesn't know is that he's pregnant -- until the night their son is born. Now everything's changing. Babies do what they want, when they want. Just like Deacon.

Only Deacon's not sure just what he does want... but he's sure what he's not willing to give up on, and that's a future. And a family. *His* family.

Now all he has to do is convince Kit he's in this for keeps.

Chapter One

Deacon came home that night as the sun came up. Oh, not his real home, Kit supposed. Deacon's only fixed address was the sleeper compartment in his eighteen-wheeler, and had been since the day he'd paid cash down for the truck. But if home was where the heart was, then when he came to Kit, Deacon *was* coming home.

And then coming, and coming again. And maybe just once more for sweet good measure.

Deacon hadn't been expected, and that made his arrival all the more perfect. Kit didn't care that he was dozy and wobbly and warm from a night in bed. Kit's bed had been too lonely but now that would change because Deacon was here, right here at last. Hair ruffled, stubble on his cheeks and a cocky grin on his lips, Deacon looked like trouble in ragged blue jeans and good leather boots, ready for anything. His Marine Corps tattoo showed where he'd rolled his sleeves up and his eyes gleamed with a taste for playing as hard as he worked.

"Deacon. *Deacon.*" Not giving a damn about standing on his front stoop in a busy neighborhood just waking up to a new day, and which would have loved a show, Kit leapt at Deacon and wound both arms around his neck.

"Now that's what I call a hello." Deacon laughed, low in his throat and pleased, and held Kit up as easily as if he wasn't a full-grown man with shoulders just as broad as the Alpha's. He bent his head to nibble at Kit's neck. "Need something, Omega?"

After all these years as lovers, he could still make Kit blush. Kit hid his face against Deacon's firm chest and shook his head, not knowing what to say. *I need you* was obvious. *I want you*, even more so. *I have to have you inside me…*

Kit peeked up from beneath his lashes, aware of just what that did to Deacon, and glad, because a look like that was all he could manage between breathless shudders of yearning. "I want you inside me," he said, winding his legs as well as his arms around Deacon. "Come inside." *In all ways*, he meant, and he knew Deacon understood him that way.

Deacon bit his lip hard and swore, dark and rough. "You'll be the death of me."

"A little death," Kit promised, twining closer. "Make love to me."

"Sweetheart, if you think you can stop me now…"

And oh, Kit liked the sound of that. He laughed as Deacon, strong as an ox, wriggled him loose and tossed him over his shoulder. A hearty smack on the ass and they were on their way up the stairs, taking them two at a time. Kit slid his hands down the back of Deacon's jeans, kneading the fine firm flesh he found there.

Deacon popped his hip again, the sting sweet and sharp. "Not playing fair there, Kit."

Kit rubbed his cheek against Deacon's shoulder. "All's fair."

"God damn, when you purr like that you make me want to bathe you in cream and lick you clean," Deacon said as he reached the top of the steps and set Kit lightly on his feet. He gave him a warm look, no less wild than his nature allowed, and tilted his head at the locked door. "Want a good fucking, Kitten? Let me in."

And didn't Kit just! He hadn't seen Deacon in weeks, far longer than they usually went between visits -- Deacon's work had taken him to California for ages, and every time he'd planned to make his way back to the East Coast, another job opened up. Every time they put their plans off, Kit retreated to his bed with a toy or two specifically designed for Omega satisfaction, but they just weren't the same.

They couldn't kiss you. They didn't have hands to run over your skin. They couldn't whisper wicked things in your ears. They couldn't...

Who cared? They didn't matter. Not when he had his favorite Alpha in his arms. Kit hurried to let them both in, and turned quick as a wink to catch Deacon by the belt. He tug-dragged the man to his bed, both of them laughing, shedding clothes as they went -- not in any particular order, and when they reached their goal Deacon still had his jeans on, if open, and one sock, and Kit still wore his pajama shirt.

Kit peeled that off with a thrill going through him at the way Deacon stopped to stare hungrily, then fell back onto his bed. He rested on his elbows, his legs splayed slightly apart with one drawn up a little to hide his cock from Deacon's view. Deacon loved a show, and he loved being the one to draw out a performance. With him -- only him -- Kit could play that sort of a part.

Deacon, he trusted.

Though Deacon had paused to frown at the bed, taking in the unplugged heating pad pushed to one side and the uncapped bottle of ibuprofen on the nightstand, along with a mostly-empty bottle of water. "You all right, hon?"

Kit shrugged. Part of the reason he hadn't slept had been a backache that just wouldn't quit, but he'd spent the previous evening helping baby-sit his friend Jory's new son, lifting and chasing and picking up after the exhausted new father. "Tweaked a muscle," he said. "Nothing to worry about."

"You sure?"

Kit clicked his tongue. A distracted Alpha wouldn't give him what he wanted, what he needed. He reached out to tickle Deacon's thigh with his bare toes and get him back on track. "You can't do much with your jeans on, love. Take those off."

His ploy worked. Deacon snorted and shook his head, reminding Kit of a horse. *Hmm.* A steel horse, perhaps, given Deacon's nature. He did ride whenever he got the chance, whenever he visited old Ranger friends who owned bikes. The notion suited Kit. Powerful, and mighty between the legs.

"Anything you ask," Deacon said, hands going to his waist, then hovering there. "But give me a show, beautiful. Warm me up."

As if Deacon needed encouragement! He'd have a tricky time working a cock that hard out of his jeans, but Kit didn't mind. Hot could always get hotter.

Where to begin? *Ah.* He traced his tongue across his lips as he nodded, then reached inside his jeans and between his legs to stroke his cock, dipping one finger into the slit beneath his balls for moisture. Deacon's nose twitched, and Kit knew he could smell the deepening of Omega pheromones.

Kit touched one fingertip to his tongue and thrilled at the sound of Deacon's deep groan. The Alpha had gotten his jeans off, and his cock jerked at the sight and smell. *Gorgeous.*

"Come inside me, now," Kit murmured again as he fingered himself. He could go deeper than usual, oddly deep, but egging Deacon on satisfied an urge he hadn't known he was suffering from, to stroke high and hard within himself. "Come inside, Deacon, come."

Deacon came -- in one sense at least, tumbling down onto the bed, on top of Kit, and smothering him in kisses, enveloping him in heavy limbs, stealing the rest of Kit's breath with his touch. Deacon couldn't wait, Kit discovered, as hot for some bed-play as Kit was, and pushed his spread legs higher, wider open, farther apart so that he could snug his groin between them. "I'll make love to you nice and sweet later," he promised, "but I have to have you now."

Kit surrendered, rocking his hips up to bring them closer. "Then *take* me."

Deacon groaned again, deep and guttural, as he slid home inside Kit's body. "Fuck, you're so wet, so open," he muttered, moving so that Kit's knees clamped his hips. "Been thinking about me?"

"What do you think?" Kit could feel his orgasm coming already, hot and eager, and before he could go on the first spasm rocked him. "*Deacon!*"

"Shit," Deacon swore, thrusting deep and slow. "What's got you this fired up? So wet, *fuck*, you almost never get this wet."

"You. The dreams I was having. I don't know." Kit arched back and raked his hands through his hair, seized by the powerful shuddering in his groin and belly. He wasn't done yet, he could tell. "Keep going. Don't stop. Don't stop until I do."

"Darlin', you try and make me," Deacon said. He put his mouth to the side of Kit's neck and all talk was forgotten then for hot, wet, long minutes where nothing existed, nothing mattered except the slide of his cock in Kit's slick, open slit and then the hard squeeze of his hand around Kit's erection. Kit often needed more than just a hand job to come, but he spasmed into orgasm at Deacon's first touch, climaxing with a clenching of the belly that nearly made his heart stop. His slit clamped down on Deacon without mercy, making the man buck atop him.

Breathless, Deacon laughed, but cords stood out in his neck and he was getting close, so close, himself. "Gonna squeeze my dick off, angel. What's gotten into you?"

Kit couldn't answer in words. Instead he surged up, caught Deacon by the back of the head, and brought their mouths together in a kiss as deep and dirty as original sin. He wrapped his legs around Deacon's thighs and rocked, needing him closer, deeper, for him to go *harder*, damn the man, and *harder* --

Deacon came with a startled shout, his arms as tight around Kit as bands of iron and his cock so deep Kit would have sworn it bumped the mouth of his womb. His penetration *hurt* but hurt *so good* that Kit came once more, with third time the charm, the room whiting out around him as he rode wave after wave of pleasure.

He came down slowly, breathlessly panting, his mouth a half inch from Deacon's and Deacon's dazed eyes staring into his own. Seeing that Kit laughed. Breathless, delighted, worn-out but so pleased that looking at him made Deacon laugh too. The Alpha draped himself bonelessly on top of Kit, breathing his breath. "If that's the welcome home I get, I ought to stay gone for longer more often."

"Don't you dare," Kit said severely, then grinned up at his lover. His stomach muscles quaked, squeezing, and his back ached again but he couldn't have cared less. The pleasure was far greater than any minor pain. "All the same, Deacon. Welcome home."

* * *

The hands on the alarm clock beside his bed showed four and six when Kit next opened his eyes. Took him a moment of bleary squinting to figure out what that actually meant in real time, but either way he and Deacon had slept for hours. *Mmmm. Must have needed that.* Kit stretched luxuriously, arms over his head and toes pointed, halfway through realizing he was being watched. He blinked his eyes all the way open and let his head fall to one side to quirk an eyebrow at Deacon.

"See something you like?" Deacon asked, using a lighter Omega register to mimic Kit's voice. Then, in his own Alpha bass answered himself, "Always."

"*Stop.*" Kit covered his face, but he was laughing. "If anyone ever told you that you were smooth, they were wrong. They were so wrong."

Deacon tucked his hands behind his head. "I think the guilty party was you, darlin'. And you weren't wrong. I'm smooth as a fresh pane of glass. As a baby's ass. As --"

Kit swatted at him, but absently. His back spasmed again, stronger than the night before, and he winced out loud as he reached to massage his sore muscles.

"Something wrong?" Deacon asked, always quick on the trigger when something set off his Spidey senses. "Cramp?"

"Maybe. Or I might have slept wrong." Kit sat up, the better to reach the small of his back with both hands. That helped a little, and the spasm faded. He nudged Deacon, who he couldn't help noticing was still naked, with his knee. "Was I tossing and turning?"

"I wasn't awake long enough to notice much, but a little. I was about to shake you and get you to turn over, see if that helped."

Odd. Kit would have expected a proper seeing-to like the one Deacon had given him to knock him out from top to toe, but life always was full of the unexpected. He stretched again, determined to ignore the twinges and kinks until they went away -- such things always did -- and swung his legs out of bed.

Ugh, what a mess! Deacon hooted laughter at the face Kit made at the mess left behind. "Wet and wild," he said lazily and proudly, grinning at Kit without an ounce of shame. "If the sheets are ruined, I'll get you a new set."

"You might have to get a new mattress." Kit wrinkled his nose. Omega slick was one thing, but heavens. The sheets were soaked. *Ugh.* He'd slept in all that? And look at Deacon, lolling contentedly as a cat in cream still. Kit swatted at him with more firmness. "Up, up. Out of bed and change the sheets at least. I'll wash these later and see if they can't be salvaged."

Deacon shrugged but did as he'd been told, kicking himself free of the sheets and rolling nimbly to his feet. "What're you going to do while I'm playing housewife?"

"Taking a shower. A hot one. And if you're very, very good, and very, very fast at making beds, I might just let you join me." Kit winked at Deacon over his shoulder and sauntered out, nice and slow, letting him enjoy the view.

A good start to the day, and a very good middle. Kit approved. *Now for that shower...*

* * *

Oh, that felt good. Kit patted the washcloth he'd soaked with the coldest water his bathroom tap could deliver across his neck. He hissed when he met a few scrapes that Deacon's teeth had left behind, but once the sting faded a rippling sense of pleasure took its place. He always had liked to be marked, and Deacon knew exactly how to leave a lasting impression on kit. Not enough to create a scar, but plenty to feel for a few days.

Another twinge in his back made Kit hiss and grip the edge of the sink. He twisted against the discomfort to work the cramp out, and scowled when the pain took longer to fade than he'd have liked. Honestly, this was getting ridiculous. He might end up having to, but he'd hate to waste time on a trip to the doctor while Deacon was in town. Every moment Deacon was here, Kit wanted to spend with *him*.

Stolen weekends with Deacon weren't enough. A purloined week once or twice a year with Deacon was never enough, but Deacon's need to wander carried him cross-country almost without ceasing. When Kit had met Deacon, he'd known falling for someone like this former Marine would lead to heartbreak. A man who couldn't stay, and a man who couldn't bear to go? Recipe for disaster.

But no. Kit wasn't a child, and he'd long since shelved his books of fairytales. He didn't need a happy-ever-after. What he needed was what he had, and if -- only rarely, ever so rarely -- the long nights alone left him yearning for more, that was his problem.

Kit re-wet his washcloth with cold water and pressed the chilly fabric to the back of his neck. *Better.* Besides, no matter what good reasons he might have once had, Kit had never been able to say no to Deacon. The tie between them was too strong, almost from the start.

So be it. Kit had made up his mind. Deacon was Deacon, and Kit loved him as he was -- as he was loved in return. So Kit wouldn't try to change him. He wouldn't be "that Omega," the one who clung and whined and stomped their feet until they had their Alpha whipped into the shape they wanted. He'd die before he deliberately made Deacon as unhappy as his parents had been.

Kit's back muscles twisted, sharp and severe enough to make him hiss and double over, clutching at the sink for balance.

"Kit?" Deacon appeared around the doorway, looking worried. Frown lines made his face severe. "I heard that. Something's wrong."

Kit waved him off, unable to speak until the spasm passed. When the cramp finally eased, he let out a breath he'd been holding. "Nothing's wrong! I'm fine."

"That is *not* fine." Deacon's worried scowl deepened as Kit stood gingerly. "I'm not joking. That happens one more time and we're going to the emergency room."

"For heaven's sake, I don't need an emergency room. My GP, *maybe*. Tomorrow," Kit bargained.

Deacon looked as if he wanted to argue, but before he could open his mouth a chorus of whoops and hollers made him startle half out of the jeans he'd pulled on but left unfastened. Kit and his Alpha automatically cocked an ear, but it didn't take much effort to make out what was being said. Thin walls, with neighbors currently banging cheerfully on them.

"Kit! Hey, Kit! Deacon! Deacon, we know you're in there, you fuckhead!"

"Zane! What are you doing here? You can't use a phone like a civilized kind of bastard?" Deacon yelled back, hammering his fist against the wall in return.

"Visiting a friend, dickweed, and I knew all that caterwauling was your fault!" Zane yelled. Kit only knew him tangentially, as a friend of a friend, but he had a rough and ready charm that made him easy to like. "I told Nathaniel, I said, you hear all the screaming? I bet you that's Deacon back in town."

Kit covered his face with one hand. He didn't know Zane well enough to be thrilled with the turn of *this* conversation. Deacon gave him an apologetic grimace, though, and that went a decent way toward soothing his embarrassment.

"Hell yeah," his actual neighbor -- Nathaniel -- went on. "You know that's about the only time there's yowling like that in these lonely-ass-bed parts. Sounds like you got him good."

"Sounds like he *got* got. Feeling the burn, pretty boy?"

Deacon hammered the wall. "Aw, piss off. You wish you were half as lucky!"

And you know what? Kit decided he could cringe himself into a ball of humiliation, or he could stand up tall and proud and claim the truth. "Damn right," Kit called back. "And I'm going to get lucky again as soon as I can!"

The delight on Deacon's face made all that worthwhile.

Kit's neighbors and their guests gave him a few more sprinklings of flak, but the teasing was all well intended, and Deacon could dish back as good as he got. Kit settled back to enjoy the show. Part of enjoying Deacon while he was in town was enjoying every bit of him, even the noisy, extroverted parts.

Kit lived every day to the fullest that he could, but only when Deacon was there did he really felt alive.

Finally, they got to the point.

"Barbecue on the roof in an hour, and beer until then, starting now," Zane yelled. "Get out here and show the rest of your friends your ugly face, would you? Come on!"

Deacon lit up with interest. He glanced at Kit. "I could eat. You up for some dinner and a cold one, babe?"

Kit's back cramped up, fiercer and sharper than before. The pain made him bite his cheek before he nodded. The thought of eating made his stomach do uncomfortable flips, but he managed to keep his smile from wavering.

Honestly, this was getting out of hand. He'd go to the doctor as soon as Deacon left town, he decided. Until then, he wouldn't dwell on the pain. Fresh air, stretching his legs, and a good distraction might even help.

"Barbecue and beer?" Kit leaned over just far enough to drop a noisy, messy kiss on Deacon's cheek and laugh when he spluttered. Perfect. "Of course we're in. Who could say no to that?"

Chapter Two

Damn, but this was the good life.

Deacon tilted back his Longneck and drained the beer to the last drop, rolled the still-cold bottle across his hot forehead, then tossed the empty into a nearby bin full of other empties. He snagged a fresh bottle from a tub of ice and cracked it open for a swig. Turned out to be hard cider and not beer, but eh, no big deal. Nothing beat cold alcohol and good friends on a hot night. He'd spent plenty of long evenings getting rowdy with his military buddies across the continental forty-eight, but this party here had the home advantage.

So he didn't technically live there. Still felt like home.

The building Kit kept his studio and apartment in had a flat roof studded with rain gutters and potted garden plants. Tonight, someone had strung every flat surface they could reach with those tiny Christmas type lights and Chinese lanterns with mosquito repellent candles inside, and a couple of Tiki torches for good measure. Music thump-thump-thumped from a stereo with decent bass in its speakers, and an almost-dangerous number of Alphas, Omegas and Betas rocked against each other to the beat. Their scent spread out in a heady cloud, creating an atmosphere of equal parts camaraderie and lust.

Kit would be upstairs to join him as soon as he'd finished getting dressed, and then they'd add their share to the miasma. Deacon drew in a deep breath, peripheral city funk be damned, and let his gathered air out in a long plume of satisfaction.

A tall, lanky figure plowed into Deacon from the side, wrapping a lean arm around his neck in a chokehold. Blue eyes and a cheeky grin both gleamed as their owner rubbed his knuckles briskly against Deacon's scalp. "You did come! Nathaniel owes me ten bucks. He bet you'd forget and stay wrapped up in Kit all night."

"Fucking asshole, knock it off!" Deacon yelped. Dude had a grip like iron. "Jeez! Uncle, uncle. I just got back in town today. Let me at least have a drink before you snuff me out like a candle." He jabbed the man in his flat stomach to make his point extra clear -- but he checked first; Zane was an old friend but also an Omega, and he'd never risk a baby.

The poke made Zane back off, though he was hooting in triumph and took a jab of his own at Deacon's ribs. "Missed you, my man. You should have been here a month ago."

"How come?"

"Could have used some big-muscle Alphas to help me heft shit around and hump boxes up two flights of stairs." Zane's grin blazed so bright and fierce that a man could cut himself on the edge of all that pride. "Finally got my own place, baby."

Deacon whooped and grabbed Zane around the neck in a hug as rough as any he'd give an Alpha. Always had thought of Zane as an honorary Alpha anyway, he was such a rowdy cutup bastard. "Hot damn! Look at you go!" he enthused.

Zane's grin went from fierce to ferocious. Pride? Hell yeah, but well deserved. Zane had meant to join the service too, but he'd had to put that dream aside and had lived with his uncle since he'd gotten pregnant by a deadbeat and refused to give up the baby. He'd made plenty of bad choices, but he'd also worked hard to turn his life around and as far as Deacon could tell, he was doing a good job.

"Good for you, man," Deacon said with a final hearty thump to Zane's back. "You need some help while I'm in town?"

"I might. But that, my friend, is for tomorrow. Tonight we eat, drink and be merry. What's your poison? Beer or hard cider?" Shameless, Zane swiped Deacon's Longneck and emptied half the contents at one pull. He made appreciative noises. "Cider! Excellent choice. Someone get you in the mood for cracking open sweet fruit and licking the rind dry?"

Deacon laughed. "Anyone ever tell you, Omega, you have a dirty mind and a dirtier mouth?"

"Plenty of people. I just don't listen to them." Zane saluted Deacon with his purloined cider. "Speaking of, are you finally here to stay or has your dumb ass still not learned when its owner has it made?"

"Fuck off." Deacon crossed his arms. He scowled down at Zane, who never let having to look up slow his roll in the slightest. "I love being here, dude, you know that. But me and Kit, we're both happy the way we are, and you know that, too. What we have is enough for both of us. Always has been, right?"

"Sure, sure," Zane agreed. "I never said otherwise. But could I direct your attention to the situation happening stage left?"

What? Deacon frowned. He scanned the left side of the roof, wondering what crack Zane might be smoking, until he lit on Kit, who'd perched himself on the side of a planter with a bottle of water so cold ice chips clung to its side. He glanced up, talking to… Ah.

"This right here is what they call a situation," Zane murmured.

Deacon punched his friend's arm without looking, all his attention on Kit and the Alpha trying to make a move on him. Kit's body language said *nope, not for sale, and by the way if you don't move back I'm going to kick you in the nuts* but the Alpha didn't look like the kind who'd take no for an answer. He leaned forward, pressing his point. Even laid a hand on Kit's arm to try and influence him.

The hell you do, asshole.

Deacon didn't realize he was growling until Zane cocked an eyebrow at him. "Well? Going to do something about that there lummox putting the moves on your man?"

Just watch his dust. Deacon thrust his cider at Zane. "Hold that for me, and don't drink a drop. I'll be right back."

"With or without blood on your hands?"

"That en-fucking-tirely depends."

* * *

"Ferdie!" Kit knocked the big lunk's hand away when he tried to make a grab for Kit's shoulder, then pointed a finger in his face. "Touch me again and I'm going to feed you that hand. Do you understand?"

Deacon wasn't close enough to do the aforementioned feeding himself -- getting through the crowd on the roof was a *bitch* -- but he one hundred percent approved of his Omega's initiative. Even so, his fists tightened. *Ferdie, eh? Shitty name for a shitty dude.* Let him get a little closer and he'd do the hand feeding himself.

Ferdie, apparently, wasn't the kind of man who learned fast. He had a broad, dull face, cheeks pitted with acne scars, and a redness to his nose that went right along with his head start on a beer belly. He smirked as he leaned closer and cupped Kit's cheek as roughly as he'd cradle a punkin' ready for the chunkin'. Not too stupid though; he let go before Kit could do more than bare his teeth.

"Feisty, I like that," he said, Deacon close enough to hear him now. Not that he was making any effort to lower his voice. "I hear you're a screamer. Bet I can make you scream good and loud, pretty boy."

Did this guy have a fucking death wish or something? The Omegas *and* Alphas who had noticed Deacon coming, the steam all but billowing from his ears, were starting to clear a path, and Ferdie hadn't noticed a damn thing yet.

Nor had Kit, but Deacon wouldn't blame him. Kit kept his teeth bared as he spoke, ferocious as a feral dog. "You couldn't make me sneeze with that needle dick of yours, Ferdie. Piss. Off."

Ferdie's face went dark with anger. "Bitch. You think you're all that?"

"I don't have to. I have an Alpha already who does everything I need for me."

"One who leaves you for weeks at a time," Ferdie scoffed. His eyes went crafty. "You learn how to talk sweet to me, I'll show you how you can get some sweet back from an Alpha who --"

Finally. Deacon was close enough to grab Ferdie's arm and twist his wrist almost far enough backward to slip its joints. "An Alpha with a needle dick and a broken arm? Doesn't sound like much of a deal to me."

Kit sagged with relief. "There you are. I didn't know where you'd gone."

"I'm here now." Deacon put himself between Kit and Ferdie. "You need me to spell the situation out for you? *Git.*"

"Ain't nobody asked for you!" Ferdie, bless his heart, had the lack of brains needed to put up a struggle. Not much of one. Odds were he never lifted anything much heavier than a glass and Deacon found it all too easy to bend his wrist a fraction more sharply.

Kit rubbed at his back, looking troubled. "If you break his wrist, do the other one so he matches."

"You heard the Omega, asshole," Deacon said. Almost pleasantly. Well, pleasantly compared to the way old drill instructors would have delivered that line. "Piss off, and piss off fast now or I'm really going to lose my temper and I just don't know what might happen then. Do you?"

Ferdie snarled at him. Deacon rolled his eyes, and gave the oaf a tug, a shove, and a boot to the backside while his teaspoonful of brains were struggling to catch up with what was going on. Ferdie yelped as he went sprawling, the sound almost lost under the roar of laughter that went up as he tumbled down. He scrambled straight back up, but Deacon still stood between him and Kit. He made *bring-it-here* gestures with his hands, daring Ferdie to try him, just try him.

Ferdie did have just enough sense to save his own hide. He barked like a dog at Deacon and turned to stumble-shove his way through the crowd.

Deacon curled his lip and let the bastard go, too busy otherwise with going to one knee in front of Kit to take his hands. "Did he hurt you?"

"No," Kit said, squeezing Deacon's hands hard. "No, he just -- he didn't scare me."

"'Course he didn't. You're tough as nails."

"I don't know about that." Kit managed a small laugh. "I don't want him, Deacon. He delivered some bookcases for the store one day and saw me and after that he just wouldn't leave me alone. I try and avoid him, but..."

"But he's slow to learn. I kind of got that."

Deacon stood, offering Kit a hand up from the planter. "And I never thought you wanted him. Not for a second."

Not even for one second? A tiny, treacherous part of his brain asked. *Ferdie wasn't wrong. Neither was Zane. You* do *leave Kit all alone for weeks at a time. Could anyone blame him if…*

Deacon told that corner of his mind to shut the fuck up, pronto, and slammed the door on it. He put his arm around Kit instead. "Come on, babe. You need some peace and quiet. Around here, to the alcove."

* * *

The alcove was a fluke of architecture leftover from the days when the apartments above the storefronts on Roanoke River's main streets all had fireplaces in regular use. Those had all been long blocked off and replaced with radiators or central heat, but no one had ever knocked down the chimneys. The one on the roof had a three by three recess that had likely been used to stack extra firewood. Made an excellent make-out spot, one they'd used before, and Deacon hurried Kit there without stopping. He put Kit's back against the wall, gently as he could, and ran his hands over Kit in a quick pat-down just to make sure Ferdie hadn't done anything more than ooze a little slime.

Kit tolerated the coddling, but not with his usual smile for Deacon's over protectiveness. He looked pale, a little sweaty, not well, and when he swallowed his throat bobbed visibly. Almost like he was in shock, but not quite. But he was brave, he was. "I'm not hurt."

"You're not well," Deacon told him frankly. He did not like Kit's color. Wax was a good shade for candles, not Omegas. "Seriously, are you coming down with something?"

Kit took a deep, frustrated breath that brought some pink back into his face and made Deacon relax a hair. "No. I slept wrong, I'm sure of it, and tensing up like that didn't help. That's all."

Kinked muscles, then? Deacon could work with that. "Turn around. I'll rub your back for you." He could work out some of the knots and soothe Kit at the same time. Win/win.

But nope, Kit had his stubborn face on, and Deacon knew from experience that once Kit had his mind made up it would take an act of God to get him to budge. "I said I'm fine."

"Sure you are, darlin'." Deacon could be stubborn too. He slipped his arms around Kit's middle, surprised at how tight his stomach muscles were -- tense as hell, poor guy, and who could blame him -- and put his hands to Kit's back to start kneading gently as his work-roughened mitts could on either side of Kit's spine.

"*Ahh.*" To his relief, Kit melted like butter on a hot stove. He leaned forward into Deacon, going limp. "Don't stop. Please."

Deacon had no plans to. He worked deftly and firmly, long sweeps and knuckle digs into the muscles that were tight as iron until they relaxed. He laughed, somewhat muffled by Kit's hair, as Kit plastered himself against Deacon's chest. "You like that, huh?"

Kit made an unintelligible noise.

"Hold on, babe, I need some leverage." Deacon adjusted Kit, like manipulating a rag doll, and nudged his legs apart to put a knee between them. He pulled Kit forward then, easing him into a straddled seat on that knee that would help take some of the weight. Ought to help, and --

Kit stiffened so quickly Deacon didn't have time

to react. His fingers hooked into claws and dug into Deacon's shoulders, his breathing jerked to a shuddering stop and a low keen slipped from his throat. Deacon was wearing jeans, good sturdy Army surplus issue, but by God if Kit didn't soak his leg with a spurt of Omega slick that smelled so strong the scent dizzied him.

Deacon jerked his head back, startled. Not displeased, but plenty startled. "Did you just --"

Kit raised his head. His eyes were so wild and dazed Deacon wasn't sure he'd heard him. "I -- what?" Those pale cheeks of his bloomed a sudden brilliant red. "Oh my God."

"You *did*," Deacon said, still baffled but delighted. "Fights get you off now, beautiful?"

"I -- I --" Kit shook his head. He bit his lip and rocked forward, grinding down on Deacon's wet knee. "I need more. More, please. More."

If he'd come at barely a touch, what was deliberate action going to do?

Deacon couldn't resist the urge to find out. He rocked his knee up, grinding into Kit's crotch, and went hot with excitement when Kit moaned and clutched at him as if he were balls-deep instead of just over-the-pants. Two more good firm rocks, and Kit cried out, trying and failing to muffle his ragged pleasure in Deacon's shoulder.

Oh, he had to know what was going on here. Deacon worked one hand beneath Kit's belt, stroked the soft/hardness of his belly -- he'd put on a couple of pounds but Deacon liked that, loved a little softness to his Omega -- and wriggled his fingers down to Kit's slit.

Good. Sweet. Lord. He'd never felt the like. Kit was so aroused he'd blossomed like a flower opening its petals, letting him right in, and deep as his fingers could stretch. Deacon curled those fingers, dragging their tips against his most sensitive spot, and barely managed to keep Kit from taking them both to the floor as a third climax rocked and rolled him. Kit's opening flexed and squeezed around his hand, clamping down hard, and be damned if feeling Kit this way wasn't almost as good as having that tightness around his dick.

One more, Deacon promised himself. One more before he asked *what the fuck*, because this shit was addictive as hell. He worked his hand to a side, barely feeling the way Kit scrabbled at him for purchase, and rubbed his thumb hard under the glans of Kit's still mostly erect cock. More slick coated them, and a jet of hot cum coated Deacon's hand as well.

Maybe just *one* more --

But no. Kit stopped, as stiff as he'd been when they started, and dazed again. He pushed at Deacon, trying to shove him back. "No," he panted. "No, I'm sorry, the sensation's too much, and my back --"

Deacon's left hand still rested at the small of Kit's back, and he could feel for himself that the muscles there had gone hard and tight as steel. Something was wrong. He cursed under his breath. "Kit, what's going on? Talk to me. Tell me what's happening."

"I --" Kit opened his mouth, then clamped his lips shut, staring over Deacon's shoulder with dismay-widened eyes. "Oh, *no*."

Now what -- Deacon turned his head so sharply he could almost hear a cartoon snap, glower ready at right around 10,000 watts.

Good thing, too. Ferdie had left the party, or at least Deacon had been sure he was headed that way, but there the needle-dicked Grand Canyon asshole was again, lurking at the top of the staircase that led down to the apartments above the shop front. Literally lurking, deliberately placing himself in the half-shadows and watching the two of them in a way that could only be described as predatory.

If, you know. Predators looked like a warthog on a bender.

Whatever. He had his eyes on Deacon's Omega like he had some naked plans going through his head, and that shit would not stand. Deacon snarled under his breath and started to push himself away from Kit, meaning to go and give Ferdie an object lesson in why that was a bad idea.

Kit caught him by the wrist before he could get more than a step away, and there was that steely grip of his again. "Don't," he warned. "I'm not going to have you spoil the party for everyone else by starting a brawl and getting the cops called."

Deacon made a sound of disbelief. "You've got to be shitting me. He's fucking stalking you, Kit. You said it yourself -- he won't leave you alone."

"No, but that's my problem. I'm the one who has to deal with him day to day when you're not here." Kit drew himself up, pale again but stubborn as hell. "I'll file a police report. Tomorrow."

Looked like he planned to say more, but any words on his tongue were cut off by a hiss of pain. Kit doubled over, catching himself against Deacon's chest, and poof, there went any thoughts of Ferdie -- who could, frankly, go fuck himself with a cactus. Deacon caught Kit and held him up until whatever was hurting him eased off, and by that time he had his own stubborn on. "File a police report? Like you're going to call your doctor tomorrow, maybe? No deal, Kit."

"It's not that bad," Kit said through gritted teeth.

"It's not that good either. Where do you hurt? Just in your back?"

"Nothing hurts. Now."

"You're a sorry liar, darlin'." Deacon patted him down, gentle as he could be, but when he got just slightly south of Kit's navel Kit gave a strangled yelp and shoved Deacon's hand away. His stomach muscles were so tight and hard Deacon could barely imagine the amount of tension required to keep them locked up so.

He prodded the spot again, hardening his heart to Kit's discomfort. "I ever tell you about my buddy Marshall? Nice guy. Fit as any other Marine. He caught a hot appendix instead of a bullet in a firefight, and I'm telling you that's what this looks and feels like."

"I don't have appendicitis," Kit said automatically, but he sounded doubtful. "I'd have other symptoms, wouldn't I?"

Deacon shook his head. "Doesn't matter. We're going downstairs now, Kit, and I'm calling 911. Only choice you get is whether or not I toss you over my shoulder again or if you can walk on your own."

Kit started to protest, but stopped. Deacon had a glare on him that, if looks could kill -- but he could see Deacon didn't care, and he wasn't budging. He was going to get Kit seen to, no matter what the cost. Kit mattered too much to him to risk losing for a second.

His Omega must have recognized that. He gave an impatient snarl and pushed past Deacon, but he was heading for the stairs and Ferdie had disappeared after making whatever point he'd wanted, so Deacon was going to count that as a win. All the same, Deacon followed him through the party and down the stairs. He loved Kit, but he could ride herd with the best of them when need be. And this? This needed to be.

Chapter Three

Deacon was right.

Though some might be surprised to learn this, Kit hated to lose an argument. He especially hated to lose because he was wrong, even if he did have enough sense to recognize the truth when he saw it. And he did.

He *hurt*. He hurt like he never had before, not even when he'd had a kidney infection -- had that bacteria come back? Was that what this was? -- and each of his steps down to the second floor was more like a lurch, awkward and ungainly. His body felt liquid in a bad way, heaviness settling where heaviness shouldn't and throwing him off balance, fear making his knees shake. Deacon hovered behind him, so plainly unsure whether he should hang back there to keep an eye on him or walk in front just in case Kit fell, *or* just save them both the trouble and carry Kit like he'd threatened, that despite everything the ridiculousness of the situation almost made Kit laugh.

He stopped long enough to reach back and lay a hand on Deacon's cheek, hoping the gesture said *I love you* better than his uncooperative lips and lungs could manage at the moment.

A flash of relief showed in Deacon's eyes. He understood. Good.

Not that such a moment was any kind of Faerieland's magic kiss that solved all their problems. By the time they reached the bottom of the steps, Kit was wishing Deacon had taken the decision out of his hands and carried him. His feet simply wouldn't hold him up. Without Deacon's quick rescue of an arm around his waist, he would have gone to the floor -- and been happy there.

He wanted to curl into a ball. He wanted to brace himself in a corner with his feet flat on the floor and -- and --

What?

He shook his head, not able to wrap his mind around the strange messages his body was sending him, and pointed instead to a comfy chair that the bookstore cat usually curled up and slept in. "There," he gasped. "Put me there. Call the ambulance. Please."

Deacon went ghost white.

Kit laughed at how easy he was to read, bless his heart; he must be thinking that such a willing surrender meant Kit was two steps from the grave. He patted the part of Deacon he could most easily reach -- his chest -- and managed a smile. "Just to be safe. I'm fine."

Relief swept into Deacon's expression, but it came with a side of raised eyebrow. Deacon could be comforted, but he wasn't going to be fooled.

It still worked. He guided Kit to the chair, escorted the bookstore cat out of its cushiony depths with a fairly admirable amount of restraint given the circumstances -- the cat hissed and spat at him, and Deacon only glowered back -- and settled him there.

"Stay." Deacon pointed a finger in Kit's face, then bent and kissed him hard, bruising-hard, and deep. "If you die on me I'll bring you back and wring your neck."

Kit laughed a third time, though he was nearly breathless. "Drama -- queen -- Marine," he panted. "Go. Call."

Deacon shook his head, but he went, digging his phone out of his pocket. He cursed and threw the device against the wall.

"Battery -- dead?"

"God *damn* it. Yes."

The drama queen Marine thing hadn't been entirely a joke. Kit pointed at the wall just past Deacon's shoulder. "Landline."

Deacon didn't waste time with even a nod of thanks. Just darted for the landline, crashing into the wall and leaving a Jarhead-sized hip-print in the drywall. "The fuck, Kit, this thing has a *rotary* dial. How fucking old is -- ? Like it matters. Never mind."

Kit didn't answer. Deacon needed to vent, so Kit let him vent. Besides, he'd been distracted by a hard fuzzy head thumping the side of his calf. The bookstore cat, a rakish black-white-and-orange spotted calico queen who everyone loved because she was so pretty, and who had left at least one scratch mark on anyone foolish enough to try and pet her. Kit blinked in disbelief as she meroweled and head butted him a second time.

"Do you just -- want up -- or are you trying to be sweet for once?"

As if he expected a cat to answer! But Kit tried scratching behind her ears just to test his luck. She flicked them both but didn't stop purring, and as if she'd been given permission scrabbled up the side of the armchair and parked herself on the top of the backrest, a looming presence over Kit's head.

Well, any port in a storm, and the noise she made, the sensation of her company, *was* soothing. Kit timed his breathing to the smoker's-rasp of her purrs and managed to get his air under control. That was better, that was --

Kit groaned and doubled over, abruptly ceasing to give a damn if he scared Deacon. God, this squeezing made it feel as if his balls were going to burst. On top of the twisting in his gut there was so much *pressure* between his legs that he --

He --

Kit went still. So very, very still, except for the tremors that shook his calves and knees. It couldn't be. There was no way. Surely not. He would have *known*. He wasn't un-self-aware for heaven's sake, he --

But --

The battered, comfortable old chair was deep and wide, made for a time when clothes were bulkier and sitting like a proper Omega was ever so important. Kit didn't give a particular damn about *that*, only that the chair had enough depth for him to draw his legs up and plant his heels on the cushion without falling off.

He closed his eyes, breathed a prayer without words or specific direction, and reached beneath his belt, his underwear, between his legs. And found what he was looking for.

Oh, *shit*. Oh, God.

"Deacon," he croaked, and then when Deacon didn't look up from shouting at the EMS to hurry their asses up, pounded the arm of the chair as hard as he could with his free hand. "Deacon! Deacon, come here!"

* * *

Shitfire and fuckballs, that did not sound good. Deacon dropped the phone, and pelted across the apartment toward Kit. He skidded to a stop on his knees in front of the chair.

What the --"What are you doing?" He started to pat Kit down. "Why are you sitting like that?"

Kit shook his head so hair his hair whipped over his eyes. He seemed to be struggling with his pants, trying to yank them down his hips, but his hands were wet with blood and something that smelled like pure Omega, and they kept slipping. Either he couldn't or wouldn't speak, and the cat sitting on top of his chair glared at Deacon as if the contrary beast would enjoy disemboweling him one claw slash at a time.

This day could not get any fucking stranger, but if Kit wanted his pants down then fine, Deacon would help. He slapped Kit's hands away as gently as he could and got a better grip on the pants than Kit could have managed. Not an easy task given the way Kit had his legs drawn up, but Deacon swore and tore and tugged and finally got the pants a decent way down, puddled around Kit's ankles. Normally he'd have found that silly enough looking to tease Kit about, but not now. Deacon hadn't seen anything like this since his blessedly brief emergency medical assistance training some years ago, but you'd have to be a bigger damn fool than Deacon was not to recognize a baby's head crowning when he saw one.

Even so, he dropped his hands in a second's worth of shock and horror. "Kit, what the *fuck*?"

"Fuck," Kit groaned. He bowed forward, and the baby well on its way to being born -- from what? From what the *fuck*, because aside from that little extra softness Deacon had noticed earlier Kit looked almost as slim as ever -- slid a little farther out.

Kit made a noise Deacon never, ever wanted to hear again, and the primal depth of it woke him up.

He didn't understand? Fine. There'd be time for explanations later. He gave himself a full-body rattling and settled down, tugging Kit's pants fully off and shoving Kit's thighs wider apart. They needed room to work, and there was no fucking time to waste, because one more spasm and somehow, God knew how, Deacon was quick enough to catch as the hard/soft roundness of a brand new person's head landed in his palm.

"Hush now, hush," he heard himself babbling. He stroked the blood-smeary insides of Kit's legs to soothe him. "Breathe. That's what you're supposed to do. I remember from my training. Just breathe, and let this happen. Can't get a thing undone when it's already half done."

A Kit in his right mind would have kicked Deacon in the face for that one, not that Deacon would have blamed him, but they were on the move again. An almighty -- something -- had Kit hard in its grasp, wringing him inside out, and with an almost audible *pop* the rest of the infant's body slid free of Kit's body.

Luck was on Deacon's side one more time, and he caught the baby without dropping him. He was still attached to Kit with a long, kinked rope of flesh, and he was covered in blood and slime and something like thick white wax. He weighed a good six or seven pounds by Deacon's automatic estimation, and he was far too damn big to have fit inside Kit's body at any point ever. Except he obviously just *had*, and by God, now he was opening dark blue eyes and a pink mouth in shock, then screwing up both to let out the most ball-shriveling shriek of indignation Deacon had *ever* heard.

Kit gaped at him, at the baby, so plainly in just as much shock that he couldn't speak -- and that made two of them. Somehow Deacon held the wriggly, flailing infant without dropping him, stared up at Kit, and felt as if he'd never manage to un-widen his eyes far enough to blink again in his life.

"What," he breathed. "Kit, *what*."

Kit could only shake his head, which would not have been a sufficient answer except that he started to shudder from top to toe and Deacon had to jump into action. Shock. Real shock, not just surprise, and he needed warmth. There was such a mess on the chair Deacon couldn't tell if he'd lost a genuinely significant amount of blood. That would have to wait for the paramedics.

But warmth he could do something about, if only on instinct. Deacon didn't realize he'd laid the baby between Kit's legs and gone bolting back up to Kit's apartment until he was there and grabbing the warm quilt they'd left all tousled over Kit's bed until he was on his knees in front of them a second time.

The world finally snapped back into focus as Deacon bundled the squirmy fragment of humanity up into his -- fucking fuck, into his bearing father's arms -- and tossed the quilt over both of them. He loosened its folds only far enough to make sure the little mite could breathe, and so he didn't have to take his eyes off either of them again.

"Don't drop him," he said, his lips numb. "Kit. How did this happen?"

Kit's lips were white, but bowed in a quick smile -- infuriating Omega -- as he said, "I guess maybe you should tell me. I didn't do this by myself."

That was *not* what Deacon had meant, not at all, but the whirling blue and orange of ambulance lights suddenly blasted through the windows from the street, and there were professionals with lots and lots of fucking wonderful professional equipment banging to be let in, and the world got even busier than it had been for a while. No time to stop and chat, but they were going to have some words later, he and Kit, and that was for damn sure.

And through the whole damn thing, that frigging cat stayed put and kneaded the top of the destroyed chair, purring fit to beat the band. No cat in the world could be happier.

Good for the cat, Deacon guessed. At least someone had things just the way they liked them.

* * *

Things only really started feeling real again when Jory got there. Up until then, Kit had the feeling he was only hanging on to reality by the barest edge of his fingernails. This couldn't have happened. He couldn't really have given birth, could he? But he had.

Unless he was dreaming? He might have been dreaming.

Yes, that was it. Maybe Ferdie had -- had thrown a bottle and Kit had taken a knock to the noggin. Or maybe he'd slipped coming down the stairs and hit his head that way. Maybe he was riding in the back of an ambulance on the way to get his appendix taken out. Or maybe he was still tucked up in his bed on a warm afternoon, curled around Deacon, with nothing more drastic to worry about than how long Deacon would stay this time.

He couldn't be sitting here in this utterly destroyed armchair with a cat wrapped defensively around his head and a wrinkled, squirming, squalling newborn flailing in his arms. He *couldn't*. It was too strange to be real.

But he remembered, so vividly, what it'd felt like to have that little body slide out of him. He recalled every second of -- his son's, dear God, his son's -- birth. "Deacon?" he asked through numbed lips. He was cold.

Deacon had his arms wrapped around Kit as best as a man could from the side -- when had that happened? -- and they tightened, but he could feel Deacon only shake his head in baffled answer to Kit's question.

And then, Jory. A commotion at the door, a

good-natured, practical Omega voice greeting paramedics -- when had they arrived? -- and shoulder-blocking his way through them as Kit lifted his head for a startled look.

"I called him," Deacon said in Kit's ear. His arms tightened a little more. "I didn't know who else."

No. That'd been perfect. Kit couldn't think of anyone he'd have wanted more, but his mouth wasn't working and his eyes had gone blurry. Why was he crying? What did he have to cry about? Jory wouldn't have cried. Look at him! Shaking hands and applying gentle elbows to get into the shop, all with his properly-carried-and-delivered son Chance strapped to his back, gumming philosophically on a Zwieback cracker and taking the rest of the world in his stride.

Kit laughed, a small thing, but the sound made Deacon relax like the air had just been let out of him.

His exhale drew Jory's attention, and Jory made quick work of the few steps toward Kit in his chair and knelt on the other side of him. If Jory gave a single damn about the mess he didn't let anything show. Just reached up and smoothed back Kit's tangled hair and grinned at him.

Kit reached for Jory's hand and took it.

Jory squeezed his fingers and winked past him at Deacon. "You know, I seem to remember back when I was still dancing around about hooking up with Darius, wondering if I could ever even could conceive, this Omega here was telling me stories about people giving birth without knowing they were pregnant. I believed you then, but you always go the extra mile to prove your point, don't you?"

"Just -- you wait until I feel better," Kit managed. Salt drops still clung to his cheeks, but Jory's calm teasing made him feel so much better. Like someone had turned the sun on in the room. Someone who understood and could help Kit make sense of things. "This is real?"

"Real as real could be, and he's beautiful. Have you looked at him yet? Really looked?" Jory reached down and somehow rearranged the bundle of squirming howls until it settled into a proper baby shape. "Look at that face! Omega or Alpha, he's going to be a heartbreaker when he grows up. Chance looked like a potato with legs when he was born, bless his heart."

Kit couldn't stop laughing now, no more than he'd been able to get control of himself earlier. "He did not! And he's right there. He can hear you."

Deacon laid his head on Kit's shoulder. He'd started muttering to himself, though Kit couldn't tell what he was saying. He could guess, though.

Kit reached, awkwardly but successfully enough, and carded his fingers through Deacon's hair. "Are you okay?"

Deacon's head came up with a jerk. "Am *I* okay?" he blurted, eyes huge. "Are you shitting me?"

"No, he's not," Jory said quietly. "Answer the man."

Both Kit and Deacon turned to stare at him, but whatever Deacon saw there had the same effect as a good hard shake. He blinked a few times, coughed, and nodded roughly. He took Kit's hand and held tight the way he always did, rough palms, gentle grasp, rubbing his thumb across the backs of Kit's knuckles. "I'm fine, darlin'. Surprised, but fine."

"Good," Kit said. "Because if you *weren't* surprised too, we'd have problems."

That made Deacon laugh too, finally, and Kit realized he'd been holding himself stiff and tense as a board as well. He bent his head, then cocked it, studying the baby. His son, too. Hesitant, as if afraid he'd break the little creature with too firm a touch, he reached out to brush a fingertip across one of its cheeks. "Look at that," he murmured. "Jory's right. He's beautiful."

The man in question made a satisfied noise and stood, dusting off his hands. "Jory is always right, and the sooner you learn that the better. Now!" he said over Deacon's automatic scoff and Kit's automatic razz. "Darius is on his way over with a truckload of all Chance's newborn things, and whatever else he can rustle up from the parents in the neighborhood."

"Hey, no, you don't have to --" Deacon started to protest. Kit could almost taste his injured pride. "I can --"

"Of course you can, and when you do, you can take all the loaner stuff back where each piece belongs. But you're not going any farther than the front steps tonight and nothing's open but Waymart anyway," Jory said, utterly unbothered. "Do you really want to go walking around Walmart right now? No, I didn't think so."

"Is this how you talk to your preschoolers?" Deacon demanded.

"When they need me to," Jory retorted. He studied them for a second, maybe two, and nodded again. "Now, about those front steps. Go downstairs and wait for Darius. He hasn't been here before. You can show him the way up and help him carry things."

"I'm not leaving Kit."

"I know you don't want to, but you need to," Jory said, and that *was* the way he spoke to his preschoolers. Kit recognized the tone. He put one hand on Deacon's shoulder, loose and casual the way an

Alpha would. "The EMTs need to check Kit over, and they haven't been able to get close enough yet. They need to check the baby too, though I can tell how healthy he is, and they need room to do all of that. You won't be going far, and I'll stay right here with Kit until they're done. All right?"

Or at least that was what Kit thought he said. The gist. He'd started having trouble tracking his surroundings again, but he got hold of himself. Lord, if he was so rattled that the cat had a set a defensive guard on him, what kind of vibes must a new father like Deacon be putting off? Jory had a clear head right now. His advice would be good. Kit would listen to him.

Deacon glanced dubiously at him. "Are you sure?" he asked Kit, not Jory.

Kit found a smile and gave it to Deacon. "Go on. I'll be here. And I'll be fine. We both will."

"You'd better be." Deacon caught Kit's hand and kissed the back of his knuckles. Oh, Kit loved him. Kit loved him so much his heart could burst from all the love inside, even if he still couldn't wrap his head around anything else. He *loved* Deacon. Even the way his knees popped like firecrackers as he stood and he didn't even wince. "I'll be downstairs. Call me if you need me. The second that you need me. I'll be here."

Deacon's words were a promise, and Kit believed him. Deacon wouldn't be there forever, that wasn't his way. But he would be here tonight.

That, he could count on.

Chapter Four

So, that'd happened.

That'd...

That...

Get your act together, Jarhead! Deacon gave himself a full-body shake, not giving a damn if doing so made him look like a wet hound dog. He took a deep, deep breath, holding the air inside until his lungs ached, and let it back out in a slow stream.

Better. Didn't help too much with the question marks swirling around in his head, but those weren't going anywhere any time soon. But he could feel his arms and legs again like proper limbs instead of sensationless pipe cleaners attached to his torso, and that wasn't nothing.

Shock, he diagnosed himself. A good old-fashioned shock. No *shit*, the events of the past hour had been something of a shock.

Maybe he'd stop repeating the same inane questions over and over inside his head if he kept breathing steady and deep. He reached into his pocket and almost pulled out a cigarette, rejected it -- bad for the -- for the -- well -- and found a toothpick he'd taken from beside the cash register at a truck stop, still wrapped in plastic. He bit the plastic off, spit it out, and wedged the toothpick between his incisors to worry at the sliver of wood.

Better still. Deacon shook his head in baffled wonder and shoved his hands in his pockets. That'd keep him while he waited for Darius. What did Darius look like? Deacon wasn't sure he remembered. They'd only met a couple of times at parties like the one they'd had tonight. Jory was the one usually hanging around, teasing the both of them and getting in the way.

Jory. Hell. When he'd been pregnant, he'd had a figure like he'd swallowed a basketball. By the end of his nine months, two basketballs, though he'd only delivered one baby. Kit had put on a pound or two of jiggle in the middle but he'd never looked like he was *pregnant*, not even when that baby slipped out of his body.

Be damned. Deacon could have lived until he was a hundred and never, ever forget what that had been like. What it felt like to catch an entirely new life in the palms of his hands. Bloody, messy, bright as a falling star.

How had he never noticed how busy this street was? Anyone could be Darius -- but no, the tall, lean black man pushing a dolly loaded to maximum capacity with a carrycot, a jumbo pack of diapers, and assorted other sundries seemed most likely. He had a vaguely familiar face, too.

Deacon raised a hand to wave at him. Alphas, he loved Alphas sometimes. No chit chat or a big to-do. Darius simply gave the dolly a shove his direction and ambled quietly to him, not speaking until he didn't have to shout to be heard.

"Jory inside? And Chance?"

"Your husband. And son. Yeah. Got here not that long ago."

Darius nodded. "Good. EMTs up there too?"

"Doing Omega things." Deacon shrugged to indicate that he'd been kicked out.

That made Darius crack a grin. "Best stay out of their way for the time being," he advised. "A baby, huh?"

Deacon flashed back to the sensation of the newborn in his hands, and the way the infant looked nestled in Kit's arms. Something -- different --

passed through him. It wasn't just that Kit was a beautiful Omega, that Omegas and babies went together like peanut butter and jelly, that the whole world just seemed right when Kit had a baby cradled to him, it was -- it was -- Deacon couldn't find the right words.

"Congratulations." Darius clapped him on the shoulder, then settled in across the stoop. "Once they say we can come up, I'll help carry." He studied Deacon for a moment. "You look like you just got knocked over by a runaway train."

"I look like hammered shit and twelve miles of bad road," Deacon said. He'd caught a glance at his reflection in the glass of the door, and he hadn't been a pretty sight. "And like I just escaped *The Shining*."

Darius laughed, a low and quiet rumble. "Yeah. Birth gets messy. Same happened to me, back when."

"You knew yours was coming."

"Even so." Darius raised one shoulder. "Next baby'll be second verse same as the first."

Deacon raised an eyebrow in question.

"Next June," Darius said. He looked abruptly both lost in thought, and like they were damned good thoughts. "Jory's something else when he's got his mind made up on what he wants."

Deacon snorted. Yeah, he could empathize. "Think we should have cigars or something?"

"I think the EMTs would skin you alive if you came back up stinking of smoke," a new voice said behind Deacon, startling him -- him, who'd been in fucking firefights -- so badly that he nearly jumped out of his skin. He twisted at the waist to glare at Zane, who could apparently walk like a fucking cat when he wanted to, and wasn't that good to know. At least he hadn't brought *his* son strapped to his back. "Where did you come from?"

"The cabbage patch, if you asked my bearer when he was sober," Zane said laconically. "Otherwise, I figure the root cause was good old fashioned fucking. From what I hear, you should be familiar."

"How in the hell did you hear?" Deacon demanded. "Did someone send out a bulletin?"

Darius cleared his throat. "This walls. Also, you've got to realize someone told Jory. Word just seems to spread after that point."

Fair enough. Deacon sighed. "Did you just come by to give me a hard time?"

"Turnabout's fair play. You must have given Kit one hell of a 'hard' time nine months ago," Zane said with one of his puckish, lopsided grins. He dug in his pockets, and pressed square packets into both Deacon and Darius's hands.

Deacon glanced down. "Candy cigarettes?"

Darius laughed again, shook his head, and tapped out a candy cigarette to tuck in the corner of his mouth. "I have never met this man before, and I already know not to argue with him," he said when Deacon frowned. "Eat one. The sugar will do you good."

Zane thumped him on the back, reminding Deacon of why he liked this contrary, un-Omega-like Omega in the first place, and settled down in a comfortable lean. Deacon eyed him, wondering how different Zane's life would have been if he had gone into the service instead of taking a single father's road. He'd have gotten endless PT for all the shit he would undoubtedly have pulled, but he was whipcord lean and strong even after having a kid, and he had a sharp mind.

"I did come to give you a hard time," Zane said. "Also to say hi to Kit and the baby. S'only polite. And to do the dishes and the laundry. Don't tell me no. Neither one of you is going to have the chance or feel up for much for the next few days." He nudged a bulging grocery store bag at his foot that Deacon hadn't noticed before. "And I'm making you like three casseroles and putting together as many sandwiches as your fridge can hold. Trust me. You'll be glad you have them."

Deacon stared. He and Zane were friends, sure, but..."Why would you do all that?"

"Because I remember how much I'd wished someone would have done this for me," Zane said. He brushed straight past any chance of Deacon or Darius reacting to that, narrowing his eyes at something across the street. "Buy me a steak dinner someday if you feel obligated and shit. There's one more reason I came by. Don't move, don't go do something stupid, but a good old fashioned death glare that-a-way might be a good idea."

Damn it to hell, what now? Deacon turned his head, and when he saw what Zane saw he bared his teeth. Fucking. Ferdie. How the devil had he even heard? Or had he just seen the ambulance lights, heard the sirens, and decided to come sniffing around?

Deacon officially did not care. The glare Zane had suggested came hand in hand with that, and naturally too, vicious as a junkyard dog.

Ferdie paled a touch under his pimples, but he'd found an ounce or two of balls somewhere. He offered Deacon a mockery of a salute, pointed up at the apartment with the kind of smug look that itched to be knocked off his face, and sauntered away.

Right about then, Deacon realized Darius had

hold of one arm, and Zane the other. He shook them off, irritated. "I'm not going after him." *At the moment.* "Ferdie's not worth the trouble." *Not worth the trouble right now, that is. When the time's right, Ferdie's worth and due an ass-kicking so intense he's gonna taste my boot leather every time he burps.* "I've got other things to worry about."

That, at least, was true. Through the glass door, Deacon could see the EMTs packing up and getting ready to head out. They must be about ready to let him back in.

He swallowed a huge knot that seemed to stick in his throat.

Zane knocked shoulders with him. "You'll be all right," he said, quiet enough that Darius might not have heard. "We'll take care of what needs taking care of, so go on, now. Kit's going to need you. Go be with your Omega."

* * *

Deacon usually took the stairs up to Kit's two or three at a time, so eager to get there he went faster with every leap. Kit would almost always hear him coming and laugh, tease him about his eagerness.

Tonight, he went slow. One step at a time.

He could do this. He could. He already was doing this, for fuck's sake, it was just...

He still hadn't wrapped his mind around what'd happened. Zane had. Darius had. Jory had. The paramedics had all clapped him on the back and congratulated him on their way out. They'd moved Kit up to the bedroom in his apartment, they'd said, where he'd be more comfortable, and gotten him settled. He'd have to come in for a follow-up with a real doctor the next day, but he was healthy. No need for a hospital tonight.

Which was good. Really.

Just.

Kit had had a baby. He was a father. *Deacon* was a father. Doubtful anyone would blame him for having butterflies fucking disco-ing in his stomach, but that wasn't going to help either of them.

Still. Would have been relaxing to hear Kit's laugh. Instead there was only silence. Deacon paused to cock his head. He wasn't unfamiliar with this kind of quiet, actually. He'd come home at odd hours every now and again and caught Kit asleep, or maybe reading, too deep in a book to notice anything but the words on the page and the pictures they made in his head.

There. That last one, that was what Deacon had noticed. The silence of total absorption, and it didn't take a genius to figure out what would have Kit so absolutely fascinated. His baby. His son.

Kit's son. *Deacon's* son. He was a *dad*. Holy *shit*.

Took more than coming in an Omega to make a father, though. Deacon knew that. So he'd better man up to the job, hadn't he? Deacon got hold of himself, steeled his balls, and his spine, and took the last few steps up to Kit's apartment door.

When he tried the knob, he found the lock wasn't engaged. The door slid open quieter than usual, or maybe it was that Deacon wasn't flinging things around like he normally did. There was something extra in that almost-silence, the sound of a second, smaller person breathing, that made him want to move slowly, quietly.

That smaller person. Deacon breathed deeply without meaning to as the door came open and got a heady whiff of things he'd mostly only experienced at a distance -- blood, shit, livery afterbirth, fecund salty

Omega bonding hormones. Milk, or was that formula? Warm skin so new its owner didn't know what to make of the air surrounding him.

Kit sat propped up in bed, all the pillows Deacon remembered him owning and some he didn't recognize tucked around him like a makeshift throne. Light from the bedside lamp didn't quite cast a halo around his head, but Deacon couldn't help feeling like he was in the presence of something just about that worthy.

There was a blanket-wrapped bundle in Kit's arms, and all Kit's attention was fixed there. Or so Deacon had thought. He glanced up when Deacon took an uncertain step forward, and there was that smile of his. Deacon let out a long, deep breath he hadn't known he was holding.

"Hi," Kit said so quietly his voice was almost a whisper.

Deacon couldn't take another step just yet, but he bowed his head in a nod. "Hi."

The bundle in Kit's arms stirred and a tiny arm poked up out of the tangle. The owner of that arm let out an unholy squawk and waved its fist as if he had a *point* to make, damn it, and they'd better shape up and listen.

Laughter burst out of Deacon, loud before he muffled the noise, but Kit's returning laugh echoed his and some sort of indefinable frozen ice between them shattered and crumbled away. "That him?" he asked, pointing with his chin.

"I'm not sure if the bookstore cat would beg to differ, but he's not a stray kitten." Kit adjusted himself, sitting up a little straighter, with only a slight wince. Tough little Omega. He beckoned with a nod. "Come here and see for yourself?"

Now or never. Deacon swallowed hard around a knot in his throat and came there. Went there. Whatever. Point was, his feet moved forward and he found himself a careful perch on the edge of the bed where he could see past those swaddling blankets.

"I thought Jory said he was beautiful. He looks like a wet gremlin," he blurted in blank surprise, then braced himself for a punch in the nose.

Didn't happen. Kit was laughing again, eyes raised to the ceiling. "I've seen your baby pictures. You didn't look any better."

"Yeah, I've seen 'em too. Wish I could disagree." Deacon stretched a tentative finger toward the baby, wondering if that little fist would grab on.

It did. Locked those tiny fingers around his and held tight.

Deacon's ribs strained under the pressure of what was happening to his heart. He swallowed again and couldn't get that knot to go down, but somehow he didn't give a damn.

"I think I know when this must have happened," Kit said, though his gaze was locked on to the tiny hand and Deacon's finger. "About thirty-seven weeks ago, when you were just coming back from that long run through Texarkana. I'd had a bug and I was on --"

"Antibiotics, I remember." Deacon hesitated. "I wore a rubber, though. I remember that too."

Kit lifted one shoulder. "Nothing works a hundred percent of the time. Maybe there was a micro-tear in the latex. Or -- you had one rough nail. Your thumb, where you'd caught the cuticle on a packing crate. I remember you scratched me by accident."

One little nick in the condom, yep, and that could have done the trick. Deacon nodded. He hadn't thought anything of the incident at the time besides being sorry he'd accidentally hurt the man he loved. But that might well have been when this whole thing started, all right.

"I didn't have any idea," Kit said. He held the bundle a little closer. "None. Do you believe me?"

Deacon frowned. "What? 'Course I do. *I* didn't have any idea and I was all over you every chance I got between then and now. Hell, Kit, no one could have laid eyes at you and known a thing was going on. How'd you manage that, anyhow?"

Kit only shook his head; no idea about that either, it seemed. "Maybe I'll put the rest of the pieces together later. I just…" He bit his lip, and he wouldn't look up at Deacon. "I remember my parents," he said, very quietly. "I remember every time one of my siblings was born we knew about the pregnancy from the start. All of us. With all the screaming and blaming, the whole neighborhood knew."

Ah. Deacon thought he was starting to get the picture, to see what was eating away at Kit. "Got no plans to scream at you," he said with a shrug. "I didn't even think about wanting to."

One corner of Kit's mouth lifted, and his shoulders relaxed a fraction. The baby made a *growf* noise and did something with his head that made Kit yelp. Before he knew what he was doing, Deacon had both hands underneath the surprisingly heavy bundle to support the baby's weight, and was looking down, and --

"Oh," he said, startled. "You're, uh…"

Kit's cheeks went red. "It's only colostrum."

"Only what, now?"

"You probably don't want to know. He had formula, to fill him up, but this has antibodies." Kit's already-red cheeks flamed. "Jory explained how it works and showed me how, with Chance." He stroked a fingertip across their son's cheek. "And we're going to leave the subject at that. Okay?"

Super-fine by Deacon. He reached out and tried a stroke on that chubby little cheek himself, amazed by how soft his son's skin was. "My parents fought too," he said. "Not like yours, but still. Seemed like they never stopped."

"I know. I wish your childhood had been better for you."

"And you."

Deacon tried another swallow, and the lump that kept forming in his throat went down easier this time. The world was starting to slot into place for him. He was beginning to see where the pieces went, or where they needed to go, and if he didn't have the full picture yet he had enough to get the gist.

Shit that happened to kids left scars. He already knew if anyone ever tried to hurt his son, there wouldn't be enough left of them to make a greasy stain on the sidewalk, where they would have landed after he'd tossed them out of a top-story window. Or blasted a handful of caps up their asses.

But of the people who could hurt his son, he had to put himself on that list. He had to do this right. Show Kit he wasn't like their parents, either set, and neither was Kit. That they hadn't expected this, but that they could rise to the occasion.

And that was where words would fail. Hell, they'd never been Deacon's strong suit anyhow.

But where words would fail, action would succeed. Or at least it should. Always had. And that? That *was* his strength. He might have to make up most of the *how* as he went along, but he could manage as much. And he would. He wouldn't leave Kit again, for one thing. Not ever again. He wondered, just for a moment, why the thought of abandoning his wandering ways didn't hurt at all, but he hardly had room in his head to dwell on that.

Deacon's heart took up too much of his attention, and he suspected that would be the status quo from now on.

Yep. He had some plans to make. This was where everything changed.

Chapter Five

Kit woke the next morning with the fiercest craving for coffee, needing caffeine like he needed air, and the absolute certainty that he wouldn't be able to have any for months. He knew exactly where he was, and remembered down to the last detail what'd happened the night before.

Having a baby still didn't seem quite real, but ye gods, did he remember the birthing, all right. His body was happy to remind him every time he shifted his legs.

He opened his eyes and reached across the mattress. Though he'd left a knot of tangled sheets and a by-now-cool depression where his body had been, there was no Deacon to be found -- Kit stuffed down a quick stab of disappointment -- but there *was* a baby's bed set up just within reach.

Lying inside, the baby -- *his* baby -- stared back at him with wide, baffled eyes. Kit's lips parted in a grin. He knew those eyes. Those were Deacon's eyes, and that was exactly the same look he gave Kit whenever the situation left him lost for words but ready to remember how to swear a blue streak until the world made sense again.

"Can't help you with that one," Kit said. He offered the baby his forefinger, marveling at how strongly he took hold. Someone had wrangled him into a green flannel onesie, adding a nightcap with a silly tassel and a set of fluffy socks. "Did Deacon get you all dressed up?"

Blink.

"I suppose it'll be a little while before we can hold a real conversation. I'm sorry I didn't know about you," Kit said, flexing his finger slightly. "And I'm not sure what to tell you about your father. I don't know when he left. He's not... he's not the kind who stays all the time. He'll love you. He does love you. I'm sure of that. He's just not going to be here every day, or most days, and I'll help you figure out that that's okay. It's better than..."

Forty weeks of fighting, like every time his parents got knocked up. Bitter shouting for years afterward, each resenting the other for the added burden, the new anchor weighing them down, pawning the rest of the work off on Kit and any of the other kids old enough to change a diaper or give a bath.

Kit shook his head, slow but determined. He would never have a life like that again, and he would never make his son feel that kind of misery. Which meant being straight with him, always. "We love your father -- Deacon -- just the way he is," Kit said firmly. "If you love people, you have to let them go. If they love you, they come back."

Mostly. Usually. But this was all so unexpected. What if Deacon had decided new fatherhood was too... much. Too soon. Too... everything. Kit cleared his throat. "If it ends up being just you and me, if that happens, then we'll be fine. You'll see. What do you say?"

The baby smacked his lips, an already familiar signal. He said he was hungry, that's what, and someone had better hop to action. Kit chuckled as he hurried to sit up, only wincing a little. Just like when he was being born, Kit's body seemed to know what to do and how. Blew his mind.

He couldn't mess this up. Maybe he hadn't had nine months of mental preparation like every other bearing Omega out there, but he was catching up fast.

He already loved this boy with so much ferocity the emotions nearly knocked him down. He *wouldn't* mess this up. Bending carefully, he scooped his son out of the bed and cradled him on his shoulder. "Let me get a glass of water," he said in the curve of that tiny ear. "And then we'll have your turn."

With the baby in careful balance, Kit padded from the bedroom through the short corridor and took the left turn toward his kitchen, and -- stopped. Stopped stock still, too surprised to take another step.

Deacon was still here. He hadn't gone anywhere. He stood in the middle of that kitchen, wrapped haphazardly in an apron liberally coated with flour, egg, possibly milk, and a few smears of things Kit couldn't identify right away. The bedroom had smelled too strongly of baby and his own body to have picked up any other odors from in there, but out here Kit could smell sausage sizzling in a frying pan, scrambled eggs with pepper, slightly scorched toast, melty butter and honey and -- tea?

He didn't own any tea bags. He would have known. And -- Deacon was still here? Making a mess, and breakfast to boot? Without being asked?

He was still *here*?

Kit hadn't stopped blinking, trying to process, when Deacon must have sensed him. He raised his head and flashed Kit a bright grin. "There you are. I was going to come wake you up next. Ready for breakfast?"

I -- what?

* * *

Two weeks in, and the way Deacon figured he was almost sort of starting to get the hang of this fatherhood business. Not too shabby! Another month or so and he might have the business down. It helped

that Felix -- they'd picked their son's name together --
was a super-chill little guy. Totally cool.

He shrugged on his jacket, taking the garment
from the hook by Kit's door where it more or less lived
these days -- just like him -- and patted the sleeve. *I feel
you, buddy. Life's not so bad though, parking in the same
place every night, huh*? He hadn't realized how tired he
was starting to get of the road going ever on and on
and on, of gas station burritos and truck stop meatloaf
and cheap motels with mildew in the showers and the
stink of skunky weed lingering in the walls.

Being a homebody wasn't bad. Not even a little.
Who knew? Deacon had jumped in early and
established himself as pretty good with a broom and
mop, as well as a duster on the high shelves, and he'd
managed not to poison either of them with his cooking
before Kit was back up to doing more than pressing
buttons on the microwave. Which they mostly still did,
having a neighborhood's worth of well meant
casseroles to get through, but whatever. Deacon liked
tuna noodle just fine and Kit made bitchin' grilled
cheeses when they wanted something fresh.

Every night he went to bed under clean sheets
that smelled of Omega and affection, curled up next to
a warm body that always ended up snuggled under his
arm by morning. Baby Dude might have a screech as
loud as an air horn when he wanted feeding or
changing or he got bored, but he was barely fourteen
days old. How else was he supposed to let them know
something wasn't right? Take three steps out of the
crib, curtsy, and say "Father, may I?"

A pretty damn good deal, if you asked Deacon.
And all these changes for the better had taken was a
baby. Who knew?

Though... hell, sometimes he did stop and

wonder. Shouldn't he miss the road more? Hadn't being a Marine, then being a trucker, been all he'd thought he ever wanted? Why didn't he yearn for that life now?

And... sometimes, not all the time but sometimes, he caught Kit looking at him as if he couldn't manage to wrap his head around what Deacon had up his sleeve, so to speak.

But Deacon figured he'd be a damn fool to not only look a gift horse in the mouth but demand to count its teeth. Kit knew he could trust Deacon, right? He'd know Deacon wasn't going to run out on them. His old family had been replaced with something worth staying for.

This whole family thing was all just new to Kit too. They'd adjust. Both of them would.

Kit popped out of the kitchen with a piece of pumping apparatus -- Deacon knew better than to ask details on the thing -- in one hand, and a drying cloth in the other, hair tousled and expression startled. "You're leaving?"

"Yeah, for a little bit." Deacon popped his collar to make Kit grin, mildly disappointed when the move didn't work. Always had before. He'd snort and ask him who he thought he was, James Dean? *Oh well. Next time.* "I've got a taste for corned beef with sauerkraut and some spicy mustard that'll burn my nose hair out. Heading down to the deli. You want one too?"

Kit did snort then, but almost as if he was confused, not amused. He recovered himself so fast Deacon didn't have a chance to ask. "Only if you want to know what colic sounds like in a newborn who's got a stomach full of secondhand horseradish. I don't think Felix would forgive either of us."

"Baby Dude," Deacon corrected.

There, that got the reaction he wanted. Kit swatted him with the drying cloth. "*Felix.*"

"Lucky," Deacon countered with a grin. "That's what Felix means, right?" He ducked in to kiss Kit on the cheek, a little more domestic than their usual kind of kiss, but he didn't know. Gentle seemed to fit. "No spicy shit, fine. Turkey club?"

Kit hesitated, but then nodded. "With bacon."

"You got it," Deacon said, cheered. "Back in fifteen or less. Keep it warm for me."

"Keep *what* warm?" Kit called after him as he started to take the stairs down at his usual three at a time.

Deacon stopped at the bottom to wink up at him. "Whatever you want, darlin'."

He left whistling, a spring in his step. See? He was getting the hang of this just *fine*.

The neighborhood was getting the hang of him being there, too. People whose names he knew and those he still hadn't learned brightened up when they saw him, waved or nodded to him, and there were a couple of "Congratulations!" still coming his way as word got around. Deacon returned every one, feeling somehow bone-deep satisfied. He liked the folks in Kit's neighborhood. Some rough, some polished, but all good people.

Except one.

Deacon didn't see him at first as he turned the corner, headed for the deli, but three steps down that particular stretch of sidewalk and he couldn't have missed the big asshole loitering in the doorway of a closed, shuttered storefront. Ferdie. He had his arms crossed and one hip cocked, so plainly thinking he was the biggest and baddest thing to roll through here since the bobcats and bulldozers that'd built the place, an ugly smirk on his face. "How's the baby?" he asked as Deacon tried to be the bigger man and pass him without engaging. "Who's he look like?"

That was too damn weird, and brought Deacon to a stop. "Say again?"

Ferdie raised one shoulder. "As gone as you are all the time, just seems you'd stop and wonder. Who's that baby look like? Kit? Or someone else?"

Oh hell no, he was not suggesting what Deacon thought. All thought of the deli forgotten, Deacon turned to face needle-dick straight on. "You want to say that again?"

Ferdie paled slightly under his red nose and cheeks, but he had as much stupidity as he had nerve. "You heard me."

Deacon worked his jaw. By God, he'd never wanted to pop someone in the face so much. He could almost feel Ferdie's nose crunching under his fist, but if he came home bloody and bruised, then Kit would blow his stack. Besides, he didn't want Felix seeing him like that. He didn't want to scare his Baby Dude.

"Piss off," Deacon said at last. "Keep pissing. Don't stop till you're out of my sight, and if you get back in it, you and I are going to be having more than words. You get me?"

"I got you. Do you get *me*?" Ferdie took a step forward. "Or maybe, you've got to wonder, did Kit get me? At least once, while you were gone?"

Deacon's fists were knotted tight by the end of that, and there was no telling what might have happened next if a warm arm as hard and sturdy as cordwood hadn't landed heavily across his shoulder just then. A scent as familiar as family surrounded him, Alpha-Marine-brotherhood-safe, and the last person he'd imagined seeing again for a while grinned at him.

Marshall, one of his platoon brothers back in the day. Marshall had gone into extreme sports when Deacon went into trucking, but they both traveled just as much and knew how to take care of themselves.

"Got a problem, brother?" Marshall asked genially. That was his specialty -- smile while you were smackin' 'em around.

"Depends." Deacon jerked his head at Ferdie. "You think he's tough enough for both of us?"

"He might think so. Or might not, since all that's left of him by now is dust."

Deacon turned to look, and sure enough Ferdie had taken to his heels. So much for the spoonful of balls he'd found the night Felix was born. Fucking chicken shit, and mouthy little ass to boot. How dared he --

"Calm down, jarhead." Marshall gave Deacon a light shake to keep him in check. "What'd he say to get you so hot under the collar, anyhow? That's a rhetorical question, by the way, I heard every word. And I heard a few things on my way into town. You got yourself a kid, man? Fucking congratulations!"

The arm around his shoulder shifted and Marshall was giving him a good hard hug, the kind anyone with weak ribs wouldn't survive. Deacon found himself grinning again, pounding on Marshall's back hard enough to drive nails through his shoulder blades. Exactly as a hug should go.

Deacon felt better when Marshall let him go. Mildly bruised, sure, but better. "You hear all the gory details?"

"Enough. You delivered him yourself? Tough as nails, my brother, I'm impressed."

Deacon wrinkled his nose. "Yeah, and next time he gets knocked up I'm driving him to the hospital two weeks before he's due. We can set up a tent on the sidewalk and wait."

Marshall roared a laugh. A big guy, four inches taller than Deacon's respectable six feet, he'd grown a Viking red beard to go with his barely contained biker hair, and he had a couple of scars that'd give a man pause, but enough good nature in his system you barely noticed them after the first glance. "You try and make him do that. I'll sell tickets and bring popcorn."

Deacon hooted. "Yeah, maybe. Doesn't mean I won't try."

"You would," Marshall agreed. He cocked his head. "You know, before I heard about all this, I was going to ask if you wanted to head down to Cozumel with me. I've got a plus one and no takers and there's a wakeboard thing going on. Figured you'd be all over that."

And for an awful, wonderful second, Deacon was. The old excitement for adventure he'd thought was sleeping blazed to life, and he opened his mouth -- and shut it. Temptations were just that -- tempting -- that was their job -- but he had bigger things now. "Can't," he said simply. "I've got responsibilities."

Marshall nodded in approval and gave Deacon a good hard thump on the shoulder. "When the kid's older, I'll bring all three of you with me somewhere. Give you a good beach vacation. But I'm sticking around for a few days, and you'd better have me over to dinner one night. Or come out, whichever. You've got my number."

"Man, it's a deal," Deacon said. He traded grips with Marshall. "See you around, brother. Keep yourself out of trouble between then and now."

Marshall's gaze had shifted to a lithe, pretty Omega with long red hair, walking the opposite direction. "You better believe I will. Go on home, now. Enjoy your good luck."

Deacon planned to. As soon as he had sandwiches. He couldn't wait to tell Kit about this. Surely that'd soothe a few of his doubts, wouldn't it?

Chapter Six

No one could have done a better job of learning to be a father. No Alpha in Kit's experience, anyway, not even Darius, and Darius was, as Jory would have the world know, a prince among men. And domesticity wasn't what Kit had expected of Deacon, not at all.

He knew this couldn't last forever. Sooner or later Deacon's nature would get the better of him, and he'd be off again. Kit was ready for that day. He'd prepared his heart, even if the stubborn thing *would* still jump into his throat every time he saw Deacon pick up his keys or put on his coat.

It was practice, he told himself. The day Deacon left to be true to himself, he'd let Deacon go with a smile, and wait for him to come back. He would never tie the man down against his will. That didn't mean he couldn't show his appreciation for what Deacon had done so far, and while Deacon had been off getting them sandwiches, Kit had gotten busy making preparations of another sort.

He waited, breathless, in the living room, listening for the sound of Deacon's tread on the stairs with his heart in his throat. This, if he had his way, was going to be a night to remember. He knew he'd gotten everything exactly right when Deacon threw open the door, dropped his bag of sandwiches on the floor, and gaped at him without blinking.

Kit stood from the ottoman where he'd perched to wait, bare of any stitch of clothing, and let his arms fall to his sides without trying to hide his bearer's body. He'd healed as well as he'd carried and delivered, and he was a little softer around the middle than he had been before, a little fuller in his pecs, but that only made him more of an Omega. He stood still, not breaking eye contact, letting Deacon see his nakedness, every bit that Kit could offer him, and his willingness to offer and be taken. "Welcome home," he murmured. "I've been waiting for you."

"You…" Deacon started. He stopped and shook his head hard. "What?"

Kit walked toward him, slow and easy to avoid aggravating the last little aches that still hung on. "I think you know what," he said, so quietly he wouldn't have woken a mouse, much less the infant tucked up milk-drunk and asleep in his bed. "I think you know exactly what." He came close enough to smell Deacon's rich Alpha scent, for their chests to touch when they breathed in and out. "I think you want what I want too."

And yes, he did. Kit knew that look in a man's eye. In Deacon's eye. Yet Deacon tried, bless his heart, to take a step back. "You can't be healed up enough."

"But I can. Mostly. And if you're worried, there's more than one way to please a Kit."

"Thought the phrase was 'skin a cat'."

"I'm already skinned," Kit said, taking another step closer. If he'd been a real cat and had a tail he would have wound its length about Deacon's legs. "Breathe me, Deacon. Know that I want you. Will you have me?"

There was no more unfair question to ask an Alpha, and Kit wasn't the least bit ashamed of asking. He did want this. So much. As much as he loved Deacon, and that was enough to overflow the world and everything in it.

He knew he'd won when Deacon groaned, and exulted in the sensation when Deacon's arms went around him. Deacon set the edge of his teeth to Kit's throat. "Anything hurts, you tell me. Promise me."

Kit swooned into him, dizzy with pleasure. "I promise."

"What you want, you tell me. Or show me. No guessing."

"I promise." Kit wound his arms around Deacon's neck and drew him up, down, deep into a kiss. "I want this."

And that was what it took. That was what he got. And more, so much more... Almost as much as his heart wanted.

"And I want *this*, too."

Kit had positioned them just where he wanted them, and one light little push was all he needed to topple Deacon backwards onto his bed. Deacon's arms windmilled as he fell and he landed with a startled "Oof!" but he bounced back up to rest his weight on his elbows. The grin he gave Kit was a delighted one.

"When you make your mind up about something you don't mess around, do you, darlin'?"

Kit gave him grin for grin, his own feeling a little feral and a lot hungry. Maybe this hunger was down to all the hormones. Maybe it came from being near Deacon for the last two weeks, but not *with* Deacon. The man was a walking temptation no matter the circumstance. "And here I haven't even gotten started yet."

"Well then." Deacon cocked his head. "Far be it from me to stand in your way."

"You're lying down."

"So I am." Deacon's hot gaze asked, *going to do something about that, Kit?*

Damned right he was. Kit put one knee on the edge of the bed, nudging Deacon's legs apart so he'd have room to crawl between them, and settled between Deacon's thighs. Deacon winced slightly, no doubt not used to having to spread so wide, but Kit had plans that needed room. He settled on his heels and leaned over Deacon to capture his mouth in a hard, deep, hungry kiss.

Mmm. Deacon dropped one arm and lifted his head to return the kiss with interest. He caught at Kit's bottom lip with the edge of his sharp teeth and nibbled, angling them to one side so he could take control again.

Or try to. Kit put a hand over Deacon's sternum and pressed down, gentle but firm. When he was sure Deacon would lie still -- humoring him, but that was fine -- he let his fingers drift downward. The thin material of Deacon's Raglan tee wrinkled up into ridges that allowed Kit to slid his palm beneath and caress warm bare skin that was hard with muscles that flexed slightly with each breath and hitched as Kit's hand drifted lower.

Kit hooked up the waist of Deacon's jeans, just far enough to tease inside and to give himself room to draw his zipper down. He paused to admire Deacon's underwear choice -- simple navy cotton tight enough to support and display a package worthy of admiration.

"Darlin', you're killing me here," Deacon said hoarsely.

Kit bent his head and put his lips to the furry trail just below Deacon's navel, murmuring against his skin, "I know."

Deacon groaned, but Kit detected appreciation therein. He nipped Deacon's skin, catching a thin pinch between his teeth, and slid his wandering hand down the open fly of Deacon's jeans. He cradled Deacon's balls, finding them full and firm, smelling of Ivory soap and spicy Alpha musk. *Delicious.* They rolled gently in his palm, and his cock jerked when Kit squeezed ever so gently.

"This is a murder in progress," Deacon declared. "Help, help, baby, I'm being repressed."

If he'd meant to make Kit laugh with that, it worked. If he'd meant to distract him, it failed. Kit hooked two fingers under the waistband of Deacon's briefs, now gratifyingly damp over the head of his cock, and pulled them down out of the way. His mouth watered at the sight of Alpha cock, hard as rock purely from wanting *him*, and he almost swallowed before changing his mind. He dropped his head and engulfed Deacon's cock in one filthy, dripping-wet gulp that made Deacon arch off the bed and shout fit to make the windows rattle.

Deacon clapped a hand over his mouth before Kit could do as much for him, and for a second they waited in breathless silence. They'd made a nursery out of the room Kit had mostly used for storage before. It wasn't big and so far it wasn't much, but Felix liked it, and it was right next door. The walls weren't thick.

Silence answered them. Felix hadn't woken up. *Thank God.* Relief and desire both made Kit ferocious when he got back to the serious business of sucking dick as if Deacon were a banquet and he'd been starving. He had. He needed this. Needed Deacon, so much. So, so much.

Kit tamped that down carefully and reached for Deacon's balls again, wanting to feel them go tighter and harder as he pushed Deacon toward orgasm -- but before he could do more than take hold, Deacon reached down and seized his shoulder. When he looked up, Deacon's face glowed red with arousal and barely-repressed cravings, and the arm that held him was strong as iron.

"It's occurring to me that this is all a little one-sided, darlin'." Deacon raised himself to a sitting position, his heels hooking momentarily around Kit's ass in a way that made Kit's hardening cock jump with interest. They almost never did this the other way around, but --

But that wasn't what Deacon had in mind. He pulled at Kit's shoulders, guiding him down. Pushing him this way, prodding him that, even tugging at his ankles until Kit got the idea and lay down next to Deacon, upside down so that they must have resembled a pair of commas curled against one another. His mouth was still at Deacon's groin, but now Deacon's was at *his* and Deacon's hands were busy freeing Kit's cock.

Kit moaned and thrust toward the first press of Deacon's mouth over his still-covered erection. "Yes," he said in a hurry, before Deacon could even ask. "Yes, Deacon. I want this. I promise."

Deacon licked at Kit's channel and purred -- there was no other word for the sound. "Good." Then his mouth sealed around Kit's cock, and all Kit's ability to think flew straight out the window. Kit gasped and thrust forward, seeking *more*, more wetness, more heat, more friction. His channel clenched hard, almost hurting for a second before mild discomfort blossomed into something just one breath shy of coming.

"More," he begged, trying to remember how to suck while being sucked, and managing only to mouth uselessly as a baby bird at Deacon's thighs, his balls, his cock. "Deacon! More."

Deacon slapped his hip, sparking another of those near-orgasmic surges. Kit could feel wetness trickling out of him, and gasped when Deacon caught the liquid on his tongue and swallowed. More, he wanted? More, he'd get. A finger tracing the soft furrow that led to his channel, a slow slide inside on the slickness that leaked in a slow, steady patter. He was *so* gentle on tissues that were still a little sore that his touch turned everything to bliss, and from bliss the growing sense of something big, something that would split him open, and all the while wet heat surrounded his cock. His thoughts flashed back to what it'd felt like to *be* split apart, swelling wider open than he'd ever thought possible, the intense pain and pressure and the *release*, and he was coming, he was --

Kit burrowed his head against Deacon's abdomen and muffled a hoarse scream in Deacon's smooth skin, soft tickling hair, rigid muscle. The muscles in his channel flexed hard around Deacon's fingers as if Kit was giving birth all over again. Deacon's fingers slid out and he thrust them back in, driving a second spasm of orgasm out of Kit that wrung him dry. He didn't even have the breath left to scream again, but his throat let out a long rattling rasp of air. His head spun and sparkling lights dazzled his eyes as he went limp -- but not too limp.

Kit dimly recognized what Deacon wanted when Deacon pulled at him to arrange him a second time, and he went with what Deacon was asking of him with his movements. Up the bed he went, wondering how his planned seduction had gotten turned so topsy-turvy -- Alphas! -- and settled on his side with plenty of room for Deacon to slide up behind him. He plastered himself to Kit, his front to Kit's back, his cock nestled between the crux of Kit's thighs without sliding inside him.

"You can," Kit whispered, raising one leg and bracing his foot on the bed. He knew from Deacon's sharply indrawn breath that he could see the mouth of

Kit's channel, and knew his flesh would be red, swollen, pouting, hungry. "Deacon, you can. You won't hurt me."

"God, Kit. Don't want to hurt you," was what Deacon said. But his fingers sought out that entrance again and teased around its opening, pulling with his thumb, letting out still more of his slick, thick with Omega scent.

"Please," Kit begged. He wasn't proud right now. "I want you, and you won't hurt me. I promise."

Deacon crushed the roughest of kisses to Kit's temple. "Never hurt you," he swore. "Never, on my life."

His cock already rested against Kit's opening. With his thumb to open Kit just a little, he slid inside, smooth and hard and hot and everything good in the world. Deacon filled Kit's emptiness the way Kit only just now knew he wanted, and having him inside did hurt, but not in the way Deacon needed to worry about, only in the way that made a third climax build and build and --

Deacon clapped a hand around Kit's mouth, letting him howl out his satisfaction, and thrust deep, fast, hard. His breath came in great heavy chuffs that made Kit's back hot and damp between his shoulder blades, and their sweat mixed in a giant tangle of *want* and *need* and *mine*. He stopped, his hips stuttering in tiny thrusts.

"Love you," he said fiercely in Kit's ear. "You're mine."

Kit bucked forward and back, unable to stop himself, and neither could he stop Deacon. Deacon froze, shuddered hard, and stifled his own shout in Kit's back.

"Love you," he said over and over again, his

mouth moving over Kit's back in hot, open kisses. "Mine. Yours *mine*. Always, yours, mine."

And oh, to believe him! To believe him! Kit hid his face in the pillow of his arm and wished, wished, wished his words could be true.

Wished so hard that he almost believed.

* * *

Kit spent half the next morning humming happily to himself. Okay, maybe not a whole half -- Deacon had only been awake for half an hour or so -- but whenever Kit was happy that happiness had a way of spreading itself out like a melted butter on sweet pancakes, like sunlight. And wasn't that just too damn poetic for a Jarhead trucker?

"What are you laughing at?" Kit paused long enough to ask, his head tilted in curiosity. "No, really, what? You've been sitting in bed just watching me and grinning since you woke up."

Deacon tilted his head to mirror Kit, teasing him, and drank him in. His Omega had figured out the knack of showering while their son snoozed in his carrier, and he looked clean and smelled fresh, dressed in comfortably careless flannel and denim with a white tank top underneath. His hair, still damp, curled around his collar, and his skin glowed with whatever happened to new bearing fathers. He held Felix cradled against him, one hand cupping their son's baseball head, and joggled him gently as he waited for Deacon to answer.

"Darlin'," Deacon said at last. "If you even have to ask why I'm feeling glad to be here, go take a look in the mirror."

Kit's cheeks bloomed a brilliant pink. He shook his head, muttered something about Alphas and chocolate-box romance, and ducked around the corner out of sight. But not ten seconds later Deacon heard the humming start back up again, so that was all right.

Still chuckling to himself, he swung his legs out of bed and reached for the jeans he'd discarded the night before -- considered, reconsidered, and headed for the shower himself. Least he could do was keep up to Kit's standards. When he emerged, clean and combed and even shaved, Kit's approving nod made a pretty good reward for the effort. Kit's light touch at the back of his head, and Kit's not-so-light-at-all kiss, made better rewards still.

"Better hurry," Kit said, his lips brushing Deacon's on each word, before he let go. "We'll be late."

Deacon shrugged and found his boots, shoving his feet into them, but asking anyway, "Late for what? Thought we were just going for a walk."

"We are. With a two-week-old. Who is then coming with me to my follow-up appointment, where they're going to poke and prod both of us and ask me for the hundredth time in a few hundred different ways *how* I didn't know I was pregnant." Kit grimaced. "And then they'll tell me all the things that *could* have gone wrong and give me a whole new bucket of nightmare fuel."

"You've been having nightmares?"

Kit brushed that aside. "That's not the point."

"Kind of is the point, or at least one of them, from where I'm standing." Deacon frowned as he crossed his arms. "You didn't say."

"Because they're just bad dreams. They're nothing to worry about. And the doctors are just covering their asses. Look at him! Isn't he healthy? And look at me. Aren't I, too?"

Well, no one with working senses could deny

that. Deacon still didn't like the idea that Kit having bad dreams, and promised himself he'd stay awake after Kit fell asleep that night. Keep a watch out, see for himself how things seemed from the outside, and figure out a way to fix the problem. He'd always been better with his hands, but he could learn new things.

Kit was rushing around again, gathering up this and that, but he stopped long enough to tousle Deacon's wet hair. "Stop. Worrying. I'm fine. If you want to do something useful, find the baby wipes, and those mittens Jory bought. And a bib. If we have any that aren't dirty."

"What's he need a bib for? All he eats is..." Deacon made a vague gesture toward Kit's pecs.

"Yes, and he's just like his father," Kit said primly, his cheeks pink again. "A messy eater."

Deacon hooted. Fair enough. He cast about and rummaged through the gathering mess babies just seemed to generate, finding socks and plastic keys and hats, but not the other things. "You want to get lunch at the diner after your appointment?"

Kit was in the other room, but he made an approving noise. "I could go for their chicken salad."

Or a cheeseburger, something good and fatty to keep his strength up, but they'd have that argument then, Deacon decided. An idea sparked in his head. "Hey, do you remember Marshall? He's in town. You mind if I ask him to join us for lunch?"

Silence. The quiet lasted longer than a moment, then two, and then Kit came back around the corner, a faint frown on his face. "Is Marshall the deep sea diver?"

"Diver, surfer, wakeboarder, skier, poker player, whatever he can make some money at," Deacon agreed. "He's in town for a few days. Asked me to go to Cozumel with him when he heads out, you know how he is." He shrugged to indicate that he'd said no.

He wasn't sure Kit had heard that. Kit had turned his head to stare into the distance, and he didn't look too happy about what he saw there -- but before Deacon could ask him what was up, he blinked back to the real world and gave Deacon one of his pretty smiles. "We can have lunch with him. Of course."

"You sure?" Deacon asked, dubious. Did Kit not like Marshall for some reason?

"Positive." Kit's smile didn't falter, so maybe Deacon had read that wrong. "Baby wipes. Did you find them? I have a packet in the bag, but I don't want to run out."

"How many do we need?" Deacon asked skeptically.

"Hmm. How many diapers have you changed by now?"

Deacon eyed the hundred-count box sticking out of the quilted bag Kit carried everywhere now. It had duckies and bunnies on the sides. What even was his life, and what the fuck, he loved every part. Except for the diapers. "Yeah, that might not be enough."

Kit burst into laughter, tipping his head back, and yeah, okay, there was no hint of his earlier weirdness lingering there. Deacon figured he must have been imagining things. He offered Kit his hand. "I think we'll manage with what we've got. Let's go, darlin'."

Chapter Seven

Walks were a whole different animal, Deacon discovered, when you had a baby in tow. Kit wore Felix so bundled up and strapped so snugly to his chest that Deacon kinda wondered how anyone could *tell* he was a baby and not some kind of overstuffed forward-facing knapsack, but apparently people had a nose for that kind of thing.

He didn't mind. Hell, he almost glowed with pride every time someone's head whiplashed their way, zeroing in on "baby." They rushed over to say hello, crooning over the bits of Felix that showed through his swaddling, the Omegas petting Kit as if he were an actual cat and the Alphas thumping Deacon warmly on the back. He figured he'd end up with a handprint-shaped bruise right between his shoulder blades before the day was over, and did he mind? No, he did not.

Kit noticed, and his nose crinkled with amusement during one rare spell they had to themselves. "I'll rub something on that tonight."

Deacon arched an eyebrow, wicked as he could manage. "Rather you rub something else."

"And isn't that how we got into this situation in the first place?" Kit asked pertly, turning them both to face two preteen Omegas who'd caught their scent and a mighty case of baby fever. They descended like a plague of locusts chirping "cute, cute." Kit shook his head but let them have their fun, though Deacon could almost read his mind and hear him wondering *was I ever that young?*

Some neighborhood planning committee or another had recently mounted clocks on corner light poles, which did come in all kinds of handy. Deacon glanced up at one as they passed beneath and elbowed Kit on his non-Felix-bearing side. "Isn't your well-visit appointment at eleven?"

Kit glanced up at the clock -- ten forty-five -- and made a noise halfway between a squeak and a yelp. He clutched Felix to him. "I've got to run."

"Are you sure you don't want me with you?"

"You're meeting Marshall soon, and those exam rooms are small. You don't need to come. I'll see you for lunch!"

One quick kiss on the cheek and he was gone. Deacon watched him till he was out of sight, half worried they'd take a tumble from trotting so fast, but maybe part of being pregnant was developing internal stabilizers. Kit didn't wobble once.

Ah well. He'd count his blessings. And... somehow... figure out what to do. He hadn't gotten around to that the night before, somehow, when he'd normally make his plans for the day. Getting jumped and seduced within an inch of his life did tend to distract a man.

Deacon smirked and started walking. This was Roanoke River, after all. Might not be a happening hotbed of clubs and hemp stores and foodie heavens, but there was plenty to look at and poke his nose into if he took the time to look around. And with nothing else to do, why not? Felt good to stretch his legs, too.

He ambled, taking his time. Down side streets that looked interesting but held nothing more than dumpsters and stray raccoons, and others that held little indie brick and mortar stores still holding out against a world flooded with big box stores and online ordering. He poked his head into the ones that were more interesting than others and picked up enough odds and ends to stuff his pockets with. He called

Marshall, who cussed him out cheerfully for waking him up before noon, but got the good old son of a bitch to agree to meet them for lunch.

When he'd finished all that, Deacon checked his watch. Eleven-fifteen. Kit wasn't meant to be out of his appointment until noon at the earliest. *Damn*. So, what roads hadn't he walked down? Deacon turned in a slow circle, picked one at random, and started ambling.

This road wasn't as clean and tidy as some, but not as tumbledown as others. A couple of houses, turn of the previous century models that somehow hadn't been converted into chiropractor's offices or accounting firms, scarred and beaten but still standing. A little taqueria stood cheek-by-jowl with a grocery so full of fresh produce they were spilling over, baskets of tomatoes and peppers displayed on the sidewalk.

And next to that? A garage. Deacon's amble slowed to a stop as he took a gander. He'd seen plenty of mechanic shops on the road, mostly rundown or overrun with bikers, but this appeared to be a going concern. Only two mechanics, one a grizzled old Alpha and one a middle-aged probably-Beta with a spare tire around his waist, but they moved at a good clip and he could tell they knew what they were doing.

The old Omega spotted him -- old buzzards like that did tend to have eagle eyes. He raised his hand, then beckoned Deacon over.

Why not? Deacon moseyed over, curious, and when he got closer he recognized the Alpha in a vague sort of way. "You fixed the brakes on my rig once, didn't you?" he asked, trading grips with the old man -- who had hands like iron, damn. "Last year."

"Year before," the old Alpha corrected. "Bert."

"Deacon." He got his hand back, only mildly bruised, and grinned at the man. "I started carrying a kit like you told me. Fixed 'em again myself when they tried to fuck me over out in New Mexico this spring. And gave the engine a tune-up while I was at it."

"Huh." Bert eyed him. "Have any trouble?"

"Nah. Not once I knew what I was doing." He'd liked the work, Deacon remembered. There'd been something deeply satisfying about being up to the elbow in engine grease, putting parts together and patching others back to fighting fitness. "I keep listening for noises so I'll have an excuse to dig back in."

Bert's chuckle sounded like an old chainsaw trying to start on a cold morning. "Not so much lately, from what I heard. Got yourself a son now?"

Deacon straightened his back and there he went again, glowing like Rudolph's nose with pride. "Felix."

"Unh." Bert turned his back, but beckoned for Deacon to follow him to the engine he'd been working on before. He tossed Deacon a pair of work gloves sitting on the car's hood and donned a pair of his own. "What do you think, the carburetor?"

Odd, but maybe the old man had forgotten his glasses or something, and Deacon kind of liked the way Bert didn't bullshit around with social niceties. He tugged on the gloves and leaned over the engine for a moment, then shook his head. "No. The fuel line's shot. See here, and here? There's cracks under all that built-up oil."

"Unh," Bert grunted again. "Figured. Buy a car, never take the damn thing for so much as a tune-up, then act all sur-fucking-prized Pikachu when she breaks down." He snorted at Deacon's side-eye. "I got grandkids, I know memes, shut up. You need a job?"

Deacon's ears heard Bert, but it took his brain a second to catch up. "Come again?"

"Don't stare at me like I just shit in your shoes. You heard." Bert leaned against the car they'd been poking around in. "You got a son now to keep you in one place, and there ain't much hauling business in town to bring in your daily bread with. You're decent with this kind of shit. I could use you. So?"

Swear to God, Deacon didn't know what to say. He opened and closed his mouth a few times before coming out with, "You don't even know me, old man."

Bert pointed at him. "And that's the last time you get to call me 'old man.' I know enough, and if you fuck up I'll kick you to the curb, so what've I got to lose? Except I don't think you will fuck up. I've got a nose for this. But, eh." He waved a hand. "You gotta talk to your Omega first? I've been widowed so long I forget they like that kind of thing. Ask him, see what he says, see if he had anything else in mind."

"Why would he?"

Bert shrugged. "Omegas, you never know. Maybe he likes being a trucker's partner. Sometimes they do, they like their space. Offer still stands though. Come back tomorrow, the next day, and let me know."

"Yeah. Yeah, I'll do that. Thanks, man. Sir." Deacon stuck out his hand and traded grips with the old man a second time, then turned to walk away. He'd spent enough time at the garage that now he'd have to jog to get to the diner on time.

And he did. But as he went, he couldn't get those words out of his head. *Omegas. You never know.*

Would that be what Kit wanted? Deacon had never asked himself the question before. Would Kit be happy about him taking a job? Would Kit *want* him to stay, or…

* * *

"… couldn't be better, considering the

circumstances." The nurse practitioner hadn't let Kit and Felix leave his office on their own like usual, choosing instead to walk them back out to the lobby. He chattered as they wound their way through the corridors -- why were medical clinics always such a maze? -- and kept a guiding hand very nearly too close to the small of Kit's back. "You're both as healthy as can be. You and your son are amazing. If you ever do change your mind about being part of that article we're working on, let me know."

Kit kept a smile on his face. Just. His baby, and his pregnancy, were his affair. And Deacon's. He didn't want the OB-GYN world to gawk over him. He just wanted to go home.

But he was being unfair, wasn't he? When he shook his head *no*, the nurse practitioner gave in with a graceful shrug of acceptance and used that guiding hand of his to usher Kit into the lobby, where he smelled… caramel shortbread? At his curious look, the nurse practitioner slapped a hand to his forehead and said, "I forgot! The hospital volunteers come around once a week with tea and cookies as a treat. You landed on the lucky day." He winked. "Caffeine free, but they make a good cup."

He *was* being unfair. Embarrassment made Kit's face hot as he balanced Felix in one arm and reached to shake hands with the other. "Thank you. I'll try some."

"All anyone can ever do is try," was the nurse practitioner's philosophical judgment. "I'll see you and Felix next time. Keep up the good work!"

All anyone can ever to is try. And he would. Day by day, he would.

But today…

Kit hung back from the tables that must have been set up while he was in the back getting poked and prodded. He wasn't normally shy -- maybe a little -- but somehow he didn't quite feel like he could join the group. Why hadn't he let Deacon come with him when he'd asked? He should have. But no, Kit had wanted to test his independence, and now look where he was. Alone in the middle of a crowd. Omegas with their babies and toddlers jockeyed for position around the table, but *they* were joined by their Alphas. Some by more than one Alpha, which raised an eyebrow but not in disapproval.

Something more like wistfulness, maybe. They all seemed so *happy*. But Kit had been able to tell just by looking at Deacon that morning how excited Deacon was at the thought of having his buddy in town. If he tried to cut Deacon off from that pleasure, he'd be no better than either of his parents, always out to spoil whatever they could for the other. He wouldn't do that. He'd be damned first. Loneliness could go take a flying leap; it wasn't wanted.

Kit's phone chimed in his pocket, the volume set on low but audible nonetheless. *Speak of the devil.* He slipped the phone out and pressed it to his ear. "Deacon? Is everything all right?"

"Kit!" Deacon boomed, the noise of the diner they both liked a raucous if muted roar in the background. "We're great here, but we're *here* and you're not. Doc appointment run over?"

Kit could hear an unfamiliar male voice so clearly that its owner had to be sitting in the same booth as Deacon; that'd be his friend Marshall, who was going to take him out of town and all the way to Cozumel for -- Kit had forgotten what for. Hot jealousy burned for a moment before he stuffed the sensation down.

"Yes," he said. He was getting some odd looks

from the Omegas around the tea table now, easily interpreted. They'd glance to his side, note the lack of any Alpha, and either turn pitying or faintly judgmental. Kit kept his own face as neutral as he could. "Sorry."

"Everything okay?"

"A-plus, they said." Kit cuddled Felix a little closer, his baby weight and warmth a comfort. "Tell Marshall I said hello."

"Sure, but you could do that yourself. We're waiting for you. Come on over."

He could, but suddenly going for lunch was the last thing Kit wanted. He couldn't bear to go and sit in a booth across from the man who was going to take Deacon away sooner or later, to smile and nod and keep himself absolutely pleasant when what he really wanted to do was rage and throw plates and -- and -- tie Deacon to the bedpost by his ankles until he decided he'd rather stay.

Hormones. But he'd best not indulge them. Kit took a swipe at his eyes with his forearm and managed to smile, so Deacon would be able to hear that in his voice. "I'll pass this time. Felix needs a nap, and they've got tea and cookies here. I'll grab one of those and make myself a sandwich at home."

A baffled pause answered him. Then, "What's wrong?"

"Wrong? Nothing at all," Kit answered, knowing he sounded too bright, too cheerful. He had to end this call, and now. "Stop worrying about me. I'll see you when you get back." Whenever that might be. "Enjoy your time with Marshall, okay? Have fun!"

He ended the call before he could say something he might regret, and turned his ringer to silent for good measure before slipping his phone back into his pocket. *There*. Deacon was free.

A cookie and some tea didn't sound too bad, actually. He'd wait for the crowd around the tables to thin out a bit, and --

And he hadn't noticed Zane among the gathered parents, which was odd considering how Zane tended to stick out, but then again Kit had been distracted. Zane had noticed *him* though and was meandering his way, his toddler balanced on one lean hip. The boy was old enough to babble in what sounded mostly like English and only a little like baby talk, and he looked so much like Zane except for his dandelion cloud of blond curls that the resemblance was almost startling.

For once in his life, Zane didn't say anything. He put one arm around Kit's shoulders instead and gave him a light shake that Kit guessed was meant to be a hug. He meant to nod, but somehow he ended up putting his head on Zane's shoulder instead.

Zane let out a quiet breath, something like a sigh. "Don't be a stubborn ass."

Kit reared back, stung. He might have lashed out if not for the toddler that stared at him with an exact copy of Zane's curious gaze. "What's that supposed to mean?"

"That you're not the only one who's here alone. But you're probably the only one who doesn't have to be. And if I had what you have? I'd fight for it."

Kit stared at him, not knowing what to say.

Zane raised one shoulder. "Just saying," he said. "Come have a cookie. They're still warm, and they're good. Food for the body, food for thought. You could use both, so come on. This way."

* * *

Deacon swiped his phone off and held it in front of him, giving the device a narrow-eyed glare as if that'd help produce some answers to questions that made no sense.

Across the booth from him, Marshall cleared his throat. When Deacon glared at him he held up one hand in a *not my circus, not my monkeys, not unless you buy me a ticket* gesture.

Which Deacon fully planned to do, because what else were friends for? He cleared his throat and pinned Marshall with a harder stare. "So," he said deliberately. "That was weird."

"Little bit." Marshall pointed at him with a French fry, going along with it, God bless his jarhead heart. "I don't even know Kit, and I could tell that was weird."

Deacon snorted. Munchy bastard couldn't wait long enough for the whole party to get there, not that that was going to be a thing now. "You could tell, how, now?"

"For one, you couldn't shut up about how much your Omega loves this place, how he always says he's going to get the chicken salad but ends up with something breaded and deep-fried and/or dripping with cheese. For another, you have a very expressive face, my friend." Marshall ate his fry in two bites and reached for another, rolling the fry in the puddle of ketchup on his plate until it looked more like a tomato-based cigar with a salty, greasy center, and damn, could fathers get morning sickness after the fact?

"Eat that or give the damn thing a decent burial," Deacon said, queasy. "Jeez. No one ever taught you manners?"

Marshall leered cheerfully at him, chewing open-mouthed.

Deacon kicked him under the table. Boots weren't just good for walking. Marshall yipped and kicked back.

Now that both of them were nursing bruises and on a more even keel, Deacon could let a little of his tension go. He blew out a breath and leaned heavily back in his booth. "You think he got bad news? No, he'd have told me that. He doesn't fuck around when it comes to Felix."

"He didn't let you know he was having a baby until Felix was halfway out of his --"

Deacon pointed sharply at him. "Careful how you finish that sentence. Also, he didn't know until then either."

Marshall made a *fair enough* gesture. "Though I still don't get how neither of you noticed. How is that even possible?"

"Him, I don't know. He's usually sharper than that. Me, not so much." Deacon sighed. He'd done this before, go over and over in his head over things he could have picked up on but hadn't. His fault for not being around as much as he should have been, could have been. "But I swear, he didn't look pregnant to anyone. That's what everyone swears."

"Then it's not your fault. Except for how it is. You knocked him up and from the pictures you showed me Felix is a little mini-me if I ever saw one, but aside from that."

"You're just a whole bushel of help, brother."

Marshall relented, lightening up on the teasing. He pushed his plate to one side and folded his hands. "What do you want to do? Go home and check on him? I'm cool here. Always plenty to keep busy with if you know who to look at."

"Thought that was 'where to look'?"

Marshall grinned. "Not if you're me."

Deacon threw a napkin at him. "The fact that

you're a horndog is already a well established fact, Marsh. Stay on target. I shouldn't go home, probably. He sounded like he wanted a few."

"But you still want to?" Marshall guessed. He raised one shoulder. "Then maybe you should. Tell him you've got a job, see if that perks him up."

No, not like this. Deacon shook his head. He wanted to share good news like that when Kit was in a receptive mood, not a keep-away one.

"You want to go to Cozumel with me after all?" Marshall asked. "I could still make a twofer happen."

Looking at him, Deacon could see he genuinely was trying to help. "No. I made myself a promise I was staying, and I'm staying."

And that, for a man solely accustomed to one night stands, was visibly where they hit the limit of Marshall's ability to give relationship advice. It was almost funny, watching him frown and search for words. He cast about a few times, opening and closing his mouth.

Deacon waited, curious to see what he might come up with, the whole thing perversely making him feel better. He might fuck up from time to time, but when it came to loving an Omega he was miles ahead of at least this one. He and Kit had worked through things before, whatever this was they could --

Both he and Marshall jumped hard enough to knock their knees on the underside of the booth table when a sharp, startling *crack!* sounded right next to their fucking heads. Deacon nearly shoved Marshall out of the line of fire when he realizes what he'd seen and heard. A beer can. Someone had thrown a half full can of shitty beer at the window outside the booth where they were seated, visible from the street. Skunky foam dripped down the plate glass and the can itself teetered on the window ledge.

"Son of a bitch!" Marshall swore, but Deacon barely heard him. He angled forward, straining for a look at the culprit, and yeah, they were exactly who he'd imagined as the most likely suspect. Ferdie, not even bothering to hurry his lumber along the sidewalk. Bastard even turned back and smirked, like he'd done something clever by half scaring the shit out of a couple of veterans.

Marshall saw Ferdie too, and Deacon had described him well enough that he could tell Marshall had made an ID himself. Marshall's jaw tightened in a way that used to mean whoever had pissed him off was in for a world of trouble. "That the lowlife Alpha who's been sniffing around your Omega?"

Deacon growled a reply. "That's the prick."

"Okay." Marshall pushed his plate to one side, dug a twenty out of his pocket and tossed the bill on the table. "Okay, fine. Your Omega wants space, we can give him some space, but that? I'd say that's the textbook definition of fucking *asking* for a lesson in manners, and that? That we could do a thing about. You wanna?"

Fuck yes. Deacon cracked his knuckles as he stood, the booth seat screeching out slantwise behind him. "Let's go."

Chapter Eight

Ferdie hadn't been walking all that fast. Deacon expected to catch up to the slimeball pretty damn quick, but he was a slippery little -- not so little -- weasel. He and Marshall spent a good fifteen, twenty minutes tracking him down, and only got lucky when they doubled back. Ferdie had hidden in the alley next to the diner, but now that he'd sent them on their goose chase, he apparently felt smug enough to stand outside the window he'd hit and smirk at them.

"Jog, boys, jog!" he jeered. "Hup, two, three, four."

"Ever think maybe you should try?" Deacon demanded. He jabbed a finger at Ferdie's beer belly and jerked his chin in the direction of Ferdie's jowly neck. Looked like the better part of what he didn't spill from a twelve-pack went down his gullet on a daily basis. "Maybe stop pickling your liver? Or you know what? Never mind. Keep going. Get yourself out of my way all the sooner, that'd suit me fine."

Marshall took up position at Deacon's side, arms crossed and glare focused. "What is your fucking problem?" he asked, more direct than Deacon.

Ferdie ignored Marshall -- further proof that he just wasn't too bright -- and curled his lip at Deacon. "You don't deserve him."

Aaand there they had it. Not that Deacon had expected anything different. "Says you, but you don't get a say, so how's that taste? Good and bitter?"

"I get a say." Ferdie's jaw jutted out, mulish as well as lumpish. "I get all the say I want."

Deacon barked a laugh. "Says who?"

Ferdie's smirk turned devious. "Said Kit, last time I was balls deep and nutting in him."

Deacon's stomach flipped. He took two steps closer, near enough to smell spilled Budweiser. "You want to smile when you say that, motherfucker?"

"Smile? I was, and so was he. Couldn't get enough," Ferdie boasted. "Says he loves my cock. Wants me on him all the time."

And wasn't that just richer than rich? Deacon had had enough. "I've never heard such bullshit, and that's saying something. Leave Kit alone," he ordered, crisp and harsh. Plenty of authority in that tone of voice, and anyone sensible would pick up on the warning. "If you pester him again, or if your stupid ass even thinks about throwing a Goddamn beer can at me a second time, I'm not going to let you off with a warning. Get me?"

Get him? Ferdie hadn't even been listening. Too busy cooking up a second salvo of stupid. "Stupid? I knew he was pregnant," he said. "You're the stupid one, if you never saw it."

For the love of fuck. Deacon shook his head. "Not even he knew."

"He knew. He just didn't want anyone else to know. He's an Omega! They always know."

The tiniest, tiniest spark of doubt flickered in Deacon's mind. He rooted the nasty little bastard out, stamped on it, and let his already-hot anger stoke the fires higher. "And?" he asked Ferdie. "That all you got, needle dick?"

Ferdie was dark purple enough now to throw an embolism, not that they'd get that lucky, and spitting mad. "You're never here! You leave him alone like he's a puppy you throw in the doghouse whenever you get tired of him. I'm gonna claim him, and that baby, and once he's mine I'm gonna show him what's what. Not like you. And he'll learn to love me. I can make him love me."

Deacon *almost* felt sorry for Ferdie then. Sounded too much like Ferdie was talking from personal experience -- but stalking an Omega who didn't want him crossed a line there wasn't any coming back from.

Ferdie must have sensed he was losing. He curled his meaty fists up. "I'll fight you for him."

And that was just sad. "Listen, dickweed," Deacon said, almost gently. "Kit. Doesn't. Want. You. I know you've heard him say so. And Felix is *mine*. So is Kit, as Kit chooses to be. He's a person, not a fucking first prize ribbon at a county fair. He makes his own choices, and they aren't you. So piss off. Last warning."

Anyone with sense would have listened. Not Ferdie. Ferdie snarled like a mad dog, himself. "Scared? I'll whip your ass."

"You and what army, piss ant?" Deacon said with a scoff.

Ferdie repaid the insult with a sucker punch Deacon didn't see coming. Apparently Ferdie could move fast when he wanted to. He hit like a toddler, though. All fury, and fists as weak as his ideas of romance.

Deacon shook his head. *All right then. Game on.* He gave Marshall a pointed look. "Watch my back."

Marshall showed his teeth in a savage grin. "I don't mind sloppy seconds. Let's do this."

Ferdie had thrown the first punch, but Deacon threw the second. Felt good. Felt damned good. He just hoped Kit would understand.

* * *

Kit... did *not* understand.

Or maybe it was that he didn't *want* to understand. If he did, his head just might explode and that would leave Felix with only one idiot for a father, and what kind of childhood would that be? He swallowed his anger, counted to ten inside his head while he sponged patiently away at the blood smeared around Deacon's purpling-black eye, and once he was sure he could speak without yelling, said, "Go over what happened one more time."

Deacon glanced over Kit's shoulder to where Marshall loomed uncertainly, but loyally, in the bathroom doorway. Exchanging looks, no doubt, trying to telegraph *what do I say* and *I don't know, he's your Omega* with three and a half working eyes.

Kit counted to ten in Spanish this time and dabbed at Deacon's face just a little harder than he needed to. "Go over what happened. Again. Slowly. Not both of you, just one. Preferably Marshall."

"Why him?" Deacon blurted.

He'd moved his face to speak. Kit moved him back. Firmly. "Because I'm about to make sure none of your teeth are loose," he said, as levelly and patiently as before. "And then I'm going to make you gargle with salt water. And you're hard enough to understand when you don't have your mouth full. You *idiot*."

The two men exchanged glances again, this set full of *damn* and *oh shit*, but Marshall manned up to the task. He did keep a wary eye on Kit as Kit ran a finger around the inside of Deacon's mouth, but Kit supposed that was only to be expected of a friend. "We ran into Ferdie. Ferdie started the fight, by the way. Threw a beer can at us."

"Noted," Kit said. He turned to run warm water into a bathroom cup. "And?"

Marshall exhaled. "And, we went after him. Come on, Kit, you didn't expect Deacon to let that stand, did you?"

Kit made a noncommittal noise and added a generous palmful of salt to the cup of warm water.

"Fucking fuck," Marshall muttered under his breath. "Deacon, you owe me."

Kit turned his head slowly, only his head, to fix Marshall with a look that must have been ferocious. The jarhead went pale.

"Fine!" Marshall rattled through the rest of the story, picking up speed as he went, until he was nearly as hard to understand as Deacon talking around a finger and a mouthful of blood. "We exchanged words. Rude ones. He had some things to say about you…"

Deacon pushed the cup of salt water away before Kit could pour the whole mess down his gullet. "He called you a loose Omega. Insinuated he'd had you," he said quietly, hand firm on Kit's wrist. "I wasn't going to let him get away with that. I couldn't. I had to defend your honor."

A string in Kit's heart twanged plaintively. He resolutely ignored the tug, and pressed the cup of water to Deacon's lips. "Ferdie lies like he breathes, and anyone with any sense would ignore him."

"Not when he's willing to back up what he dishes out. Or spread rumors around town like horseshit after a hayride," Deacon insisted. "I won't let him do that to you."

While you're here. When you're there to hear them. But what happens when you're gone again? What then, Deacon? Kit pressed the cup firmly against the split in Deacon's lip, making him swear but also open his mouth. "Swish. Marshall?"

Marshall made a complicated gesture reflected in the bathroom mirror. "He got in a few lucky swings, mostly at Deacon's face, but then he ran out of steam. Purple face, puffing like a steam engine, grabbing his chest. I think it was just fat meets fight, not a heart attack, but we ended up calling an ambulance for him just in case."

"And if a doctor realizes he'd been brawling and he points a finger at the two of you in court?" Kit asked.

"He won't," Deacon said, cheeking his salt water for a second. "Not when we can counter sue for libel. Slander. Whatever."

"Or just pulp him again," Marshall added cheerfully.

"You'll be in Cozumel. I doubt your reach is quite that long," Kit said. *While I'll be here, and don't you see you've just made things worse?* "So you beat him up. He made a valiant effort at beating you up. No one won --"

"Fuck that. I won," Deacon insisted.

"Good job. Well done." Kit took the cup away and tossed it in the trash, lobbed the bloody washcloth he'd been using on Deacon into the sink, dusted off his hands, and turned to Marshall. "Thank you for coming along to help explain. You're a good friend."

Marshall frowned. "That doesn't sound like a compliment."

"In this case, no." Kit studied him. That tiny, stubborn bit of his heart that sighed with pleasure over being defended burned briefly bright with pride before Kit stamped it out and returned his focus to Deacon's friend. "If you don't mind, I'd like some privacy to discuss the evening's events with Deacon."

Deacon and Marshall shared another set of *aw hell* looks, but Deacon squared up and set his jaw. "Go on, Marsh, I'll be cool. Call you tomorrow."

Kit was sure he would. They'd probably leave for Cozumel early now just to get away from him.

No, thinking like that was being as sour as his parents, and he wouldn't do that. If only he could stop being so *angry* about this! "Goodnight, Marshall," he said instead. "You know your way to the door." He turned his back to wash the cloth out, and kept it turned until he heard the door close.

Deacon reached out to capture Kit's hand. "Kit, what the -- what's going on? All I did was try and take care of you."

Kit's temper cracked. Gently, like an egg tap-tap-tapped on the edge of a counter, but cracked all the same. "I know!" He threw the washcloth across the room in a flurry of pale pink water and wet terrycloth and stalked out, even if he had no idea where he was going.

He knew *why*.

He couldn't stay in that small space with Deacon any longer. If he did he'd let everything out, every word he'd kept bitten back: *if you're going, why can't you just go? Why do you have to make things more difficult? Why can't you just leave and make this easier? I'm used to waiting for you to come back, knowing that you might not. But having you here, every day, every night, doing things like this, oh, Deacon. My heart can't take this. You'll split me in two.*

But of course Deacon followed him. That was Deacon. He took hold of Kit's shoulder, and ignoring his split lip and the pain he had to be feeling, asked gently, "What's wrong, darlin'? Talk to me."

Chapter Nine

Kit couldn't do that. He wouldn't. So he did the only other thing possible. He whirled on Deacon, seized his face in both hands, and kissed him as if the world was ending tonight.

Deacon broke free only long enough for Kit to catch a glimpse of wide, startled eyes -- even the purpling one, which must have hurt -- and to say, "Kit, what the hell?"

No. No talking just now. Kit crushed his mouth back against Deacon's, careless of his split lip. He tasted coppery blood in the kiss, but Deacon had delivered their son. What was a little blood now?

Deacon struggled for one second more, maybe two, then groaned deep in his throat and wrapped his arms around Kit, squeezing as if he wanted to smash the breath out of him, and just in that second Kit wouldn't have cared if he did. He'd already broken his heart, the lungs might as well go too.

Deacon pushed them backward, landing them against the corridor wall just outside the bathroom. Kit could smell the salt and blood and faint chlorine of their tap water as clearly as he felt the prints of Deacon's hands on his arms, his waist, his hips and his ass, searching for somewhere to hang on and stay hung. And the way he kissed! Deacon kissed Kit as if he never, ever meant to let go. As if they'd go to their graves locked together like this if he had his way.

Making everything all worse, worse, worse.

Kit thrust his hands through Deacon's hair, and he wasn't gentle at all. Short strands came away in his fingers, bristly and rough, and Deacon made a noise of protest but he didn't pull away. His tongue slicked past the parting of Kit's lips, reminding Kit so vividly of when Deacon had his mouth between Kit's legs that Kit's cock began to stiffen and his channel grow damp with the beginnings of slick. The scent sprang up between them, intoxicating as witchcraft, and either Deacon or Kit moaned. Kit couldn't tell which.

But it was Deacon who slid his hand between Kit's legs and rubbed at his opening, just as roughly as Kit had tugged at his hair. He was mostly healed, but it still hurt a little. It also made Kit cry out with the want for more, too. He ached to have Deacon inside him, fucking him hard and fast and raw, not stopping until he'd planted another baby inside him. He *wanted* this. Almost so much that he almost let it happen.

He pulled away at the last possible second, the span of a breath before Deacon would have jerked open his jeans and thrust his hand inside them. "Stop," he said, ragged and out of breath. "Stop, Deacon, stop."

"You started this round," Deacon said, his black eye mostly closed again but both eyes dazed with confusion and lust. "You're making me crazy, Kit." But he stopped. He stopped, and that gave Kit the drop of courage he needed to do this. What he should have done all along. Should have said.

"I can't do this anymore." Kit wrapped his arms around his chest as if they could keep him warm and stepped back, away. "I can't keep waiting for the other shoe to drop."

Deacon started to struggle up from the wall, no doubt meaning to follow him. "Kit, what are you even talking about?"

Kit held up a hand to stop him and spoke as quickly as Marshall had before, understanding him better now. "I *know* you, Deacon. I know you need to be free, and that I tied you down without meaning to.

You've been trying and I love you for all you've done, but I *won't* toss you into a cage and shut the door. So. You need to go, Deacon. You need to leave. Now. Tonight."

Deacon's mouth opened, but he only stared at Kit instead of speaking.

Desperate to make him understand -- why wasn't he? -- Kit pressed on. "Don't you see? I have to move out of this holding pattern. Stop waiting to wake up and find you gone. If I send you, then I know what's happened, and I can still hope you'll come back. Just like always. I want to love you forever, Deacon, and I will, and that's why you need to get. Out. Now. Get it over with!" He stopped and held his breath, waiting for Deacon to say something. Do something. *Please, Deacon. Do* something. At least then the ground would be secure under his feet again. At least then he could move on.

He stared back at Deacon, begging him without words. *Now, Deacon. Please, Deacon. Now.*

* * *

For a moment, all Deacon could do was stare. That, and watch half-formed thoughts go racing through his head. *What the... He can't be serious, he... Did he hit his head or... What?* He blinked and shook his head several times, hoping maybe he'd dislodge something that'd gotten stuck in his ears and worked its way up to his brain, because that was the only way this was going to make sense to him.

"I'm sorry," Kit said. Possibly again, or for a third time. Deacon hadn't been listening too closely to anything but the shock buzzing in his own head. "Please don't stare at me like that. You don't have to explain yourself, Deacon. I understand. I always have. It's okay." His voice wobbled on that last bit, as good as a neon sign that read *I am lying* in twenty-four foot high letters. "I'll -- I'll go get that duffel you like. I'll be fine. I am fine."

An abrupt, piercing wail split the air and made them both jump. Kit bit his lip, still swollen and pink from kissing, and dithered briefly before making tracks for the bedroom next door. Whether Kit was going to get Felix or the duffel, Deacon didn't know. He didn't move from where he was planted, not that he could have. His feet seemed to be stuck to the ground as if with quick-set concrete. And he couldn't grant Kit the courtesy of not staring. He couldn't stop.

He thinks I'm -- what the fuck, *even.* He was staying, for Pete's sake. For *Kit's* sake, and for Felix's too. So why didn't Kit see that?

After all, he'd --

Deacon stopped. Stiller than before. Even held his breath as his brain gently, but thoroughly and mercilessly, exploded inside his head and bounced around the inside of his skull. He had, but he *hadn't* after all, had he?

Deacon, you fucking idiot.

Had he *said* so? Out loud? Even once? Hell no. He'd pounded on a bully and figured the permanent ringing Ferdie would have in his cauliflower ears was as good as a dozen roses. Which under other circumstances might have been, but --

Don't get distracted. But you can cuss Kit's stubborn death-grip on the past, maybe, just a little. Damn. Deacon knew better, or would have if he'd been thinking straight. He'd heard so many times how Kit's parents had stayed together for the sake of the children and made everyone miserable until they could escape. With all the shocks he'd been through, and with Deacon's own previous habit of hitting the road every time the notion took him, why would Kit ever think any differently about them?

Especially when Deacon hadn't told him. Not directly. Nor had he shown him. Not truly. He'd assumed, that was all.

So then.

No shame to Kit for not being able to read his mind, but it was well past time to do something about the state of affairs. Deacon shook his head again, this time to get things to settle into place, and gave a decided nod.

Across from him, standing in the doorway that led to his bedroom -- their bedroom -- Kit drew in a deep, miserable-sounding breath. Deacon hadn't noticed him coming back, but he'd dropped Deacon's empty duffel at his feet while he cuddled Felix to him, and hugged the baby tighter. *Now,* Deacon could see the difference, and figure exactly what Kit thought that meant. That he'd decided to cut his losses, skip town, fulfill every last of the worst possible outcomes. It'd break a stone's heart.

Yeah, well. Screw that noise.

Deacon held up one finger to stop Kit from speaking, or even worse, starting to fill that duffel bag. He'd punt the damn thing out the window first chance he got, but he had things to do first.

He just hoped Kit would take a turn at standing still and paying attention while he did them.

Step one: fire up his phone and let his fingers do some walking. He had to look up the number, but one quick Google search and he had the digits to the garage where he'd been offered a job.

One ring. Two rings. Three.

"Bert's," growled a two-pack-a-day voice. "I'm closed right now, so this better be good."

"I hope so too," Deacon said. He fixed his gaze on Kit and kept it there. "You offered me a job this morning. Offer still good?"

"Who the hell are you?" Bert asked blankly.

Deacon's heart sank. Until Bert let loose with a wheezing cackle like an old steam locomotive trying to blow its whistle. Relief made Deacon's knees wobble, but the thought hit him that he ought to be on speaker for this. He hit the button just in time for Bert's raspy squawk to sound out good and loud and clear. "I'm just shitting you, son. You're the jarhead with the new baby, right? Job's still open if you want, but you better show up at the ass-crack of dawn tomorrow ready to work. Deal?"

"Deal," Deacon said. "I'll be there. Thank you, sir."

"*Sir* my ass. Call me Bert or I'll kick *your* ass."

Deacon couldn't help grinning. "Yes sir, Bert."

"So that's how it's going to be," Bert grumbled. He didn't sound displeased. More like the opposite. "Tomorrow morning." He disconnected without another word, but that was good enough.

Kit stared at Deacon, eyes round as saucers and mouth open in an O.

But that was only step one. Step two: a number Deacon had saved on auto-dial. He hit the button, still without breaking eye contact, and waited for the connection.

"Marshall," his friend answered. Loud, rowdy honky-tonk blared in the background, making Deacon and Kit wince and Felix swivel his head around with a surprised sound like a startled goose. "Deacon? You okay?"

"Getting better," Deacon said. He hoped. "You remember you asked me if I wanted to go to Cozumel?

Don't answer that, I know you do. You remember what I told you?"

"You said no, you had better things to do keeping you here, and I said 'good for you'. Or something to that effect. We both got the gist." Marshal sounded baffled, and also like he had a horny Omega on his lap busy distracting him. "What's going on?"

"Explain later."

"You'd better. But," Marshall added, "Much later. Like tomorrow morning."

"Starting a new job tomorrow. Enjoy Cozumel, brother. Get in touch when you're back stateside."

Deacon disconnected this time. One more call, and he'd be done. He had to hit up Google again, but he knew the name of the dealership and it was easy to find. Before they could get through their opening spiel, he asked, "Do you all buy used rigs?"

"Is it in good condition?"

"Like a baby's bottom."

The voice on the other end turned dry. "I have children. Try again."

"Like the whole thing just rolled off a showroom floor, or as good as. Maintained like a work of art."

"And you're looking to sell?"

"I am," Deacon said. "When can I bring it by for you to look at?"

"Tomorrow," the voice said. "Afternoon or evening's best."

Thank God. Deacon couldn't have jammed another thing into the morning, especially since he'd decided if this worked he was going to wake Kit up and keep him busy before he left -- for the day only. "I'll be there," he said.

"I'll look for the miracle on wheels," the voice said, drier still. "See you then."

And there. Steps one, two and three completed. Kit hadn't budged. His eyes and mouth were going to dry out, but Felix had settled, had even gone halfway back to sleep, his baby fists near his mouth and his legs kicking idly. Which was good. It meant Deacon could cross the room, take him gently out of Kit's arms, and settle him snugly on the couch with a pillow to keep him from falling off, and move on to step four.

Which was, in sum, a kiss.

But not just one kiss. Oh, no. One kiss wouldn't go nearly far enough in showing Kit what Deacon wanted him to see -- that he was wanted, he was loved, and he was worth staying for. That from the second he'd looked into Felix's face, all his dreams had changed in a snap of the fingers.

That'd take years of saying, over and over, and Deacon could do that.

But first -- the kisses.

Deacon tipped Kit's chin up and stroked his thumb over Kit's full lower lip. Kit closed his mouth on reflex and licked where Deacon's thumb had touched, making the skin shine. He parted them again, maybe to speak, but Deacon silenced him by bringing their mouths together again.

He lingered there for the space of one breath, two breaths, three, not pushing, not trying to part Kit's lips and lick inside his pretty mouth the way he wanted. When the count of three finished, he let go -- but not for long. A second kiss, just as sweet, and a third, *almost* the same but for a light little bite at the end, a nip at the fullest part that made Kit gasp. Not in a bad way. His body, warming and going pliant, pressed toward Deacon at that.

Not bad for a start. Deacon kissed him again, deeper, but gentle, slow and sweet, and guided Kit backward step by careful step until Kit's back was to the side of the doorframe and Kit's hand had stolen up to riffle through his short-cropped hair. A finger under the chin, and Kit tipped his head back to rest against the doorframe as well while Deacon went lower. He put his mouth to the soft skin beneath Kit's ear, then the hollow where his jawbones met. Over the hard-hammering beat of Kit's pulse, then to the dip where his collarbones met. Mapping him, inch by inch and kiss by kiss, never pushing, only showing in the way he should have done all along.

His hands weren't idle while his mouth was busy. He slid them under Kit's shirt and splayed his fingers wide over the new, erotic softness of his belly, then up where hard muscle still dominated, and then to the tender-swollen fullness of his pecs. He took Kit's nipples lightly between two fingers each and rolled, tugged, coaxed out beads of milk. The movement made Kit moan deep and throaty, and he arched forward then back as if he couldn't decide if he wanted more or less or both.

Deacon pushed Kit's shirt up as high as the shirt would go and put his mouth to each nipple in its turn, large and soft and sweet-tasting, and made Kit cry out. Though he pressed his arm to his face to muffle his cries, Deacon could still hear them, and feel the yearning, the desire and love in them, right down to his bones.

He bit lightly over Kit's sternum, where his heart hammered like a drum, and settled his hands on Kit's hips. Panting, Kit lowered his arm. He still stared at Deacon as if he couldn't believe his senses -- but as if he *wanted* to, and that was half the battle right there.

Deacon bent his head and pressed his forehead to Kit's. "You didn't know before, and that's on me.

But you do now. I've told, and I've shown, and I'll promise you here and now and I'm going to mean this forever."

"You," Kit said, sounding dazed, but *still* wanting to believe. "You really… But…"

Deacon let go of one hip and took Kit's hand in his, lacing their fingers together. He squeezed lightly, no plans to release him. "I am never going to run out on you, Kit. Not again. I am not your parents, and neither are you. You're not mine, either, and nor am I. We can do this, and we can do better, and you know why?"

Kit shook his head, the movement rocking their foreheads together. His breathing came quicker, as if he was on the verge of tears. Deacon bowed his head to kiss the salt away, and said, with his fierce grin in his voice, "Because we fucking *rock*, that's why, and we are going to be the best damn family on the whole damn block, you watch and see."

His lover, the father of his baby, his Kit, laughed, a little shaky, but finally there, finally believing him.

"That's right," Deacon said, taking Kit's other hand and standing back to enjoy the look of him. "That's always been true, you know? Even when we were too dumb to see so. And it's not about to change now."

Kit smiled at him, a little afraid, but willing. There with him. The duffel forgotten, and his courage roused to action. "All right," he said, almost too quietly to hear, and then, louder, "All right."

All fucking right! Deacon whooped before wrapping his arms around Kit and whirling him away from the doorframe, into the middle of the room where he could fucking dip Kit just because he wanted to, and bring him up into a kiss as deep and dirty as the others hadn't been.

"I love you," he said, before Kit could make a peep. "I know you know. But just so you really, truly know."

Kit wound his arms around Deacon's neck. He had determination in his eyes now, and Deacon couldn't get enough. "I love you too," he said. "But -- Deacon -- for the long term, for always? How do we make that work?"

"I've got an idea. Hear me out?"

Kit tilted his head, curiosity bright. He was listening.

So here went nothing. Deacon took a breath, opened his mouth, and spoke. Laid everything on the line, and with just one question.

And Kit?

Epilogue

I said yes. Of course I said yes! With one question, and all the promises implicit in it, Kit had suddenly had everything he'd never quite dared to dream about land squarely in the palm of his hands. What else was he going to say, but yes?

"… and by the power vested in me, I now pronounce you mates," the cheerful officiant he and Deacon had chosen together said, beaming at the both of them as if, should he really try, he actually could make his grin stretch from ear to ear. A few of the audience members sighed, and not for the wedding romance. As well as being cheerful, the officiant was as cute as a Botticelli angel with the Italian good looks and tumbling ebony ringlets to match. If Kit wasn't marrying Deacon --

But he was, he was. Or, no. He was married. Mates! Kit turned his own bright grin on Deacon, who held his hands in a loose, easy grip, and squeezed them as he grinned back. "You heard the man."

"Damn right I did." Kit wound his arms around Deacon's neck. "So make this business official."

The officiant cleared his throat. "I didn't actually say -- no, never mind, I'm just pulling your leg. Kiss, already!"

And kiss they did. Light and sweet until Deacon put his arms around Kit's middle and lifted him off his feet to swing him around in circles. Laughter poured from their audience of Alphas, Omegas and Betas in their bright springtime best, drenched in warm noon light, all there to celebrate a wedding.

Deacon eased Kit down to his feet just before he got the head spins and laid a smacking kiss on his lips that made Kit laugh again and feint a swat at him.

Deacon did not feint the swat he laid on Kit's ass, for which they got more than a few wolf whistles. Kit couldn't see Felix, but he could hear his now ten-month-old son's loud shriek of excitement from his babysitter's arms.

"Mister and mister," Deacon said, lifting Kit's hand to his lips. "For good. For always. What do you say we walk back down the aisle before everyone who came here to watch this dog piles us on the altar for a chance to say congratulations, darlin'?"

Kit's heart, already soft as warm wax with romance and love, melted like butter in the warm light. He gave Deacon his own smacking kiss and caught him with the hand he'd kissed. "Race you."

"Oh, you're on."

But they didn't run down the aisle they'd walked up minutes before, not for more than a few steps, before the onslaught of well-wishers Deacon had predicted landed on them like an avalanche of hugs, backslaps, and happy words pouring down on them like rain. Everyone was there except for Ferdie. No one had seen Ferdie since the day Deacon and Marshall had made their point with their fists, and good riddance.

The others put Ferdie and his nonsense securely out of Kit's mind. Jory caught and squeezed him in a hard hug, saying, "I knew it! I knew all along."

Darius, shaking his head patiently, pumped Deacon's hand and patted Kit's back. His friend Grant, short for an Alpha but tough and resilient, become a friend by association, socked them both lightly in the ribs. "Good job, you two."

"Good job," Darius agreed. "Jory did know all along, though. Come by MacInnes's later and we'll buy you both a shot of the best."

Marshall hung back, grinning, until Deacon side-tackled him like a rugby player and nearly took them both off their feet. "Cozumel was good," he said. "This is better. Good job, brother."

"Anyone ever going to tie you down?" Kit asked, pert and perky.

"They'd have to be fast, and know tricks they don't in Tijuana," Marshall replied. He offered Kit his hand. "Keep him in line."

"I'll do my best."

"It won't take much," Deacon said, his chin up, but with a wink. "Eh, Kit wouldn't like me if I got too well-mannered."

"True."

Bert, Deacon's boss at the garage, wasn't the hugging sort. He kept his gnarled hands firmly stuffed in his pockets, but he gave them both a firm nod of approval. He was the one Felix had chosen to stick to like glue, and waved at both his parents from where his carrycot rested between Bert's rugged old boots.

Kit blew Bert a kiss, just to watch his eyes pop and his weathered cheeks turn red.

"You keep him in line!" Bert blustered, jabbing a finger at Deacon.

Deacon only laughed. "I wouldn't like him if he was a hundred percent well-mannered."

"Fine thing to say to someone you just married! Be at work next week on time, or I'll whip your smart ass."

Kit grinned at the old man, who wasn't fooling anyone with his grouchiness anymore and hadn't for months, and made his way to the next guest. There were so many! The bearers he'd met at the Omega clinic, the doctors and nurses who worked there, bookstore staff who'd finally forgiven him for the destruction wrought to the chair Felix had been born in, and even the cantankerous bookstore cat, unbothered by the leash and harness he wore, purring so loudly Kit could almost hear her over the roar and hum of a hundred-odd voices going all at once.

At the end of the row, Kit gave Deacon's hand one more squeeze. "I have to go make sure the cupcakes don't all get eaten before we get our hands on one."

"Already put some aside, but you go do your thing, darlin'." Deacon hugged Kit to him and said in his ear, "Always."

"Always yours," Kit whispered back. Then he swatted Deacon on the ass. "Go rescue Baby Dude from Bert."

Deacon took off, walking backward, grinning all the way. "*Felix.* I see how this is going to be."

Kit winked at him, and made tracks for the cake table. He hadn't been joking about wanting to safeguard the cupcakes. Deacon might have put aside a couple, but Kit had his eye on a particular couple of flavors -- Key West limonade and cinnamon mocha -- that he wanted to at least get a taste of the icing on.

To his surprise, but also his pleasure, Zane was already there. His lanky frame and his hip lean against the side of the table said casual, but Kit knew better. Once you had Zane's trust, he'd be loyal to the end. And he'd bribed his toddler son with a plain vanilla cupcake.

"Congratulations on not being an idiot," Zane said in a lazy drawl as Kit drew apace. He offered his hand for a shake, then a fist bump. "Good job. Good happy ending."

Kit knocked elbows with him. Darius's old buddy, the unusual Omega Zane had become a good friend in recent months, and Kit knew how to read between the man's lines. Zane couldn't have been more pleased about the whole thing, and his long lean lines were softened by the romance of the day, too.

Kit couldn't resist just a little teasing. "So what about you? Do you want a happy ending of your own now that you've seen one?"

Zane snorted. "Honey, all I want is to get laid." He nodded at the crowd. "Speaking of. Who's that short Alpha giving your husband's head a knuckle rub?"

Kit craned his neck to look. "Grant?"

"Grant," Zane repeated thoughtfully. He picked up a strawberry-cherry cupcake and took a contemplative bite. "I'll remember that name."

Kit was certain that he would. He knew a certain look in an Omega's eye when he saw one, and Zane might say he wasn't in the market for a happy ending, but they did have a way of happening.

Deacon had come back when Kit wasn't looking, Felix babbling happily in his arms, and he wound Kit back against him. Kit leaned his head backward for a kiss, eyes closed, content as any Omega could ever hope to be.

Happily ever after, after all, as happy as a tale of Faerieland. Even -- especially -- for them.

Combustible (Roanoke River Omegas 3)
Will Okati

Long, lean, wild and unconventional for an Omega, Zane rocks *and* rolls Alpha Grant's world. Zane can't be predicted. He can't be contained. And Grant freaking loves it.

But it's not all beer and BJs, even for these two. Grant's never wanted to have kids of his own. His family is *Legacy Tattoo*, the business he finally reclaimed after his grandfather's death. He's dedicating his life to making it not just flourish but thrive. And he doesn't know -- yet -- about Zane's status as a single father to a rambunctious pre-K rebel.

Their love affair is gonna be complicated. And -- downright combustible.

Chapter One

Every story has to start somewhere.

"You think you're tough?" Grant cracked his neck from side to side, rolling his shoulders until they were nice and loose, warm and easy. He sized up his opponent with one long hard stare.

Hmm. Might be a harder bite to chew than he'd first thought, actually. Better free up his arms. He shrugged off the battered aviator jacket he wore out of convenience rather than desire and let it fall in a crumple to the worn city sidewalk under his feet.

Better. Grant kept an eye on the prize as he picked up the crowbar, then bounced it once, twice, against the palm of his left hand. The solid *smack* it made was visceral, meaty, and sent vibrations down his chest and toward his groin. It made him think of his first ride on the back of a Harley, the way the roar of the motor made him feel like he was riding a tiger at full gallop. Like the world was his and anything could happen.

Now he was ready.

"Let's see what you're made of." He'd lost the first round -- silly him, expecting the key to work after all these years -- but fortunately he'd come prepared with a full toolbox -- one of the few things he'd inherited from his grandfather -- stuffed with no end of helpful objects for a man on a mission. Which was a good thing, because you couldn't really ask customers to go 'round back to the delivery door.

Grant wedged the crowbar under the edge of the hasp that held the shop doors shut. Looked like no one had put a key in that rusted old padlock since his grandfather's business partner had passed away. Place had been left standing just the way it was, locked up tight.

Not anymore. The building was Grant's now, back in the family once more, and he was damn well going to get *Legacy Tattoo*, freshly renamed, open and ready for business.

Grant leaned forward, adding the weight of his body to the leverage on his crowbar, and muttered to himself in annoyance when nothing happened. Wasn't too surprising. The way the lock had rusted, they might as well have been welded shut.

So he'd try again. Life had taught him the value of not giving up, no matter what. He stood five feet three inches tall in his sock feet, and everyone had been sure he would be an Omega before he hit puberty. Had he? Had he, hell. Alpha. Alpha all the way, even if he'd never grown past petite. God knew how he'd survived adolescence. Skinny, short and willing to take a swing at anything didn't usually come with a long life expectancy, yet here he was. Someone must have been looking out for him.

So he'd pay that investment back and do his damnedest with this.

"Come on, come on," Grant muttered between his teeth as he put his back into the job. He'd love to have the doors open and the dust on its way to settling before heading to the toasted sub place for lunch. A little corner shop that looked like a hole in the actual wall, they made the best damn *Cubanos* in town. Grant's mouth watered, thinking about sinking his teeth into tender meat, homemade sauce and spicy pickles that bit back.

The thought distracted him. The crowbar slipped sideways in his hand, making him yelp in surprise and over correct. He stumbled back just in time to avoid getting clocked on the nose, while the crowbar itself clattered to a noisy halt at the tip of his duct-taped Docs.

Rattle-rattle-rattle-ronnnnnnnng.

Right. Grant narrowed his eyes at the stubborn thing. "You think you're cute, huh?" Frustrated, he shoved a hand through his hair. "Well, fuck me."

"Be happy to, sweetheart, but you could at least buy a man dinner first."

Grant looked up, eyebrow raised.

An Omega, tall, whip-thin, and with *trouble* written over him from stem to stern, grinned back at Grant. "Offer stands."

"Uh-huh," Grant said, amused despite himself. Some Alphas would pounce on anything that moved, but Grant had a particular set of preferences. This Omega ticked all of them off the checklist. Slim as a dancer, smooth and supple as a willow tree, suntanned limbs decorated in bracelets and woven bangles. Skinny jeans tight enough to hint at his religion and a soft suede jacket worn over nothing but the bare skin of his chest. A few bare-knuckle-fight scars on his knuckles, and a sultry mouth made as much for kissing as it was for smart remarks. Taken altogether it made him one damned *odd* Omega, but it made him fascinating.

"See anything you like?" the Omega asked, returning once-over for once-over. "I do. I'm Zane, by the way. Just so you know what name you're going to be screaming."

Grant barked out a laugh. "Cheeky son of a bitch, aren't you?"

"I am." Zane leaned on the railing, grinning shamelessly. "What's the name I'm going to scream? Fair's fair."

Grant wiped his forehead, smelling the strong

tang of rust from the padlock. "Grant," he said. Then, "Any of those lines ever work for you?"

"Nope," Zane replied cheerfully. "But I live in hope. How about it?"

Damn. Grant lost the battle with his own grin. Tight body, smart mouth, and sass for days. Just his type, usually, but... No. *Legacy Tattoo* was his only sweetheart right now. It had to be, until they were up and running.

"Aww. I lost you somewhere in there, didn't I?" Zane cocked his head. "Anything I can do to change your mind?"

"As an Omega sniffing up an Alpha, nope." Grant laid the useless crowbar aside. "But if you're a friendly neighborhood lay-about who happens to be passing by and you have any WD-40..."

"Oh, so you think I'm the kind of guy who knows where to lay his hands on a little extra lubricant when it's needed?" Zane's grin grew sharper. "You're right. Back in a second. You won't even notice I'm gone."

He leaped over the stairwell, easy as a cat convinced it'd land on its feet with all nine lives fully intact, and loped lightly down the sidewalk leading away from *Legacy*. Grant cocked his head to enjoy the view. This'd always been a lively neighborhood. He remembered it from back in the days when Granddad had manned a foot-powered machine and specialized in ship's anchors and LOVE + OMEGA hearts. Nice to know that some things might change, but others never did.

His phone jangled to life in his hip pocket. When Grant checked it, the readout said *Marshall*. They'd met a few weeks ago at a block party on the roof of Kit's building -- right before Kit unexpectedly gave birth to the son he hadn't known he was carrying. The miraculous weirdness of it all still made Grant blink.

As for Grant and Marshall, they'd clicked as soon as they'd met, and Marshall was like the pain-in-the-ass brother he'd never known he wanted. A new friend, and one with a little time on his hands, he'd offered to help.

"I'll be there in twenty," Marshall said, sounding sleepy. Which didn't surprise Grant. Marshall worked hard at whatever he set himself to, but he played even harder. Rare was the night that Marshall didn't host one or two Omegas in his bed. "You need anything from the hardware store?"

Grant lifted his chin in surprise as Zane reappeared around the corner, can of WD-40 in hand. A man of his word, then. "Grenades, if they sell them. Otherwise I think I've got what I need."

"I could lay my hands on a grenade or two," Marshall offered, and as far as Grant could tell he meant it. Wouldn't surprise him. "I'll put out some feelers. See you in twenty."

Grant shook his head at the phone, but he tucked it back in his pocket and had his hands free in time to catch the familiar blue and yellow aerosol can Zane tossed him. "This do you?"

Hmm. Grant studied the can of WD-40 and found it grimy and festooned with the remnants of cobwebs. Still, it beat grenades. At least for now. "It'll do."

"Aren't you the sweet-talking Alpha," Zane teased. "Go to it."

Zane leaned one hip against the wall beside the door to watch Grant apply lubricant where it would prove most instructive. Jeez, Zane had Grant making double and triple entendres in his own head now. Grant clicked his tongue at himself.

Zane chuckled. "Word on the street is your grandfather used to own this place."

"Word's right. My granddad built this building from the ground up. Ran the shop here for 62 years before he passed. Been closed since his business partner died. Took some legal wrangling and a lot of saving, but I finally got the place back."

"What're you going to do with the space? Same? Ink and metal?"

"Like it's in my blood, which it is." Grant tucked the can of WD-40 under his arm and wiped his hands on his thighs before shoving his cuffs up to show off the tattoos that stretched from wrist to elbow. They went higher, but his jacket didn't. Bold blackwork and bright jewel colors, dragons breathing sinuous fire and silvery smoke. Granddad had started it, and Grant had honored his memory by finishing the work. For an encore, he gestured to one ear and the ladder of silver hoops that ringed the cartilage. "All that and more."

A shrug sent his sleeves back down. Grant took a breath, fished the key back out his pocket, and tried the freshly lubed lock again. And again. Finally, with a small squeal of protest, the key turned. One more twist of the crowbar and the hasp popped open. Grant squared his shoulders, and gave the door a shove. It opened, emitting a breath of old leather and older ink. Grant breathed deeply, greedily, and if he happened to catch another deep whiff of Zane's spicy-sweet scent, well, that was a pure bonus.

Zane craned his head to look past Grant and let out a whistle. "What a mess."

He wasn't wrong. Years of abandonment hadn't done the place any favors. Still..."I'm not afraid of hard work."

"For that, you'll need help."

Grant shook his head. "Got a buddy of mine with a strong back already lined up. And there are others I could call on." Darius would come, even if he had a toddler and a pregnant mate, but Grant wouldn't ask him unless the situation got dire. Family came first.

"No matter how much help you think you need for a job like this, you need more," Zane said with certainty. "Lucky for you I've got plenty of time on my hands and I could use some gainful employment." He grinned, shameless, when Grant gave him a flat look. "Hey, you're the one who called me a lay-about, Alpha. The least you could do is give me an honest day's work. I'm good with my hands. See?" He held them up for examination.

"*You're* dangerous, is what you are," Grant replied, but he took Zane's hand before thinking -- which he should have. A thrill of sensation made him draw in a sharp breath when skin pressed skin. The sweetness of the air between them grew stronger, like walking face-first into a bakery on rum and spice cake morning, and Grant's skin felt suddenly too tight for his bones. A deep ache started in his balls and his cock twitched, ready and willing to go hard for a willing partner. Zane had to be close to a fertile spell. Grant wondered if he knew it or not.

If he hadn't before, he sure did now. His pupils were dilated to dark suns and his skin warming with a dusky, lusty blush. His hand spasmed once around Grant's. Tempting, so tempting, but… no. Not happening. He had a business of his own to run. He didn't have a drop of attention to spare and the last thing he needed, no matter what his dick wanted, was a lap full of warm, wet, willing Omega.

Damn, damn, and damn again.

"No." Grant eased his hand and Zane's apart.

"I'd love a bite, but my plate's already full."

Zane had to know how tempting he looked, and he plainly wasn't ashamed to use it. He leaned in, giving Grant another breath of his scent. "Sure about that?"

"Sure as I have to be," Grant said. His cock was proving him a liar, straining at his zipper. "Sure enough."

Zane glanced down and lingered, hot with lust. The kind of look that made Grant want to grab a double handful of his pert ass and hold tight. He traced the tip of his tongue across his lower lip. "Really sure?"

"Sure as I'm going to get, and that's the last answer I'm going to give you," Grant said. "So scram, would you? Before we do something stupid."

Zane laughed. "Where's the fun in that?"

He turned as casually as he'd come to walk away, Omega scent trailing behind him in a tempting cloud. He got a few steps down the street, maybe fifteen, before he turned for one last shot. He licked his lips again, maybe tasting Grant's scent in return, then -- grinned. "Hey, Alpha. You know something?"

Oh, that wasn't foreshadowing or anything. Grant had seen that look on more than one face right before its owner came out with a heaping helping of mischief to manage. He folded his arms, trying not to return the grin and invite the devil out to play. "What?"

"You're moving into *my* neighborhood," Zane said, his gaze wicked in all sorts of ways. "No matter what else opening this place back up brings, I doubt we're done yet, you and me."

He probably wasn't wrong. Scratch that. He definitely wasn't.. And so help him if Grant wasn't looking forward to it.

Chapter Two

Best breakfast in the world? If anyone had asked Zane in college, he would have voted for a black coffee big enough to swim in but strong enough to float on, and a cigarette for dessert. Maybe a roll or a doughnut if he was feeling fancy or flush with cash.

Hell, that'd been his breakfast of choice up until right around five years ago.

After that his tastes had changed -- part necessity, part maturity. He might still *want* to crawl over broken glass for a smoke but he hadn't tasted one in ages. He'd given up doughnuts and black coffee for the sake of decaffeinated tea, but he still took it black as sin, without a grain of sugar. Bitter, bottomless, beautiful.

Zane blew across the top of the paper cup he'd bought at the little cafe situated catty-cornered from *Legacy Tattoo*, or what would be *Legacy* once Grant put in all the elbow grease and backbreaking work he'd need to get it up and running.

Exhales led to inhales, and on the breath back in Zane's nose was flooded with the scent of Alpha. Not just any Alpha. He'd spent five? ten? minutes with the guy one day ago, and Zane could have picked Grant out of a coal cellar at midnight by his scent alone. Spicy, like cloves. Strong, like espresso. Ink. Rubbing alcohol. The tang of iron.

A shiver worked its way down Zane's spine -- a good one. *Mmm.* He pressed his thighs together and savored the sensation, flickers of fantasy dancing through his head. Oh, he'd cracked a grin at first at the sight of the fierce little Alpha trying to crowbar his way into the old abandoned shop. He'd meant to stop in for half a second and have a little fun, nothing more.

He hadn't been at all prepared for a fucking briefcase-bomb of a man.

His favorite kind. Wind 'em up and watch 'em go off. *Tick, tick, boom.*

Mmm. Worth pursuing? *Could be.* He'd seemed pretty set on that "no" he'd given Zane, and that was as interesting as it was frustrating -- and challenging. In Zane's life experience, it wasn't often that a randy Alpha -- and he'd smelled the pheromones on Grant, he knew Grant wanted him -- turned a willing Omega down. So why had he done it? *Curiouser and curiouser.*

Zane licked the taste of Grant's scent off his lips, swallowed it with a gulp of hot tea, and kicked back in his chair. He'd picked a seat near the cafe window, a little apart and away from a crowd of regulars who loved nothing better than lounging around and talking about everything. And everyone. Especially anyone new.

Spilling tea wasn't his usual thing, but there was no doubt it could come in handy. For example, he wanted more information about Grant and his family. Sitting here, all he had to do was open his ears and listen.

A sturdy, square-shouldered Alpha waiting for his breakfast sandwich -- to wit, Grant -- addressed the tall, rangy Alpha at his elbow -- someone Zane didn't know, but who looked vaguely familiar. "How long do you think it'll take to clean out the mess and get the shop up to code?"

Ahh. There we are. Zane tilted his head in their direction. *Must be that buddy he was talking about. Give it up, mi cariño.*

"God knows, I don't." Rangy shrugged. "Good intentions only get you so far. Two months at least. I'll bet three."

"Not that long!" Grant objected. "Maybe a month, at most. Three weeks. I can make it happen. The new autoclave should be here next week. Got it online, military surplus, shipping from Switzerland. I have my own tools, too. Two tattoo machines, plenty of inks, gloves, disinfectants, the works. So we don't have to wait on those."

"Still. *Three weeks?* Maybe. If we work around the clock," Rangy said. "You'll wear yourself out."

Grant made a gesture of dismissal. "Not me. I'm tough enough. You saying you don't feel up to a little scrubbing, a little painting?"

"Hell no, I've got nothing going for weeks and I can't stand to get bored. If that means we scrub floors, then we scrub floors. We paint until the whole place sparkles good enough to pass inspection and we hang your sign out front."

"Uh-huh. See, that's what you say, Marshall," Grant said, eyeing Rangy. "Until you decide you want to go wandering again."

Ah. A name. Good. Zane had been getting tired of calling him *Rangy.* Were they brothers? They didn't look a thing alike, one short and compact and one tall and broad as a Viking, but they sure acted like brothers.

"Not until we're done here," Marshall said firmly. "I promised."

"Who?"

Marshall stuck his jaw out. "Myself."

Which seemed to settle the point for both Alphas. They collected cardboard trays full of paper cups of coffee and brown paper bags full of breakfast sandwiches, already spotted with grease, and elbowed their way out of the shop, bickering amiably as they went.

Zane watched them go. A few more things made sense now. His come-ons were rare, but they didn't usually fall flat. Given the job Grant had taken on with the shop, that'd send anyone's libido into second place. *Though it shouldn't.* In Zane's opinion, with plenty of experience to back it up, nothing beat a good, old-fashioned, rough, hard, balls against the wall, heels pointed to heaven, no-holds-barred fuck for stress relief.

From its place in his pocket, his phone trilled. Zane frowned at the sound. No one should have been calling him at that hour, and when he glanced at the number of the incoming call his frown deepened. He answered before it could ring again. "Something wrong?"

A rusty chuckle answered him. His neighbor, Eduardo, sixty and spry as he'd been at sixteen. "Not unless you consider someone wanting cookies for breakfast a problem, but *mijo* wouldn't give me any peace until I called to get your answer."

Zane snorted. "Are you serious? No, I know you are, and I know my boy. Put him on."

Jostling noises indicated the phone had been taken by force. "But they're Wardo's, they got fiver in them!" a little voice piped.

"Hadrian..." Zane started, trying not to grin. He'd named his son after the legendary wall in Scotland, hoping he'd be just as sturdy, and he'd turned out just as hard-headed instead.

Zane wasn't complaining. The son of a single Omega needed to be tough. Besides, now he could call the kid Hades when he really acted up, or shout *Hell!* and not worry about corrupting a little mind. Win/win.

"Fiber," Eduardo corrected in the background.

"So? You want fiber? How about a prune for breakfast? I can give you a hot buttered prune on toast."

"Gross," Zane and Hadrian said at the same time, making Hadrian laugh. Zane too. "Do what Wardo says, and you can have a real cookie after dinner. Chocolate chips and everything."

That satisfied all demands, and Hadrian hung up without complaint. Or another word, but that was his boy. *Why waste many word when little word will do.* Zane laughed quietly to himself. He'd never planned on being a single father, but he wouldn't have traded his son -- too young yet to know if he'd end up an Alpha or an Omega -- for the world on a silver plate and all the kingdoms thereof for seconds. Grant probably felt the same way about his family legacy.

Zane liked a family man almost as much as he liked a fierce one.

Though his heat cycle wasn't far off, he remembered with a sudden shock of arousal, and he'd better be wary of that. Probably half of why he wanted Grant as much as he did, come to think of it. And that should have cooled his ardor, but should-have never had lit Zane's fuse. The notion just made it burn hotter, and Zane pressed his thighs together again to ease the kindling ache between them.

Mmm. Risky, that. Dangerous. He knew how it went. Get a little too involved, get a little careless, end up pregnant.

Zane toyed with his nearly empty cup, thinking hard. A smart man would walk away. It'd be safest, smartest.

Thing was… Zane never had been able to resist playing with matches, and the Alpha in his sights was a damn spitfire. Renovating a storefront in such rough shape was more than even two willing Alphas could manage in a month. They'd need help, and Zane needed a job. Needed a job badly. He usually did contract work, but jobs had been thin on the ground for a couple of weeks now. Eduardo wouldn't take a cent for babysitting unless Zane was employed or he'd have had to tote Hadrian around wherever he went while he looked for work.

But if he could convince Grant to hire him… well now. That'd pad his pocket *and* set him and the Alpha up for a sweet bit of quid pro quo.

Question answered, decision made.

He'd just set off across the street and see what kind of spark he could catch.

* * *

By the time he and Marshall strode through *Legacy Tattoo's* doors with the vast quantities of breakfast two working Alphas required, Grant was more than ready to eat. His stomach rumbled and roared in appreciation of the savory, salty, greasy smells topped off with the rich fragrance of strong coffee.

"One of almost everything, and two of the rest," Marshall said in satisfaction. "Where do you want it?"

Grant pushed his tools aside and wiped his hands on his hips. "In my stomach. But for right now, put it on the front counter." It was still sturdy enough to serve as a table. "And grab whatever works for chairs."

Marshall raised an eyebrow at him -- *you're not my CO, asshole* -- but did as he'd been told. Grant pitched in to help while Marshall scattered bags of food in a haphazard imitation of plating up a feast, and together they parked their asses to tear into the goods. Some things never changed, Grant thought, amused. Alphas always ate this way, more like a pack of starved piranhas than a horde of men, one of them small and skinny. Every time he turned around he half expected to hear David Attenborough narrating the feeding frenzy. Coffee, ham and egg breakfast burritos with crispy hash browns, pancakes, and a cup of mixed fruit to keep his arteries from clanging shut on the spot. He took a taste of each, then nodded in approval. "Good job."

Marshall grinned at him. He took a massive bite of a bear claw and asked around it, "So who's the Omega eye-fucking you while we were in line?"

He whooped with laughter while Grant face-palmed. Might have known he wouldn't get away with that one for long. "Just an Omega," he said before Marshall could jump in with a Greek chorus of perverted commentary. "A guy from the neighborhood who loaned me a hand."

"That all he offered?"

Grant whipped a tortilla crust down the counter at his friend. It bounced off Marshall's forehead, but didn't stop him from being highly entertained at Grant's expense. "Alpha's got his temper up, huh? He must have made an impression."

"Marshall, shut it."

"Nah." Marshall kicked back, still gnawing at his pastry. "You, my friend, need an Omega to cool you off. How long's it been since you got laid, buddy? A year? Two?"

More like twenty-three months specifically, but Marshall didn't need to know that.

And he still didn't take the hint and stop. "Looked like that Omega wouldn't mind volunteering for the job. You're thirty and you don't have a serious squeeze to tap on the regular. Thirty! If you're not careful it'll dry up and fall off."

Well now, that couldn't go unanswered. Grant gestured at a plastic cup of syrup provided for their pancakes. "Is that hot?"

"Hot enough it made my fingertips all red. Why?"

"Because if you don't shut it I'm gonna dump the whole thing on your crotch."

Marshall yelped and covered his dick with both hands, one of which still held half a bear claw. Grant's turn to laugh, then, which was good. Come on. Thirty wasn't senior citizenry. He growled under his breath. Dry up and fall off, his ass.

At least, it'd better not.

"Let me make this clear," Grant said while he had Marshall's full attention. "That long tall drink of Omega is not my concern, and he's not any of your business either. And my sex life is def-i-fucking-nitely not up for discussion. I'm married to the shop until it turns a profit, and so are you, so finish your breakfast and get moving. We've got a long day ahead of us and you're gonna need the energy."

He got a muttered gripe, a glower, and a grumble for that, but it was followed by the sound of speed-eating so Grant decided to call it a win. He put his chin in his hand and sighed. Marshall might be a mannerless heathen and a hellion bastard, but his heart *was* in the right place.

Food. Work ethic. Focus. Check, check, and check.

Now all they needed was luck.

Grant crumpled up his rubbish, dropped it in a bin, and started wandering the shop front to go over his mental plans for the day. He glanced over his shoulder as he paced, making sure Marshall stayed on track. He seemed bent on scraping the box for any stray crumb, but so far so good.

Just Grant and his friend, and an empty storefront.

So who, Grant wondered, was whistling to himself in the back room?

Grant detoured by the crowbar and strolled toward the noise. They'd left the back door unlocked for unimpeded access to a rented industrial dumpster parked there -- granddad's old partner had been a bit of a hoarder, and the work rooms in the back were packed to the rafters with assorted crap -- but now he suspected that might have been a mistake. Unless whoever was in there wanted to steal any of the rubbish, in which case they were welcome to it.

But when he got there, the source turned out to be neither.

Grant stood in the doorway, blindsided for the first time in years, staring at his unexpected guest. Zane, who had exchanged his studded vest for worn-in workman's gear, busy hefting an armload of assorted debris. A path through the diminished mess showed that he'd been doing it for a while now, possibly during the whole breakfast break. He gleamed with the sweat of hard work and looked good enough to eat.

Zane must have felt Grant's gaze on him. He looked up and winked at him. "Took you long enough."

"The fuck," Grant said, too baffled for words. "What are you doing?"

"Me? Working." Zane nodded down at his armload. "We haven't talked about pay yet, but I figure you're the kind of man who'll offer a fair wage for a good job done."

"There is no job."

"No?" Zane gestured around himself, turning in

a slow circle for emphasis and finishing by facing Grant without a drop of shame. Giving him a good look at cobblestoned stomach muscles under the ripped band shirt, and a fine gander at firmly muscled arms, too. "Then what am I doing?"

The noise must have drawn Marshall, who leaned over Grant's shoulder and did some whistling of his own. "Damn, Omega, you've got some guns on you. I can't lift that much."

"Just takes practice." Zane grinned. "Lots of opportunity for that here. I've carried five loads to the dumpster while you two were hoovering up enough breakfast for five. See the difference I made already?"

"Mm-hmm." Grant folded his arms. "And your point is?"

"That he needs a job, and he's already doing a good one. What? Don't turn that glare on me, friend." Marshall was enjoying this far too much. "Give him a trial, see if he can keep up. What've you got to lose? Your dry streak?"

That got another hand bounced off the back of his head, but not Grant's. Zane's.

Marshall boggled at him. "Excuse the fuck out of you, asshole? Did you miss the part where I'm on your side?"

"Nope." Zane wiped his forehead on his arm and came up cheekier than Marshall had ever dreamed of being. "Mind your mouth, and I'll mind mine."

Zane paused for a second, in which Grant was one hundred percent sure he wasn't finished. He was right. A wicked twinkle lit in Zane's eye. He waggled his tongue at the pack. "And while I'm at it, I'll mind Grant's too."

Oh yeah. Marshall loved Zane after that. He'd won himself a fan for life.

Grant gave in. "Fine!" he told Zane, who brightened up brilliantly. "One trial for one day, with a fair wage paid at quitting time. Tomorrow is up for discussion *if* you earn it. Deal?"

Zane slapped a hand into his. "Deal. You won't be sorry."

Yeah, well, that remained to be seen. "Stay with me. We'll keep clearing out the debris." That ought to sort out his willingness to work long term. And besides… while Grant still wasn't planning to go there, if the scenery insisted on being present then there was no harm in looking while keeping his hands to himself. No one ever died from just looking.

Zane bent fluidly at the waist to scoop up another armload. Smooth muscles flexed, lean and springy and inviting of naked taste tests. Grant bit his tongue instead. No, no one ever died from just looking. Except maybe from a raging case of blue balls. *Fuck.*

* * *

Eight Hours Later

Had Grant worried that Zane wouldn't hold up his end of the bargain? Not a chance. He was everywhere, sweeping up sawdust, applying elbow grease to the windows and scraping off enough grime to make them see-through again, levering up cracked squares of linoleum and wielding a ruler around ragged corners in need of repair. He seemed to know what was junk and what might be worth up cycling, recycling, or sold. A very effective worker bee. Grant almost wanted to see what'd happen if he handed Zane a plunger and pointed him toward the old broken toilet.

Zane beat him to it. Even got the damned thing running again.

And had he wondered if Zane would lay off the flirting for the sake of working?

Not a chance.

Oh, he put his back into the job. Grant couldn't fault him on that. Always moving, but always glancing over his shoulder too, with a wicked look aimed just at Grant. He put a little extra sway into his hips every time he caught Grant looking back, and though Zane smelled of sweat and hard work, a hint of Omega musk still teased Grant's nose at every turn.

"Are you like this with every Alpha, or am I just special?" he asked when the work brought him and Zane within arm's reach of each other.

Zane's eyes danced. "You make me sound like a flirt."

"No. Really?" Grant asked, dry.

Zane laughed at that, a little more scent coming through as he did. "Everybody should be allowed one vice."

"That's not an answer."

"Isn't it?" Zane knelt to scoop up an armload of what looked like old coupon sheets, faded and cracking at their corners. He glanced up at Grant and winked. "Are you like this with every Omega?"

Grant shook his head, but for all that he couldn't help grinning back at him. Zane's humor was infectious.

Marshall noticed all the banter, of course. "Not interested in him, huh?" his friend murmured, setting down icy cold bottles of water for all three of them.

Grant took his with a hiss, the bottle so *very* cold that chips of ice clung to its sides. "Shut your cakehole."

"I told you so," Marshall sang. "You do have good taste, I'll give you that."

At least Zane overheard that one and tossed a ratty old magazine at Marshall as payback. Grant approved.

"Forgive me for the ass crack?" Marshall asked Zane, with a straight face, even, which even Grant had to admire the ballsiness of. So to speak.

"I'll lick it over," Zane replied without batting an eyelash. "Oops, did I say lick? I meant think. I'll think it over. Real hard."

Grant's jaw ached, and he realized he'd been grinding his teeth. He eased his jaw open carefully, frowning at himself. He shouldn't care if Marshall and Zane flirted with each other. Neither should it bother him that Zane willingly shared his rakish charm with anyone willing to banter back.

And yet... and yet. It grated. Made something deep and primal inside Grant want to snarl and say *No. Mine!* So. What was he going to do about that? He knew what he *wanted* to do. Even if the larger of his two heads knew better. But...

Marshall and Grant were still going. "Thinking does a body good. Lots of thinking does a body even better. I --" Marshall stopped mid-sentence and glanced his way, delight written across his face. "Grant. Buddy. Were you growling?"

"You know, I think he might have been. Not sure." Zane cocked his head. "Do it again, gorgeous."

This time a genuine growl did escape Grant, and not accidentally. "Back to work," he said, using the *Voice of God* that these two better know meant business. "Now."

Marshall beat a hasty retreat, cackling all the way, but Zane wasn't done yet. "Are you two brothers? You sure act like you're related."

"God no. I don't have any family left. Forget him

for now." Grant impatiently brushed Marshall's existence aside -- and as for what he said next, the devil must have made Grant do it. He added, in a low voice meant for Zane alone, "What if I held you to that working hard thing? What then?"

Zane's jaw dropped, as loose as Grant's was tight. "Did you just..."

Grant shrugged, feeling oddly light and free, enjoying himself. "Maybe. Not sure. What do you think?" He turned his back then and strolled back to his corner of the junk pile, whistling under his breath. He could feel Zane's gaze on him, intent and just a little bit delighted, and heard the Omega murmur something indistinguishable but approving under his breath.

Zane one, Grant one. Grant grinned to himself, fierce and pleased. *Let the good times roll.*

Chapter Three

Another day, another dollar. First day, first dollar? Not bad for line-jumping past the usual hiring process. While his Alpha's pain in the ass buddy trailed out of the shop, filthy from tip to toe and cheerfully dishing out one final helping of shit to Grant as he went, Zane raised his arms over his head for a good hard stretch of satisfaction. He arched his back for more of the same, then twisted his hips for the *piece de resistance.* Joints popped, clicked and stretched with a deep, delicious ache that made him sigh in relief.

He sensed a curious gaze fixed on him from the side, and cocked his head that way. "See something you like, Alpha?"

Grant snorted quietly. He'd washed his hands and was drying them with an old but clean cloth. Idly curious, idly satisfied, Zane watched him in the light of the storm lanterns that had to serve until the shop's power was connected. He wouldn't have thought Grant was the type to dry his hands on his T-shirt or hips, and it was always nice to be proved right.

"You're staring."

"Am I?" Zane asked, innocent. "Tsk, tsk. Shame on me."

He felt a spark of pride when Grant rolled his eyes and laughed, even if it was a quiet, gruff sort of laugh. "You're incorrigible, aren't you? And by the way, you still don't work here."

"Oh no?" Zane thought Grant was teasing -- he'd better be. He knew hard work when he saw it, knew how to do it, and he'd be damned if he gave up either the paycheck or the man who would write it. "What do you call what I did today, then?"

"Making trouble. Am I wrong?"

"Wrong?" Zane then bent his head and looked up through his eyelashes, a handy trick he'd learned long ago. A wicked look, a come hither, and..."Oh no. You're not wrong."

"Good lord." Grant tossed the towel at him. "Stop trying so hard, Omega. You've got the job, for as long as it lasts. Which might not be that long if you keep working at the pace you were running today. You always go this hard after what you want?"

Grant made tracks for a stack of newer-looking boxes behind the front counter while Zane stayed back and gawked at him -- a gawk that faded to a brilliant grin. Things were coming up roses, now. Zane *liked* it when that happened.

Even if he did have to remember to be careful around this time of his cycle. "I might," he said. "I've been known to."

"Color me surprised," Grant murmured, shaking his head. He flipped open the lid of two boxes. From one, he brought out a sheaf of plastic-sheathed papers. From the other, a matched set of longneck beers, one of which he slid across the table. "Reward for a job well done."

Zane cackled, took the offering and gulped, savoring the bitter yeastiness and the round earthiness of hops. *Delicious.* The deep, warm ache drifted from the small of his back to his groin, slippery and musky-sweet. Zane breathed deep -- he'd never been one to be put off by the scent of his own kind -- and quirked an eyebrow as, across the shop, Grant's nostrils flared. Probably unconsciously. Alpha responded to Omega, always. It was the way they'd been made, and that was no bad way at all.

He wasn't immune, himself. Zane rolled the neck of the beer across his lower lip and enjoyed the view. It was, to his mind, unique to the man before him. The short, tough Alpha didn't seem to know when to quit any more than Zane did.

Case in point, Zane opening his mouth. "You really don't have any family? No one?"

"It's just me," Grant said shortly. He still missed his grandfather so much it hurt sometimes, and family was a sore point with him -- for more than one reason. One of which he hoped Zane wouldn't bring up.

Which, of course, Zane immediately did, looking deeply invested in his potential answer as he spoke. "No siblings? No kids? No one?"

"No siblings. No parents or grandparents left," Grant said. "And God no, no kids. Not now. Probably not ever."

Silence.

Grant glanced up at Zane to find him looking -- perturbed? He scowled at the Omega. "It's not unnatural. Lots of Alphas are childless by choice."

"Yeah, but..." Zane still seemed troubled. Weirdly so. He shook his head. "Why? A man like you, there's got to be a reason."

"Oh yeah?"

Zane snorted. "I've known you right about 24 hours now, Grant, and I can already tell you're the kind of man who lives or dies by a mission. So it's a mission of yours not to bear fruit. How come?"

"You don't know when to quit, do you?"

Zane only grinned toothily in answer, but that was better than his worried look.

Grant sighed. He took his armload of laminated papers and started tacking them to the cleanest of the walls. "I don't have kids or want kids because what I already have -- this place, *Legacy Tattoo*, is all the family I'm going to have time and energy for, for months.

Maybe years."

"So you're not ever going to have a family of your own? Would it be the worst thing in the world if you had a kid?"

Grant's temper flared. "You're not getting it, Zane. This place *is* my family. It's what I've *got* from family. It's my responsibility to make it live again -- no, make it thrive. That's my mission. I don't have time for anything else. I can't."

Zane frowned, but whatever he was thinking, he kept it to himself. Grant trained a watchful eye on him until he was sure Zane was keeping mum for the moment, then shrugged and got back to work. When he finished, he'd tacked up all the laminated designs, not haphazardly, but in a cascading pattern. He nodded in satisfaction at the result.

Fascinated, Zane drifted closer. "What are they?"

Grant glanced up as if surprised to be asked. Or maybe surprised at Zane's tone, bereft for once of teasing. He hesitated a beat before answering. "Flash."

"And that means..."

"McInk, the fast food of this world," Grant said with another quick, wry quirk of the lips. "Love hearts, barbed wire, dolphins and innocent cartoons engaged in nasty business. Quick and dirty, walk in off the street and get it done on a whim. I mean, some people love them. Nothing wrong with that. Artists just like a little more chance to exercise their creativity."

Zane wrinkled his nose. "So why put them up?"

Grant shrugged. "When you're saving every penny you can, you get the job that's in front of you done and you learn how to do it with a smile."

Fair point. "Or at least not with a glare?" Zane asked. "What do you *like* to do, then, when you're given the choice?"

Again, the curious stare. Zane stood still and let Grant scan him, though he did wonder what the Alpha was looking for and whether he was finding it there. He must have passed some kind of test. The bare hint of Alpha pheromones, which Grant kept mostly tamped down, expanded to tease at Zane with its spiciness, and he saw Grant's pupils dilate slightly.

Note to self: you can turn an artist on just by asking to see their etchings. Zane curled his tongue around the neck of his beer, enjoying the moment.

Grant held up a finger. He dug deeper in the box and unearthed a heavy three-ring binder which he laid on the table. Zane came closer and touched the cover. Battered, edges curling. It'd seen some hard use over the years, and it was stuffed with pages to the point of bursting.

Why not get a new one? he might have asked. If he'd needed to. Grant liked things with history. Look at this shop. Anyone sane would wash their hands of the tumbledown old disaster, but not this Alpha.

Zane liked that too.

He lifted the cover carefully, and oh yeah. This wasn't bread and butter. This was heart and soul. Page after page after page of photos and sketches -- fantastical and fascinating designs with dragons and weird, wonderful beasts with eyes of flame. Knots intricate they made him momentarily dizzy, and Viking designs so bold he could almost smell the sea. Portraits as real as life, and cartoons that almost popped off the pages, and the *colors* -- He drew in a breath to break the spell over himself. "These are amazing, Grant."

That got him a sharp look that wasn't hard to interpret.

Zane drew an X over his heart. "For real, Alpha,

no joke. I wouldn't joke about something like this. I've been known to doodle, but this, this is art. You *are* an artist."

The faintest hint of color showed on Grant's cheeks. He looked... pleased. "Doodle, huh?"

"Nothing like this." Zane turned a careful page, his attention divided between Alpha and art. Felt like something interesting, something important, something good was about to happen, and he wanted to make sure he was on top of it. "Just scribbles when I'm bored."

"Got any I could see?"

"Not on me, Alpha." Zane grinned at him. "And as it happens, I don't have a single drop of ink on me. Or anything pierced."

"Hmm. Might be we could do something about that," Grant murmured -- and if that wasn't enough of a delicious jolt, the notion of being marked by this man -- he kept going. One more rummage in the box brought out a set of markers that looked pricier than a month's rent. "Ever *thought* about a tattoo? Giving or receiving?"

"It's crossed my mind," Zane said. Since he'd met Grant, that was.

Grant nodded as if satisfied. "Good." He offered the pack of markers to Zane, and as nonchalantly as if he were in a massage parlor, hopped his tight little ass up onto the counter.

Zane looked from the markers to Grant and back again, confused. Turned on, but confused. "You lost me, Alpha."

Grant laughed. Still sitting upright, he skinned off his shirt and tossed it into a corner. Underneath he had a barrel chest that tapered to a narrow waist, liberally furred with dark blond. He leaned back on his hands, and the spicy scent of aroused Alpha rose stronger than before. He met Zane's gaze without pretense. "Bring those over here, and let's see what you've got."

Oh, that was an invitation. When Grant gave in, he did it with style. Zane's scent mingled with his, equally strong, and he knew his pupils had gone wide and dark. "And if you like what I've got?"

"Then you'll like what *I've* got." Grant slipped back off the table and held out his arms half in challenge, half in a dare. "Well?"

Zane could resist anything but temptation, and he never had been able to say no to a dare. He licked his lips. "Or I could skip the markers."

Grant's lips parted over a fierce grin. "Or that." He crooked his fingers, beckoning Zane on. And -- what was a horny Omega to do? How was Zane to say no? He *wasn't*, that's what. And how. And oh boy, oh boy, oh *man*.

Zane bared his teeth in reply to Grant's display, wicked and wanton. He rolled his hips and strolled toward Grant pelvis first, showing off his loose Omega joints and long, slender legs that wrapped so nicely around a man's back. He ran his palms up his chest and cupped his pecs as if they were sore and swollen, full of milk, and moaned. Oh, that might have been a step too far even in the name of temptation. Hot, hard, almost too tender to touch, electrified, wired to his cock. He jerked, thrusting against the air without meaning to, and groaned at the lack of friction.

Grant's beckoning hands fell as his pupils dilated, but the Alpha had mighty self-control. "Clothes off," was all he rasped, not taking one step closer. "Now."

Zane held back, eyes half open, drinking him in.

"And?"

"And get your ass over here."

Zane's lips parted on a long purr. Yes, yes, *yes*. He wrestled his way free of his shirt, let his jeans fall off his hips, stepped out of the rest and stood naked in the middle of the shop floor. They hadn't locked the door or drawn the blinds, if there were even blinds to draw anymore. Marshall could have walked back in any second. Anyone walking past would have gotten a hell of a view.

So let them.

Zane got his ass over to Grant, buttery between his thighs, Omega scent strong even to his nose. He could see Grant expected to be plastered with an armful of man, maybe even tipped over backward in a playful pounce -- and that *would* be fun, so noted for future adventures -- but even more fun would be keeping him wide awake.

He went to his knees and pressed his open mouth to Grant's denim-covered cock with a groan.

Grant loosed a rough, strangled shout and thrust his fingers through Zane's hair. He canted forward and back, half smothering Zane with cock that hadn't even made it past the zipper, and gasped when Zane followed him and scraped against the hardness inside with the edge of his teeth. "Like it rough, do you?"

"Rougher the better," Zane said between playful bites, firm enough to feel, sharp enough to invite retribution. He caught Grant's zipper between his teeth and, carefully, drew it down a couple clicks. Nosing into the opening, he breathed deep. "You want me."

"You think I was pretending up till now?"

"Nope." He let go and leaned back on his heels, looking up, drinking Grant in. Could *he* resist a dare? Zane had to find out. "You want me, and I want you.

Do something about it, Alpha."

And Grant did.

He lifted one foot and rested it against Zane's breastbone. Careful, sure, but unyielding as steel, he pushed so that Zane had no choice but to lean back, then to lie down, and not even when his shoulder blades kissed the hardwood floor did Grant ease up. He leaned over, staring at Zane, pinning him fast. "Rules," he said. "Not negotiable. You have protection?"

Wordless, Zane shook his head. "Didn't figure on getting this lucky this early. You?"

"No."

"As much as you talk about not wanting kids, you don't carry a Johnson cover in your pocket?"

"Fuck off, I wasn't planning on getting lucky today. Just working." Grant considered him a moment, then nodded decisively. "I can work around what we've got. What we don't have. Whatever. I won't fuck you without a condom, but I've got a mouth and I've got hands, and I know how to grind a man until he begs for mercy."

Zane couldn't help it -- he arched up, moaning.

"You like that," Grant murmured. "Say please."

"Oh, you bastard," Zane said on another moan. "You're serious?"

Grant's gaze went dark and proud and dangerous. "As I can be. Say it, Zane. Say please."

Giving in was almost as sweet as dancing with the devil, sometimes. Zane grinned up at Grant, and let him have it. "Please, Alpha. Have me."

Grant growled, the same growl Zane had heard when they were teasing him, and fell on him as if he were a meal and Grant hadn't eaten in years. Zane let his arms and legs fall open to welcome Grant as he came down, wrapping around him to hold him tight and give him a foundation to work with. Open-mouthed kisses came sharp against his neck, his collarbone and his shoulder, making Zane cry out -- but not as loudly as he did when Grant shoved a hand between his legs and squeezed.

He tried to grab back, but Grant took hold of his arms and pushed them against the floor. "No. My show. Keep them there."

Zane writhed beneath him, but managed -- just -- to do as he'd been told, and only because of how much he wanted to. "Yes, fuck yes."

Grant brought his mouth down to graze over Zane's chest, his hand still busy between Zane's legs. He cupped Zane's balls and rolled them just the wrong side of gently, wrapped his fingers around Zane's cock and squeezed just the right side of too hard. Artist's fingers, long and nimble and utterly knowing, found his hot spots and worked them without a drop of mercy, not stopping until Zane was a mess of writhing frustration. Not without a drop of exertion, though. Grant's skin glowed with sweat, salty drops falling off him, and his eyes were nearly all pupil.

As Zane watched, Grant backed off far enough to give Zane a good view. *Bastard*. Zane loved it.

Clearly fully focused on his audience, Grant moved his narrow hips as sinuously as a snake. His jeans fell off in a careless slide of denim that he stepped easily out of. Next went a pair of black boxer briefs that clung like a second skin with the sweat of the day's work. Those took more work, but the reward was worth the effort. This skinny little Alpha had a cock like the most ripped of all bodybuilders would envy, thick and long and hard as a cudgel. He took himself in hand to display his goods to Zane. "You like?"

Was he kidding? Fucking hell, Zane's mouth watered at the sight of that monster. He disobeyed orders to wrap his arms around Grant's back, and his legs around Grant's waist, but Grant didn't complain. He put his mouth against Zane's ear and breathed. "Use your nails."

Oh fuck. Zane drew his nails down Grant's back once, just once, and came in a great shuddering rush. His thighs squeezed Grant's so hard he felt the same happen to the Alpha, his muscles seizing and locking as he drove down against Zane. His spunk mingled with Zane's, hot and messy and nasty and fan-fucking-tastic, and cords of muscle stood out on his tight chest as he rode it through.

Pleased, fucked-out, Zane arched his neck up and bit the blade of Grant's jaw, marking him just so with his teeth.

Grant bit back. "Knew you were trouble," he murmured, sounding equally pleased. "I was right."

Chapter Four

"What're you drawing?"

Grant tried to raise his head and peer at his chest, but Zane pushed him back down with a gentle -- gentle-ish -- *thunk*. "Lie still. You'll fuck up my lines."

"Heaven forbid," Grant murmured. He crossed his arms behind his head. They'd ended up moving the makeshift table off its legs and laying it on the floor, giving them at least some measure of protection against who-knew-what lurked down there. It wasn't any kind of feather bed, but it'd do. And it'd gotten Zane drawing, which so help him, Grant had developed a powerful curiosity about. Doodles, hmm? What kind? There was just something about Zane that spoke to the untapped potential of some real creativity, and Grant wanted to see it. "So what are you drawing?"

"Are you like this with Marshall, with your other friends? You must have some, and they must be wild."

"I never said they were wild. Some of them are steadier than me. Mostly they're parents. Tough."

"And that's a judgment coming from you?" Zane snorted. "They must be made out of actual concrete and rebar."

Grant laughed deep and from the belly. He didn't have any fat to jiggle, but his muscles flexed in ways that would have distracted a less dedicated artist than Zane. Zane snorted with wry amusement and laid his arm over Grant's waist to hold him still.

"Don't fuck up the lines, I got it," Grant said, eyes half shut. Damn, but he looked tasty like that.

Zane caught his lower lip between his teeth. "Changed my mind. Get to fucking."

The pretty blue eyes under those hooded lids

rolled up and back. "Nice try. Some of us need five minutes."

"I'll start the countdown." Zane lowered his mouth to Grant's chest and bit at one small, cherry-red nipple. "Four minutes fifty-nine seconds. And counting. Van Gogh."

Grant quirked an eyebrow without opening his eyes. "Come again?"

"Oh, I plan to," Zane said. He nipped the skin beneath Grant's collarbone, then reluctantly let go. He *did* want to finish his drawing. It'd been -- what, years? -- since he'd done more than scribble on a receipt while on hold. Or help with Hadrian's coloring books. And there was something to be said for the reward of coloring outside the lines, after all.

"Van Gogh," he said again, laying down the cerulean blue marker he'd chosen and picking up one in dark saffron. Nice markers, these. Beat the hell out of Crayola. "That starry night shit. Swirls and lights."

"I know the one. You can do that from memory?"

Zane shrugged one shoulder. He shifted to lie fully on his side, the better to make use of the canvas laid out so temptingly before him. "I used to have the poster on my ceiling when I was younger. Watching it was good for relaxing, dreaming."

Grant made a thoughtful noise. "You have siblings to keep you awake?"

"Not a one. Not for lack of trying. My sire and bearer tried for years. Just never happened." Zane capped his marker, equally thoughtful. He'd wondered if he'd end up miscarrying one kit after another when it was his turn. He'd dreaded sex as much as he'd craved it at first, but when he'd conceived his kit he'd known, *known* from the start how strong he was. And all he'd need to conceive another was open legs and a willing Alpha at the right time of the year.

Strange world they lived in.

Speaking of which... Zane propped his chin on Grant's chest and gave him a nudge. "I lost a bet against myself earlier."

"Hmm?"

"Most Alphas would have had me spread eagled and stuffed with their cock before they even thought about protection," Zane said candidly. "Even if they could tell I wasn't fertile *just* yet." Even if that would be soon and he had to keep reminding himself to be careful, damn it. "And I wouldn't have minded it at all tonight. So why didn't you?"

"I'm not an asshole, for one. And for another?"

He fell silent. Zane laid his head on Grant's chest and watched him, curious. Grant kept his gaze fixed on the ceiling, his fingers gentle in Zane's hair but his mind clearly a million miles away. Zane's libido began to ebb, recognizing the look of a man who'd shifted gears for the night even if he didn't know it yet.

"For another?" he prompted.

"I can't be a dad right now," Grant said. His jaw set as he spoke. "Not while I've got the shop to take care of. I like kits, cubs, chicks, pups, babies. They're fine. But this is my legacy, and I'll be damned if I get derailed now. Marshall might take chances left and right -- though as much as he fucks around, he's probably shooting blanks -- but me, I use protection, I keep it surface, or I do without. And this, what we seem to be growing here? It can't go farther than fucking, Zane. It just can't. Do you understand me?"

His words had the ring of utter finality to them, and disappointment made Zane's stomach plummet. He didn't let it show, though, maintaining his image of idle thinking. He hadn't been looking for forever, no, but he *liked* Grant. He liked Grant's toughness, his unexpected kindnesses, his sense of humor, his hellcat lovemaking, all of it.

Damn. Real shame. Would have been nice, Zane thought before reluctantly letting go of the idea. Not that he planned to let go of *Grant*. He just wouldn't ever let the Alpha know about those barely-formed daydreams. And he'd be more careful than a monk when it came to -- er, bad comparison. He'd double down on protection and make sure Grant did too, and when the riskiest day in his cycle came around, he'd lock himself in a room with a selection of fine rubber phalluses and a subscription to X Tube. He'd done *that* before, too.

"Hey." Grant tugged a little less gently at his hair. "You went quiet. You actually know how to go quiet?"

Zane laughed, glad when the mood shattered with a little electric crackle. "Bite me, Alpha. You're gonna regret asking that tomorrow."

Grant watched him sit up and sling one leg over, balancing himself astraddle. His hands came down lightly to cradle Zane's hips. "Tomorrow, is it?"

"Tomorrow," Zane said, sticking his chin out. "At my job. Here."

Grant watched him a little longer. He craned his neck to look down at Zane's artwork on his chest, and made a noise that sounded impressed, that made Zane's blood sizzle. He touched the lines thoughtfully. "It isn't because of the sex," he said at last. "But okay, Omega. You win. I said it before, but I'll say it again. You're hired."

Zane couldn't have stopped the triumphant blaze of a grin that broke over his face if he'd tried, and he didn't want to.

Beneath him, Grant's hips shifted. Zane could feel the start of a promising erection prodding at him, and wasn't above -- ha-ha -- a little hip-based encouragement. His grin widened, sharper and hungrier.

Grant caught his breath. "Fuck me." He reached for Zane. "No, I'm serious. Smile like that and fuck me again."

Zane checked himself over quick-fast. He still wasn't fertile, not yet, and he could trust an Alpha as iron-willed as Grant. "With the restrictions you mentioned in place?"

"Non-negotiable."

Ah well. Zane could work with that. If this was all he got, he'd make the most of it. "Lie back, big man," he said, draping himself over Grant, reaching between them to take hold of their cocks and squeeze them together. "And let me put your money where your mouth is."

* * *

Grant wasn't surprised that it was Marshall who came back to check up on him. He *was* surprised it took him almost an hour after Zane had left.

Though it was odd, the way Zane had gone. Grant's forehead furrowed briefly. After their second round, he'd glanced at his watch and jumped up, and gotten into his clothes almost as fast as he'd gotten out of them, barely pausing to clean up, and bolted out into the night like he'd been stung.

Then again, Zane was an odd sort of guy. The good sort of odd, but still.

Grant heard Marshall coming long before he actually popped into view. He knew Marshall's step, the way he breathed, his giveaway tells when he tried to be sneaky. He probably succeeded with other people, but Grant knew him too well. Even with his back turned, he could tell his friend lurked in the doorway behind him, sniffing the air and jumping to all kinds of conclusions.

Eh. Let him. Grant was too bonelessly pleased, too fucked-out, to even think about caring. He carried on tacking flash and other placeholders on the walls, mostly just wanting to get an idea for how the place could look once it was all done, and waited for Marshall to crack first.

Which he would. And did.

"How?" Marshall demanded right about when Grant had anticipated he would. "How do you know every damned time?"

"Hmm?"

Marshall made a spluttering noise of indignation. Grant grinned to himself, and turned in time to dodge the crinkled-up ball of paper Marshall whipped at him. He caught it up and whipped it straight back, bouncing it off the tips of Marshall's spiked haircut.

Marshall glowered at him. "Asshole."

"Look who's talking." Grant grinned in the face of his friend's irritation. "Need something? Forget something? Can't imagine what would have brought you back here tonight otherwise."

That one didn't work as planned. Marshall shifted gears from annoyed to smirking in the twinkle of an eye. "Oh, can't you? I'll give you a hint. Four letters, sounds like Z-A-N-E."

Grant kept his expression bland and calm. "Your point being?"

"I can tell, you know," Marshall pressed. "I have a nose."

"Good. Keep it in your own business."

"What?" Marshall snorted. "Pull the other one.

There's enough Omega smell in here to cut like a piece of chocolate cake."

Which made Grant's stomach rumble. And Marshall's. Grant laughed at the both of them, and balled up a piece of tacky flash to toss at Marshall in a gesture of affection. "Go home, would you? I don't need checking up on. I know what I'm doing."

Marshall shook his head, but with a grin. "Oh, I can tell that. Whatever happened, you must have enjoyed it. Planning to keep enjoying it?"

Grant hesitated. He shouldn't have, though. Marshall pounced. "Yes? No? Maybe? I need to know if the good times are going to keep on rolling, here, or if I've got to prepare for cleanup duty."

"I..." Grant stopped and shook his head. "If I tell you the truth will you can it and go home? My home, even, if you still want to be a dick and you're hungry. There's half a chocolate cake in the fridge. Go nuts."

Marshall said nothing. Just raised an eyebrow at Grant.

Grant groaned and ran a hand through his hair. "You know I don't get involved. I'm not looking to break that streak, especially not right now. If I did have anything going on with Zane -- which I'm not saying I do -- it's just for fun, and just as long as it's fun. Nothing more."

"Uh-huh." Marshall looked far too amused. "Whatever you say. Because it's absolutely in your nature to jump an Omega the day after you meet him. Or to let him in your world as fast as that. Or to get all prickly whenever I say anything about him."

"I don't --"

Marshall cackled when Grant stopped short. "My point exactly." He waved at Grant with his middle finger, a salute Grant returned. "I'll see you tomorrow, though I am gonna stop by your place and raid your fridge on my way home. I want that cake, baby. Just like you."

"Fuck you. I changed my mind."

Marshall laughed on. "I'll leave you a few crumbs. By the way? Nice Van Gogh on your tits. You draw that yourself? Upside down and backward? Or does our Zane have some hidden artistic abilities? Thinking about training him so he'll have a marketable job skill?"

Grant reached for the nearest throwable thing at hand, found only markers, and zinged them at Marshall one after another until Marshall covered his face with his arms and booked it, hitting the street running. He watched Marshall go, not sure if he was more frustrated or entertained or baffled by the whole hootenanny in three acts that'd just played out. Marshall, the matchmaking romantic? Where had that come from? Who'd have thought it? Deacon would be fascinated to hear about this new development. *If* Grant wanted to be bastard enough to tell him, which...

Eh, he decided. He'd rather let it go, at least for tonight, and get back to enjoying the afterglow.

It was almost too bad, though. If he had ever thought about settling down with an Omega, it would have been with someone just like Zane. Who did have artistic talent, damn it. Ten minutes with some Copic markers and he'd done a damn fine job on a human canvas. He'd be worth teaching. Could make one hell of an artist...

Yeah. Too bad.

That said, nothing wrong with looking forward to tomorrow...

Chapter Five

Two Weeks Later

"And then, and then he showed me, and it was a *frog*!" Hadrian boggled up at Zane with eyes as big as that poor bastard frog's must have been.

Crouched in front of him, Zane managed to keep a straight face. "No kidding?" Poor frog. Zane didn't envy him, being traded back and forth between two four year olds not exactly known for their fine muscle control. "Did you let him go?"

"He got away," Hadrian admitted. "But we're gonna catch another one today, so it's okay. I'll bring it home an' show you."

Eduardo, standing behind them where the kid couldn't see his face, winced and drew one hand in a flat line across his neck. Message received: no slimy, warty reptiles in the apartment, please and thank you or they'd be having frog legs for dinner, see if they didn't.

Zane laughed despite himself, and dropped a kiss on Hadrian's head before the kid could question him. "Go on, go play. Build me a sandcastle instead, would you? I'd rather have a sandcastle to look at than a frog."

Hadrian brightened up. "Okay!"

Fond, Zane watched him go. Took so little to please them at that age, didn't it? Hadrian was too young to tell whether he'd grow up Alpha or Omega, but either way he was a son to be proud of.

Now, Eduardo, he had different views on Zane. Which Zane could understand. He'd known Zane almost all his life, after all. Zane could almost see his ears swiveling to keep track of Hadrian while at the same time he crossed his arms and fixed Zane with a gimlet stare. Skillz, the old man had them. "Don't think I don't know what's going on at that tattoo parlor, *mijo*."

Uh-oh. Zane tried for an innocent look, gave it up almost immediately as a poor choice, and stuck his hands in his pockets. "And?"

"And." Eduardo narrowed his eyes. "Are you being careful?"

"Yes," Zane answered honestly. He didn't take suppressants -- they didn't agree with his system -- but Grant wouldn't come near him without his dick damn near triple-wrapped. Not that he'd gotten Grant inside him yet, which was getting ever more frustrating with each successive day. Couldn't get much more careful than that.

"Hmm. Your body, you're being careful. But are you being smart with your heart?"

"Probably not," Zane admitted. "But I'm trying to be smart about being stupid."

Eduardo rolled his eyes, but let that one go. "Do you know what you're doing?"

"Maybe?"

"One out of three," Eduardo said with a sigh. He shoved a sack lunch, fragrant with cumin and oregano, at Zane, who took it automatically. "I scold because I care, boy. If you come home pregnant, we'll make it work. Just -- and I say this because *I* was a young Omega, once, too -- don't let your hormones overtake your good sense. All right?"

Zane gave the older man's fist a pound. "I'll do my best."

"Can't say fairer than that," Eduardo decided. "Go on, then. Get to work."

* * *

Work, Grant had hired Zane for? Work he did.

Zane had heard from Marshall that Grant had never known an Omega so hell-bent on doing a good job, and extrapolating on that to make it a great job. Zane did suspect -- hoped? -- Grant was sneakily teaching him how to set designs on human bodies, so he put his all into learning everything Grant had to teach about that too. And learning everything he could about piercing, too.

He even convinced Marshall to pierce one tit, and that was a feat worth remarking on. Marshall hated needles.

But -- work, yes. Work, Zane did, even when that consisted of parking his ass at the new drafting table in the back room while a coat of floor finish dried and practicing drawing what Grant had asked him for. Grant had meant business with that, turned out, and he'd turn into a proper little thundercloud if he caught Zane trying to cut corners there.

Not that it wasn't fun -- more than -- to deal with Grant in a temper, but a wise Omega picked his battles. That particular brand was best saved for just before lunch or late evenings, when they could be guaranteed some time alone. *Mmm.* But in the mornings, Zane did as he'd been told.

Honestly, that was almost as much fun as civil disobedience. You could see the wheels spinning in their heads as people waited for you to misbehave.

Also, not that Zane *could* go anywhere at the moment. Grant, spreading sealer over the freshly sanded hardwood floors, had threatened to have his guts for garters if he walked on the new finish before it had dried completely. "Garters tied in a pretty bow and hooked to the ceiling so you can twist on them," he warned, pointing a finger at Zane.

"Threat or promise, sunshine?" Zane asked,

blowing him a kiss.

Grant only rolled his eyes at that, but from Grant that was as good as a kiss in return, and hell, Zane just about liked it better.

Grant.

Zane shook his head. Sometimes he wondered if Grant had Adderall instead of blood in his veins. That Alpha could flat *work.* Less than a month after breaking down the doors, and the shop had started to look like a real place of business. Electricians had been coaxed and browbeaten in equal parts to get *Legacy Tattoo's* wiring up to code, and plumbers had been barked at until they went dumbly to work, one eye on the pipes and one on Grant's watchful stare.

Individual work spaces were coming together, and the displays on the wall weren't just placeholders any longer.

And Zane could sketch it all out in a few lines, clear and smooth. He'd never had so much time to draw, or so much scope for the imagination, and it showed. He was good at it. He could do this.

As proof to himself, Zane held his spiral-bound sketchpad out at arm's length, gazing critically at the design he'd been working on. He'd seen some embroidery on an old Omega's messenger bag and hadn't been able to get the stitching, the colors, out of his thoughts. Was it possible to recreate it with ink and paper? Or on skin? You could cover scars with those. Stitches of a prettier sort.

Lost in thought, Zane didn't hear Grant padding up behind him, and jumped half a city block when Grant put one cold hand on the back of his neck and whispered in his ear, "*Boo.*"

Zane swiveled at the hips and thwacked the Alpha with his sketchpad hard enough to bounce it off his noggin. "See if I blow you tonight, asshole."

"Yes, you will," Grant said with absolute assurance.

Zane couldn't argue. He was right. Besides, Grant had already moved on. Careless of how Zane had disarranged his hair, he scooped the fallen sketchpad up off the floor and flipped the cover open before Zane could even think about stopping him.

Still, he tried. "Do you mind, Alpha?"

"Nope," Grant said absently, keeping the sketchpad firmly in his thieving paws. He studied each page of Zane's book before turning to the next, mostly stone faced but with the occasional quirk of an eyebrow or tilt of the head. He hummed once or twice, though whether that was a good sound or a bad one, there was no telling.

Just before Zane would have lost patience and flung himself on Grant to wrestle the pad out of his hands, Grant flipped it shut and looked up to make eye contact the way only an Alpha could. The *I Mean Business* kind of eye contact, considering him thoughtfully through narrowed eyes until he came to some sort of decided and nodded his head firmly. "You'll do."

"Super. Do for what?" Zane cocked an eyebrow.

"Tomorrow," Grant said, "You get to try the real thing."

Zane's jaw dropped.

Grant didn't quite smirk, but it was more than a grin. "You want to catch flies?"

"Fuck off," Zane said numbly. "Me? The real thing? Like…" He gestured vaguely toward Grant's arms.

"No, not human. Not yet, anyway. Pigskin. You're good enough I think you deserve a chance to prove yourself. I --"

He didn't get any farther, mostly on account of Zane having flung himself on Grant after all and taken them both to the floor. But for a kiss, not a kick. And then another kiss, and one more for good measure. A picture might be worth a thousand words, but kisses? Those were worth considerably more.

Grant grinned with half his mouth, but with glee in his eyes, and helped Zane up off the floor. "Skin should be here tomorrow. I warn you, raw hides smell like ever-loving hell, so you're going to have some serious cleanup jobs ahead of you, but you're ready. I'll teach you to use the machine and we'll see if what you do on paper looks just as good on flesh."

Zane just stared. "You're serious."

"Do I usually joke about this kind of shit?"

Fair point. Zane couldn't stop staring, but managed to close his mouth before Grant could make another crack about catching flies. "Grant, I -- thanks, man. Seriously. Thanks." If he could be an artist, he could support Hadrian the way a kid should be supported. New toys, not secondhands. Same with clothes. An actual bike with a bell and all that shit.

"I'm not being generous, I'm being practical. You're a hard worker and a fine artist. It's an investment."

"Uh-huh." Zane's mouth curved. *You're a softy deep down, Grant, that's what you are.* "And the price? There's always a price. I'll pay it, mind you, but what have you got in mind?"

"Go out with me tonight," Grant said.

* * *

"You -- say what, again?" Zane blinked big gray-green eyes at Grant, who marveled that he'd never really noticed before how catlike they were. Fitting.

Wide and baffled only briefly, and then the right eyebrow went up in an arch so sharp St. Louis wept with envy. "Might be my hearing, Alpha, but I could have sworn you just asked me out on a date."

"I did," Grant said, enjoying the second brief flash of confusion that flitted through those pretty eyes. He took pity then, grinning at the Omega. "Good looking as you are, someone must have asked you out before once or twice in your life. Maybe even three times."

"A night," Zane replied without batting an eyelash. "On slow nights." He cocked his head and eyed Grant up and down. "You're serious, aren't you?"

Grant tucked his hands in his pockets and nodded.

"Why? Not that I'm bitching about it, but -- you're already getting to tap this on the regular, my friend." Zane patted his own ass. All class, he was, and Grant couldn't have liked it more. "So why the sudden need to wine and or dine and even possibly romance?"

"Because I want to."

Zane's unimpressed look could have razed a skyscraper.

Grant hooted. "Bottle and market those, Omega. No one will ever need to manufacture weaponry again. *Why a date*? Why not a date? Seriously. I want to go out. I want to take you with me. Somewhere that isn't work, and isn't sex. Isn't *just* sex," he corrected himself.

"You think I'm that easy?" A grin slowly warmed Zane's lips. "Because I know you're even easier."

"Which makes us a pretty good match, if you ask me."

"You're not wrong," Zane admitted. He sized Grant up another moment longer, and in that heartbeat's worth of time Grant almost -- almost -- thought Zane was going to turn him down. He didn't know why he had that impression, exactly, only that he could see it written all over him. He braced himself for impact and counterattack, and had his arguments all lined up and ready to go when Zane opened his mouth, sighed, and said, "Okay."

Nonplussed, Grant blinked. "Say again?"

"Isn't that how this whole conversation started?" Zane flicked the lobe of Grant's left ear, but affectionately. "I'll go out on a date with you, Alpha. You can pick me up at eight, but on the street corner because you are way too dominant for my neighborhood, and we'll… do date things. Just as long as you remember I expect to get the hell romanced out of me before the dirty filthy monkey sex. Deal?"

Grant's grin couldn't have stretched wider, or been fiercer. "I think I can just about handle that. Deal."

Zane stuck out a hand. Okay, oddly formal, but Grant could roll with it. He slapped his hand into Zane's, and was almost tumbled off his feet when Zane -- sneaky bastard -- used it as leverage to whirl them both around. They ended with Grant's ass flush against the wall next to the window, and with Zane on his knees.

He slid his fingers through Zane's soft dark hair. "Your turn for some explaining."

"If you can't tell what's about to happen, I am definitely doing this wrong," Zane informed him cheerfully, already at work on Grant's belt and zipper. "See, you took me off guard."

"I did notice."

"And for that, there is a penalty." Zane cradled Grant's cock and balls through his jeans, bent in to breathe deep and nuzzle, and to -- holy fuck -- gently lip both out through the gap made by his open fly. Grant forgot to take in oxygen, and only a little bit out of concern for the state of his junk. No one should be that good with their mouth, and yet every time he thought Zane had peaked, the man just kept going.

A thought occurred, and Grant winced and cursed. He nudged Zane carefully away. "Wait -- shit -- let me pull the shades. Last thing we need is health inspectors shutting the place down before it opens."

Zane rolled his eyes, but settled back on his heels and gestured for Grant to do what he had to do. He kept those eyes fixed on Grant as Grant took care of the necessary blinds and locks, though, and there was something thoughtful about the feel of it.

"Something on your mind?" Grant asked.

Zane made a noncommittal noise. "You're an only child, right?"

"Mm-hmm. Just me."

"You ever wish you had siblings? Brothers? Or do you just not like kids in general?"

"What?" Grant looked over his shoulder. "No, I like kids fine -- in general. They're honest, really straight-up no matter what. And they're cute. Lots of hassle, but what isn't? No, I like kids just fine."

"Huh." Zane looked even more thoughtful, but he tucked it away fast, his grin turning even a little more feral than before. He beckoned with two fingers. "Discussion over, and windows are shut, Alpha. Get that beautiful prick back over here. Now."

Far be it from Grant to say no to an offer like that. He got, and settled where he had been, already planning what he might do to return the favor when Zane had finished. Maybe turn him on his stomach and lick him open, use his fingers if not his cock because he never fucking remembered to carry condoms in his work pants. Make him see a few stars along the way.

He'd be a keeper, if he were willing to be kept. The thought flashed through Grant's mind and was gone in a twinkling, but not so quickly he couldn't put a pin in the idea to mull over later.

For the moment -- back to business. He bit back a groan as Zane took his cockhead lightly between those pretty lips, then gave his hair a little tug, the kind that would make his scalp prickle just the way he knew Zane liked best. "As you were, Trouble."

Zane ran the edges of his teeth lightly over Grant's delicate skin, gone from half mast to fully erect.

Grant sighed happily and surrendered. "Damn right," he said, and spread his legs a little wider to give his Omega room to work. "Damn right."

Chapter Six

Now, in Grant's opinion? That had been a good ending to a good day. *Would have been*, except he'd opened his damn fool mouth when sense should have told him to keep it shut. Now here he was, scrubbed and dressed in what he hoped was his best for the occasion -- that might take some fancy talking once Zane saw him, but he'd cross that bridge when he got to it -- and walking through a neighborhood that *definitely* didn't cater to his kind. Not another Alpha in sight, and Omegas watching him narrowly from every window. Some watching him with what his great-grandbearer would have called Lascivious Intent, capitals fully audible.

What in tarnation was he *doing*? Hell, Grant still couldn't figure that out.

He didn't date. He was sure he remembered making a policy out of that. He went to clubs and bars and took the occasional flight of fancy that landed him between a willing Omega's legs. Wham, bam, neither one of them looking for more than a kiss goodbye in the morning, thank you sir. And it'd worked. For years, that'd worked. He and Marshall wouldn't have gotten along half as well without that common ground.

Well. Until Marshall had caught a case of matchmaking fever, or whatever. Grant blamed all the broody Omegas around them. All those babies being born. It gave a man Ideas.

There he went again with the capitals. Grant sighed, hitched up his collar, put his head down, and headed for Zane's place. Zane's street corner, because he was being weird for whatever reason about letting Grant pick him up the way a proper date would. Wasn't like he didn't have Zane's address in his personnel file, and he knew Zane lived at 414 Raywood. Not too far from *Legacy Tattoo*, but good God, a shit-ton of Omegas must have lived on Zane's street. Turn a corner, and suddenly the air was saturated with ground-in pheromones.

Grant plowed through it with his jaw held tight. *Raywood. Raywood.*

Why had he asked Zane out in the first place?

It didn't make sense. Like he didn't see the Omega every day and they didn't fuck at least once every time the clock went fully around? Sometimes twice, if Marshall absented himself from the shop-in-progress long enough. If they *did* have a relationship, which Grant wasn't admitting to, wasn't that enough to satisfy anyone?

Why had he felt compelled to ask Zane out on a date? From the look on Zane's face, he would have sworn it was as foreign a concept to Zane as it was to himself. Like the last thing on earth he'd expected.

To his surprise, that thought raised a prickle of indignation. Zane thought he wasn't capable of romance, or something? Did Zane figure he was all about sex, and not about the man doing the fucking?

Grant's jaw set. Say that was the case, then -- it seemed likely. Well, he'd show him then. He'd date the *hell* out of Zane.

Somewhere, somehow, Grant would swear he could hear Darius and Jory and probably Marshall, too, laughing at him.

Raywood. What the fuck kind of wood was a Ray? Probably the builder, who'd gotten a boner over getting to the damned end of all these units. Grant stopped to narrow-eye the building numbers and saw that he'd reached 400, and…

Saw Zane, loitering on the street corner just

down and across from the aforementioned building, lounging the way he did best, leaned back against a streetlamp with his hips jutted out and his chin up. He watched Grant with his usual amusement, enjoying -- or so he'd said before -- the sight of him with a full head of steam.

All that steam poured out of Grant's nostrils like a horny bull in a cartoon. *Fuck*, but Zane looked good enough to eat. He'd gone with the same look that'd turned Grant on faster than a light switch back when they'd first met, a jacket open over a bare chest and jeans that might or might not have been actually painted on. The only change was two --

Whoa, and what the fuck even. Grant was up the stairs before he realized it, and had his face two inches from Zane's nips almost as fast. He hooked one finger through the titanium hoop dangling from one and gave it an accusatory little tug. "When did you get those pierced? Where? Why didn't you let me do it?" he demanded.

Zane belly-laughed, making his piercings bounce slightly with the motion of his chest. He carded his fingers through Grant's hair, careless of the product in there. *Great.* He'd end up looking like Calvin keeping company with Pimpmaster Hobbes. "Hi honey, I'm home. How was your day?"

"That makes no sense. This is your home, or almost, anyway. I'm the one who just got here," Grant said, nose-to-tits with Zane's pecs as he studied the piercings. Nearly healed, so he'd had them for a while. They didn't always or even often get all their clothes off when they fucked, so Grant supposed he could be excused for not noticing before. But now that he did -- *hmm.* The holes were clean, symmetrical, and even. Or, no. Almost even. The right was fine, but the left just a hair crooked, as if the piercer had hesitated a touch on pushing the needle through. He raised his head in indignation. "Did you do these yourself?"

"And if I did?" Zane regarded him with the same tolerant enjoyment he always showed -- then stopped, cocked his head to one side, and gave Grant a good solid once-over. He whistled. "Fuck me, Alpha, and I do mean that as an invitation. You clean up nice."

Grant snorted. "I'm wearing jeans and a baseball shirt."

"Tight jeans hugging that sweet little ass, and a Yankees shirt. Looks nice to me." Zane gave Grant a small nudge. "Not that I mind having your face in my tits, but we either need to stop giving the neighbors a show or start charging for it."

What? Oh. Right. Grant gave himself a shake. Was this going to screw with his plans for the night? Maybe not, if Zane had --"You got any Band-Aids? Ones big enough to cover those up?" He must have bought some to protect the sensitive piercings when they were still fresh enough to chafe like hell under his shirts.

Zane arched one eyebrow high up his forehead. "So maybe I have this wrong, but you looked like you were enjoying the sight of 'em. Which was the whole-damn-point. You don't want anyone else looking? I can zip the jacket."

"No, that's not it. They need to be protected."

"From what, wolves? Other Alphas? Honey, you and I can kick anyone's ass if they feel like getting fresh."

Damn right they could, and would, but that wasn't the point. "Needs to be Band-Aids," Grant said firmly. "If you've got them, go get them, and we can be on our way. You'll need them for where we're going."

Zane's other eyebrow shot up to join the first. Still, he didn't look miffed. More like delighted, and a few dashes intrigued. "Alpha, what kind of date are you taking me on?"

* * *

So this wasn't what Zane had been expecting.

Standing on the banks of the Roanoke River, mud squishing through his bare toes, he whooped as he tugged his jacket off and wiggled out of the jeans he'd taken considerable effort to wiggle his ass into an hour ago, and didn't mind a bit. "Hellfire, Alpha!" he called to Grant, his voice booming as it echoed over the water. "If you'd told me this was going to be a naked date, we could have started out that way!"

Grant, who was already wading his own bare-assed way into the water, threw his head back and laughed. "And skipped the whole mystery part of it? Come on. I don't date, but even I know better than that."

"Don't date, Alpha? What do you call this?"

"I call it me freezing my nuts off and waiting for you." Waist deep, Grant turned to cock an eyebrow at Zane. "Are you coming or not, *Omega*?"

Zane grinned at him, enjoying the view of his -- friend -- in the water. They'd come to a small cove that a bank collapse had carved out some years past, upstream enough from any industry that it was clean enough to see the bottom during daylight hours. Zane had known it was there, remembered it from when he was a kid, but he'd forgotten.

Beat a restaurant and a movie in his opinion.

He tossed his head proudly and waded, bare as the day he'd been born, into the water. *Holyshitthat'scold*! Zane's teeth would have chattered if he hadn't clamped his jaws shut, but by the time he got within arm's reach of Grant he'd adjusted enough to speak. And if he hadn't managed, being near Grant would have done the job. His Alpha almost radiated heat enough to set the water boiling. Desire flowed from him to Zane in palpable waves.

Pleased, Zane turned in a lazy circle, arms held out to the side. He would have given his new piercings a gentle tweak if Grant hadn't insisted they be covered, but at least that made sense now. Grant's gaze still went straight to them despite their being hidden, fiercely pleased and hungry as the devil.

"You like what you see?" Zane asked, expecting a casual answer, something tossed carelessly out so that no one could read more into it than Grant wanted. It was his way, Zane had learned. When he meant it the most, he spoke about it the least. Zane could relate. How had he himself *not* told Grant?

They were more alike than they weren't, Alpha and Omega aside.

And so Zane expected an off-the-cuff compliment. What he *didn't* anticipate was Grant giving him a sudden, wicked grin, and then his dropping under the water like he had rocks attached to his tits. Zane jumped back, but before he could do more than flinch Grant had grabbed him by the ankles and given them an almighty yank. He slipped and zipped under the water too, hollering bubbles at the shock of the cold.

Zane came up still shouting, almost exactly as the same time as Grant, and didn't waste a second in thinking when he could be acting instead. He launched himself at the Alpha with a war cry and landed on him in a body-to-body belly flop that took them right back under again. He twined his arms and legs around Grant and gave him a good spin before letting go, kick-

swimming in a *come-and-chase-me* bid.

Grant rose to the occasion, and just beautifully. Foreplay in motion, that's what this was. Leave it to Grant to come up with the creative path.

And Zane loved it. Almost as much as he loved his -- *anyway*.

He ducked Grant to the bottom and rubbed his shoulders in the river mud, then closed his eyes and stroked away through the water, wondering if it would start boiling around him if he got much hotter. Slickness trickled out of him to lubricate his inner thighs regardless of the water and the inside of his lower belly pulsed in long, lazy spasms of growing arousal.

Well, this was a fine time for *that* to happen.

Zane kept his eyes closed and treaded water. He sipped breath carefully, not letting it shake or start to race, but he knew heat when he felt it. A smart man would have gone on suppressants when they took up with an Alpha who didn't want kids, damn it all. Last time he'd gone into heat around an Alpha he'd gotten knocked up. He'd sworn never again.

Funny how life had a way of making its own plans.

Zane bit his lip as a particularly lusty pulse of arousal fed the fire inside him. His body wanted Grant's cock. *He* wanted Grant buried balls-deep inside him and bathing his channel with cum. He rubbed his stomach, engulfed with the all-consuming need to have it filled, to feel that sense of life growing inside, to watch himself go round as a ball and up to his chin with child. He ached to reach between his legs and finger himself open in echo of how it'd felt to bring a baby out.

He wanted Grant's baby and he wanted it now,

damn it.

Didn't he just know how to pick them? The one Alpha that got his motor revving was the one who'd probably run as if his *vas deferens* were on fire at the thought of becoming a father. *Hell!*

Zane moaned under his breath, unable to keep it inside. Would the water hide his state from Grant? *Would it, bah.* Zane scoffed at the question as soon as he'd asked it. Still. It *was* early. Grant would be able to detect that as well as the rest. And sure enough, when Grant swam toward him he jerked to a halt, his nostrils twitching wide in a startled sniff at the scent pouring off Zane.

But. But he didn't stop for good, and he didn't back away. Instead he set his jaw the way Zane had seen him do right before attacking one job or another at the old shop, and plunged forward as if he'd just rolled up his sleeves. He caught up a handful of water and splashed it at Zane, still playful, but gentler now, as if he understood the struggle.

Even so, it was a shock when he took Zane's hand. "Come on, Omega," he said, quietly and gently for Grant. "Let's get up on the bank and look at the stars for a while."

Zane rallied. "Soaking wet like this? We'll freeze."

Grant raised a shoulder. "That'd be a bad thing, to cool down?"

No, it wouldn't. And yes, it would. Or yes, it would, if Zane planned to give in and take what he wanted. Being in the water was too fluid, it brought up too many memories of salt and blood and birth. Air was cold and unforgiving. It ought to shock him back to sense, at least for a little while, and then he could get himself back under control.

He *could.*

He nodded, and followed Grant out of the water, up onto the bank.

Out of the knapsack he'd brought Grant hauled out one of those space-age blankets, the kind that folded thin as a box of Kleenex and looked like someone had just unwrapped the world's largest baked potato, and spread it on the ground. He folded Zane's jacket into a peculiar-looking parcel and tossed it to him. "For your head," he explained, doing the same with the clothes he'd worn.

Zane frowned. "You don't want me dressed."

"You'll be lying downwind, you'll be fine." Grant eased himself down atop the blanket, which was more than large enough for one short and one skinny man to lie on without touching. "Come on. Do as you're told."

Which would normally be the surefire way to get Zane to do his own thing, but the Omega in him bowed its head and did as he'd damn well been told -- and he'd be damned if it didn't help. The cold of the earth, the startling shock of the wind over his wet skin, all cooled him to the point where he could think again with more than just his dick and womb.

He drew a deep, lusty breath that rattled on its way in and out.

"Better?" Grant asked, off to the side.

Zane took another breath and sighed it out. He nodded, but knew Grant sensed it and took his meaning.

They lay there for a few long moments, together but not, blanketed by nothing but the night sky and silence.

Though the silence came at a cost. Zane licked his lips as quietly as he could, but over and over again, struggling with the need to speak. *Would it be the worst thing in the world?* he wanted to ask. *To have a son of your own? To have someone to take over the legacy from you, in time? I'd stay to help you. Like I'm helping you now. I could stay and tattoo for you and pierce for you and either way I'm going to be an artist to be proud of. You know I am because you taught me how. We could do this together. We could have it all.*

It was a good argument. One that made sense. And one that a stubborn dick, love him though Zane might, would never agree to. Because it wasn't what the plan was supposed to be when he'd thought it up. Zane toyed with the idea of getting pissed about it, but what would the point be in that? Might as well get mad at the wind for being swift.

Grant wouldn't go his way. Zane -- couldn't go his. Not for much longer. This whole thing was a powder keg about to explode. They'd have to end it. It was the only way. And he might as well do it now, while he was --

Zane opened his mouth, ready to speak no matter how little he wanted to, but startled at the touch of warm/chilly fingers brushing his without warning. He caught his breath entirely when Grant took his hand in a firm hold.

"Hush," was all Grant said, but Zane's mouth clamped itself shut. He couldn't help but roll his hips though, fresh need twisting him from the inside. He dared a sneak peek at Grant's profile but couldn't tell a damn thing about what his Alpha might be thinking. Grant had his stare fixed upward, hard at the stars that Zane couldn't bother paying attention to, and his jaw was set.

But -- but. His jaw worked, as if he were arguing with himself.

Zane's muscles went tight, unable to let go.

"It's got you good, huh?" Grant asked. "I can smell it. I can almost feel it."

Zane assayed a nod, and curiosity loosened his tongue. "Ever been in this fix with an Omega before?"

Grant barked a short laugh. "Not intentionally." He rubbed at his face. "We should go back to town. Right now."

"We should," Zane echoed. Then, somehow bolder than he'd thought he could be, "Do you want to?"

Grant's second laugh was drier, a little despairing, and a whole lot ravenous. "Do I, hell."

"Then..." Zane shuddered, but with lust, not fear. Was he going to get what he wanted? Even a taste would be enough.

"Conditions," Grant said. "I brought condoms. Spermicide. Other things."

Zane nodded, eager enough to accept the plan he saw taking shape. "I'm not on suppressants. I know you know that," he said just the same, because fair was fair.

"I can smell, Omega," Grant said wryly. He didn't ask if Zane had been expecting his heat, and for that Zane was grateful for the Alpha's practicality. Sometimes, even if not often, proximity could bring it on.

And there they were, weren't they.

Grant hesitated, and Zane was sure he was about to suggest they pack it in for the night. Instead, he said, "But if we're careful..."

Zane's mouth was dry. "If we're careful," he said around the cotton on his tongue. "Just this once. Just once."

Grant let out his breath. "Just once," he said, and

pulled hard on Zane's hand. "And no more talking about it. Deal?"

Whether he meant talking now or talking later, Zane didn't know and didn't care. "Deal," he said, and rolled himself into Grant's arms.

Just for one night, he could pretend he had everything he wanted, body and soul, and that would be good enough for him.

* * *

Oh, he'd wanted this. Even when he hadn't let himself think about wanting it, Grant had wanted Zane like the desert wanted water.

He could have sworn Zane wanted him just as much, just as hungrily, too. And it wasn't conceit, for fuck's sake. All those surprise sex-pounces at work would lead anyone to an inevitable conclusion.

Except.

Grant turned over to lie on his back and craned his neck for a better look at Zane who, nope, hadn't moved anything but his head. He stared at Grant as if he wasn't sure what to do or where to start. He'd caught his lip between his teeth and worried at it, white teeth making dents in soft flesh.

Not so much with the sexy. Grant tucked his hands behind his head. "Something wrong? Do I have river algae on my face?"

Zane cracked a grin. "Would I tell you if you did?"

"Nope. You'd leave it and laugh at me."

That drew a small, but real chuckle out of Zane, and he finally quit biting at his lip. Good thing, too. Biting those pretty red lips was *Grant's* job, thank you very much. He freed one hand and reached out to nudge Zane in the bare thigh -- which gave him a glimpse of how interested Zane's body was. Which only left the problem based in his..."Something's on your mind. Spill it."

Zane shook his head. "No," he said, suddenly so determined and damn near ferocious that it made Grant blink in surprise. "No," he said again, twisting about onto his knees and then crawling on top of Grant, straddling him. And "No," he said one more time before bending his head to crush his mouth to Grant's, stopping the words altogether.

Which Grant would have objected to, if his tongue hadn't been otherwise occupied. Good *God*, Zane could kiss when he had a mind to, and all his mind seemed bent on that right at the moment. He dipped deep, sweeping Grant's mouth with his tongue, biting at Grant's lips instead of his own, and doing filthy things Grant didn't even know the names for with his hips all the while. His body was in fact interested, boy howdy, and their erections rubbed together lubricated by the slick that dripped from Zane's Omega center.

Grant tore away for enough breath to gasp, "What the *fuck*, Omega?"

Zane bared his teeth in what wasn't a smile, but wasn't not a smile either. "Exactly. Get with the program, Alpha."

So he wasn't going to talk. Grant never would have figured he'd see the day, but under the circumstances... He gripped Zane's hips good and hard -- his Omega liked a finger bruise or two to remember the occasion by when he was particularly feisty -- and rocked his groin up. "You want to go for a ride, is that it?"

Zane's teeth stayed bared, and to be honest it was a look Grant was growing to appreciate more and more. Made him feel like he was fucking a wildcat as well as a wild man, and he liked it. Zane didn't speak, but reached between them to take hold of Grant's cock and, with just a little help from gravity and a lot of help from his slick, slid Grant inside him.

Almost.

Grant jerked back at the last second. "Condom," he said. "Condoms in my jeans pocket."

Zane let out a noise that was definitely kissing cousins with a snarl, but then he drew a deep, ragged breath and rolled off. One quick knee-walk to where Grant's jeans had ended up on the bank, a rummage through his pockets, and Zane was back, already tearing open the packet as he threw his leg back over Grant. Grant raised himself on his elbows to watch. For one, because he liked to. A hot Omega with hands all over his dick? Sweet. But for two, because Zane's hands were shaking and Grant wasn't sure he wouldn't need help.

He managed. With a growl of success, Zane glared at Grant as if daring him to come up with another objection, and when none came, let Grant guide him down, seating his cock balls-deep in Zane's channel.

They both groaned. Grant wasn't an Omega, but he had taken the occasional toy up his ass. Still, he couldn't imagine what it felt like to have a stiff dick right there in the center of you, to be so filled. *Must be pretty decent*, he thought, watching Zane's eyes flutter as he tipped his head back in a sharply curved arc of the neck. As for his part, fucking hell, there was nothing better, could never be anything better. Hot, ridged muscle that gripped his cock like a hungry python and would have held him locked there if he didn't want to move quite so much. Up -- deeper -- down -- shallower -- deep again -- watching Zane with each hungry push and pull. God, Zane was taking him so far inside. Not too far, he'd bumped the mouth of an Omega's womb once and gotten thrown halfway across the room while the Omega let out a shriek of pained indignation, but damn near close to that.

The night hadn't seemed so hot when Grant started, but sweat poured down his face and slicked his body with a fine sheet of salt. Zane's too, making him a slippery handful. Zane's cock, hard and angry-red, bobbed against his belly as he rose and fell, taking over the reins of the ride now.

Which suited Grant fine. He let go of one hip to take Zane's cock in hand, and reveled in the way Zane's eyes flew open wide, as did his mouth, in a startled gasp of arousal.

"You're on a hair trigger, aren't you," Grant murmured, enjoying this maybe more than he should, but -- what the hell. He toyed with the slit at the tip of Zane's cock. "Why isn't this pierced? This needs to be pierced. I could put the hoop in myself. Give me something to... tug." He pulled lightly at the skin there, gratified beyond words when a keening noise escaped his Omega. "And speaking of tugging..." It took some careful balancing, but he reached up and gave Zane's covered nipple piercings a good tweak that made Zane lose his rhythm and grind down hard. "You like that, oh yeah, I knew you would."

"Grant," Zane panted, hair over his eyes, in his face, but still glaring effectively. "Shut. Up. And *fuck* me."

His wish. Grant's command. No more games now. Grant set to it, driving deep as he could, only coming halfway out. It got harder, and not just the moves. His cock felt like steel, red-hot from being in a furnace, and his groin was so tight he thought it would split open from the pressure and *he did not mind one fucking bit*. He caught Zane's cock in his hand again, stroking ruthlessly and fast, driven to make sure his Omega came like never before.

Zane made a hiccupping sound, part keen and part protest and part desperate need -- his hips stuttered -- and with an elegant arch, like a dancer, he gave a great shudder and sob and came, splashing Grant's stomach with sticky white. He bit his lip so hard then that Grant saw the skin split, which he'd attend to later after he -- came --

The world whited out as Zane's channel gripped and held. If it weren't for the condom, he would have filled Zane to the depths with his seed.

And for one second -- just one -- Grant wished as fiercely as the fires of hell that it *had*.

Chapter Seven

But if wishes were horses, eh.

Grant shook his head as he dealt with the condom and pushed it aside for disposal later. After all, Zane had never shown any interest Grant had noticed of being a "typical" Omega. The occasional conversation about kids and why Grant didn't -- hadn't -- wanted to have them...

When had that changed? When Zane walked into his shop? Before?

He'd lost track of his train of thought.

Start over.

Zane didn't seem interested in having kids. Even if Grant had changed his mind, it didn't follow that Zane might have. *So keep that zipped, even if you can't keep your pants closed, and you'll be all right.*

While an Omega astride was just fine during the heat of the moment, a full-grown man did get heavy afterward. Grant nudged at Zane to get him to roll off, and turned on his side when Zane flopped as gracelessly as a dead cat onto *his* back.

No, that was overstating it. As gracelessly as someone who'd been thoroughly fucked, which was just as likely to be accurate and painted them both in a much better light.

Far more pleased with that description, Grant settled himself comfortably on his hip and bent his head to nuzzle Zane's chest. *Mmm,* smooth chest. He'd always liked guys with a little fur to them before Zane -- Omegas could be plenty hairy, it was just a matter of genetics and grooming choices, same as with Alphas. He hadn't liked getting hair between his teeth when he bit their nipples but you took the rough with the smooth in this world. And speaking of... carefully as he could, he peeled the protective covering off Zane's right nipple and touched his fingertip to the gold ring through it. It took some balls to pierce yourself, and Zane had done a nice job of it. Really was almost healed too, well enough for a gentle tug.

Huh. Grant knew from experience that Zane's nipples were hot-wired to his dick. Why else pierce them? But the tug did nothing. He might as well have yanked at an unplugged lamp cord. He tried again, frowning when Zane said nothing, did nothing, just kept staring up at the sky -- scowling at it, as if it'd cast dishonor on his cow and called his father a nasty name.

"Hey." Grant pinched the skin beside Zane's nip first lightly, then firmly. "What's eating you?"

A corner of Zane's mouth flickered. It wasn't a smile. "You were, a few minutes ago."

"Funny man. That's not what I meant." Grant sighed and lay down more fully on his side propped on one arm. He kept the other moving lightly over Zane's chest, drifting down toward his stomach, just to keep him focused. "If the sex was that bad, you're gonna crush my ego for life. Just so you know."

Flicker, flicker. "It was damned good and you know it. You were there."

"And funnily, I don't sound or look like I want to go kick a puppy." Grant poked Zane just above the navel, frowning again when he winced. A good seeing-to had damped down those rising-heat pheromones for the moment, but did Omegas get tender down there during their cycles? Funny to realize he didn't know. Never paid that much attention before. He stopped poking and splayed his fingers wide instead, lying them lightly over Zane's skin. He had a little hair there, at least, a downy trail leading to the satisfying nest of curls around his now-soft dick. "Seriously. Talk to me."

Zane only shook his head and said nothing. As far as Grant could tell he planned to maintain that status and make it quo, but Zane always did surprise him. He opened his mouth without warning. "Keep doing that."

So he liked it? Okay, fine, whatever worked. Grant obligingly stroked Zane's lower stomach, harder when Zane grunted and rocked up into his touch. "That feels good?"

"Feels like…" Zane shook his head. "Did you always not want kids? I mean, before the shop thing?"

Deja frickin' vu. "You read minds now?"

"Huh?"

"Ix-nay." Too complicated to explain. Probably. Grant kneaded Zane's belly, reminding himself of a cat -- or, no, a nursing kitten -- and tried to think. Odd how the skin was just the littlest bit loose there, as if he'd weighed more once upon a time and lost the pounds in a hurry. He prodded curiously. "To be honest, I don't remember. The shop thing was so early, and Granddad loved that store just about more than me. After he died, it went to his business partner. Then *he* died, and everything got tied up in his estate. All I could ever think about was getting it back, and that didn't leave room for anything else."

"And now that you've got it back, there's still no room for more than that," Zane said, quietly, as if to himself. "And there never will be."

I didn't say that, Grant wanted to say, but didn't. Neither did he say *For now, but not forever*, nor yet *I might not be so sure of that anymore*. Frustrated, he dug for words and kneaded harder at Zane's belly, and --

And --

Oh. *Oh*. Well, shit. He'd seen this kind of loose

skin before. The spouses of his Alpha friends, the ones who'd had kids, they had a little jiggle. Sometimes a lot of jiggle. And -- yes, stretch marks -- in the skin. Signs of pregnancies past. He'd never noticed before because he and Zane weren't much on getting all their clothes all the way off, but now --

Shit. Grant sat upright, so quickly that he jostled Zane off balance. "You have a kid," he said, too stunned to be anything but blunt. "You have a kid? Zane!"

Zane shot him one wild, defiant -- fierce, feral, *defiant* -- look, and that was all. He didn't answer, not that he had to, and he didn't stick around to be asked again. Faster than Grant would have thought possible in the midst of even semi-decent afterglow Zane scrambled to his feet and Grant would swear he was running before he hit the ground, grabbing up his clothes and pelting away as fast as a tall, long-legged drink of water like him could move. He was gone like the wind, leaving nothing but footprints and a staggering sense of *what the* fuck, *Omega?* in his wake.

Grant sagged back on his ass, staring. Zane had a kid, and he'd never said anything. Zane was a father. And he'd never told Grant.

What. Even. Grant couldn't have said, afterward, how long he sat and stared dumbly at where Zane had been, and where he'd gone. When he raised a hand to his face to rub at his mouth, his lips had gone dry, which was no mean feat sitting by a river's edge on a humid night.

But that little bit of movement helped. His brain chugged slowly into action again, long habit bringing his thoughts back into focus.

Fact one. Zane had a kid. No telling how long ago, but that didn't matter because point two: Zane had kept that kid. He wouldn't have given Grant the kind of look that might as well have dared him to say anything about it and threatened to rip his nuts off if he did, if he didn't love that kid as fiercely as a tiger loved its cubs. And then there was point three, which was that Zane had to be a single dad. Grant had never smelled any kind of Alpha mark on him besides his own.

So, taken all together: Zane had a kid, and he'd never said anything to Grant. Aside from... *aw, shit*. Grant flopped onto his back in the dirt. The first time kids had ever come up, he'd said he didn't want any, and Zane had dropped the topic like it was hot. Like it'd burned him. Hurt him. And... he'd looked at Grant a little differently, afterward. Gotten even more ferocious with his libido, sure, but kind of like a starving man would go after a buffet. All you can eat, but not forever.

Damn. Damn, and damn again. Grant sat back up and narrowed his eyes at the path Zane had taken. Thinking, and thinking hard.

Would it be the worst thing ever if he had a kid? Zane had asked him once. Grant couldn't even remember what he'd answered, it'd been tossed out so casually, but he could make an educated guess. Whatever it was, though, it'd been wrong.

Hell no, it wouldn't be the worst thing ever. No. This was *Zane*. It would be the best. *It already is, Grant, you dumbass.* He just hadn't seen it yet.

Had he let the situation go too long to be fixed?

Nah. That wasn't how Grant worked. He stood, batting river mud and old leaves off himself, his thoughts flying thick and fast. So he'd come to his senses. Now he had to do something about it, and fast, before Zane packed up and headed either up to

Canada or down to Mexico to salve his sense of protectiveness and his wounded pride.

After all, he of anyone out there could understand pride and what it cost to maintain. And what it took to break through those walls, too.

Grant set his chin, gave a determined nod, and took off at a dead sprint. He'd have to move fast, if he wanted to beat Zane home.

* * *

Zane could put the pedal to the metal when he wanted to, and in a mood like his at the moment he didn't care if that metaphor didn't make sense because he and Grant had walked to the river instead of driving. He threw his clothes back on more or less in the right order, held his head high, set his shoulders wide, and stalked back home taking huge, road-eating strides.

He went the wrong way for fifteen minutes because his head was fucked to hell and had to turn around and walk back, but fuck it.

His head still whirred as he ate up the road underfoot. He'd have to quit his job. No doubt about that. Though could you call it a job? Grant paid him, an envelope of cash once a week laid carelessly where he could find it and slip it in his pocket -- did that make him a whore? *No, don't go there.* He'd worked hard for his pay packets. Blood, sweat, tears, the whole nine.

Just like labor. Like he'd brought his son into the world, by honest toil.

Zane shook his head hard and kept walking, moving fast, the next best thing to a jog. He'd have to quit his job. Just in case that didn't make his point clear, he'd end things properly with Grant the way he should have weeks ago, when Grant told him he didn't ever want children. What had he been thinking? That he could change Grant's mind?

As if. Grant was the stubbornest Alpha that Zane had ever met, and Zane had met more than a few.

End things properly. How? With a letter? No, that was too old-fashioned... but wait, maybe that would be a good thing. Hard to doubt or question or argue with a printed sheet of paper laying out the facts in black and white.

Not that Grant wouldn't try. Or would he? No. Maybe? Zane growled as his head whirled, shoved all but certainty out of his mind, and kept walking.

He knew he'd been going fast and that he'd ache for it the next day, but still it surprised Zane how quickly he arrived on his apartment steps. He threw the door open, not giving a damn if it banged or rattled, and marched himself up the flights to the place he called home, half wondering if maybe he should pack up and move just to make things extra-clear, only he didn't have enough money saved for that and his son would miss Eduardo and -- and...

And Grant was there, *there*, sitting crisscross on the floor in front of Zane's son, caught in the act of handing a fat kid-sized pencil to him while a sheet of Pre-K homework lay on the carpet between them. To give Grant credit, he only blinked at Zane for a moment, and calmly at that, before returning his focus calmly to Zane's son. "Okay, so you have two apples, one pear, and one pineapple. That's adding up, so put them all together. What does that make?"

Zane's son gazed back at Grant just as calmly, behaving as well for the Alpha as he did for Eduardo on his best days. "Fruit salad," he said, firm as a preacher. "Can I have a bedtime snack? Please?"

* * *

Every word Zane had ever known, good or bad

or pure as the driven snow or blue as a sailor's finest phrases, flew out of his head and left him staring blankly at his son and his -- no, not his anymore -- Alpha.

Grant raised one eyebrow at him, but betrayed no other reaction to the elephant standing in the room right next to the apples, pears, and pineapples. He looked at Zane's son. "You're not going to say hi to your old man?"

Zane's son frowned. "He's not my old man. He's my papa."

"Well then. You're not going to say hi to your papa?"

Hadrian wrinkled his nose. "He smells funny. So do you."

Grant regarded him for a moment. "You are definitely your papa's son."

That made the contrary little monkey grin from ear to ear. "Yup. Hi Papa!"

A smile at his son came naturally, and Zane was glad of the reflex now. "Hiya, kiddo. Who's your friend?"

His son heaved a huge, put-upon sigh. God help him, what Zane was going to do when he hit his teenage years... love him and learn to live with it, probably. "Grant's not *my* friend."

"Hey!" Grant protested.

"He's *your* friend. He told me," Zane's son said. He clambered to his bare, still dirty from a day's playing, feet and turned to Eduardo. "Can I have a bedtime snack? I'm hungry. *Please.*"

Eduardo, who -- damn his eyes -- had been standing silently in the door to the hallway with a shit-eating grin behind his beard this whole time, tilted his head at Zane in question. Zane hesitated, then shook his head and gestured past Eduardo toward the bathroom. The kid needed cleaning before he was allowed extra eating. They'd done this bit of sign language before, and Eduardo nodded in understanding.

"Bath time first," Eduardo said in a tone of voice that Hadrian knew to pay attention to. He held out one hand. "Once you're clean, *mijo*, you can have a fruit cup. Deal?"

"I'm not *mijo*. You call Zane *mijo*. That means 'my son,'" Hadrian said, though he obediently went to Eduardo and took his hand. "You should call me *nieto*. That means 'grandson.'"

"No sh -- kidding." Eduardo shook his head as he escorted Zane's son out. "Here I thought I was the one who grew up in Tijuana."

"I watch *Dora*. Come *on*, Wardo!"

"That's *Abuelo* Eduardo to you, smarty pants. Hang on, let me clear your homework out of the way. You go think up excuses for your teacher about why it isn't done tomorrow." The old Omega came and bent to pick up the papers still on the ground. When he stood, he patted Zane on the shoulder and whispered, "Things don't have to be impossible, you know. Just try. That's what you do, isn't it?"

Oh for fuck's sake. Zane covered his face with one hand. That way he couldn't see Grant's amusement -- but he could still hear him chuckling away, quietly, almost under his breath, while first Hadrian and then Eduardo exited stage left.

Well, that was one way to deflate a good mad-on, he supposed.

"That is definitely, without a doubt, one hundred percent your kid," Grant said.

Ah. New fuel for the fire. "He's not a 'that,' he's a

'he,'" Zane snapped. "And his name is Hadrian."

"That his other father's name too?" Grant asked, too casually.

Zane wasn't anyone's fool. Most of the time. He took his hand away from his face and met Grant's gaze. "No, his other father isn't in his life. Or mine. I'm not sure where he is right now, to be honest, and neither Hades or I miss him enough to ever even think about him. That's what you were really asking, isn't it?"

Grant held up one hand. He waited, during which pause Zane picked up the sound of the bathroom door closing and water starting to run, before he started again. Eduardo would be standing right outside the closed door in case of emergency, but at least the thunder of water on porcelain would allow Zane to pretend his babysitter wasn't about to hear all of this too.

"What happened to him? His other father," Grant clarified. He stayed on the floor, fingers laced loosely across one knee. Calm, for fuck's sake. Calm as the sea on a windless day. Damn him.

Zane didn't have a choice but to do the same, or it'd put them on unequal footing, which would be Grant's entire plan. He had to pick not just a stubborn Alpha, but a smart, shrewd one, didn't he?

He sighed as he sat, but firmly refrained from giving anything else away about the turmoil bubbling inside him. "Before you ask, Eduardo's not my papa by blood. He's just a friend. An Omega whose mate is dead and whose kids live half a world away."

Grant only nodded. "He told me. Real forthcoming, Eduardo was."

Oh, Zane would just bet. "What else did he say?"

Grant's nod turned into a shake of the head.

"Things only I was supposed to hear."

Zane resisted the urge to tear at his hair, more so when Grant's grin widened. "Stop enjoying this. No one is supposed to be enjoying this. This is the breakup fight, Grant, so why are you acting like you're having fun?"

"No one told me it was the breakup fight," Grant said with a shrug. "'Just try,' Wardo said. 'That's what you do.' Cool. I fight *for* things, not against them. That's what *I* do. We don't need to fight, Zane. What we need is to have a talk."

* * *

Talk? Okay, fine. Zane could do that. "You need to know that I am not ashamed of being a single father. I'm a fucking fantastic dad. I've fought people who thought I should be, so don't go there, and don't you dare ever make Hadrian think it."

"Wasn't planning to. What do you think I am, a monster?"

No. Zane thought Grant was the best Alpha he could ever have hoped to meet. One who *didn't want kids.*

Grant sighed. "Okay, let's get some basics out of the way first. Mind you, this still isn't a breakup fight, this is just -- clearing the air."

Zane reserved the right to decide on that, but he let Grant go on.

"I get why you didn't tell me about Hadrian, you know," Grant said. "I was a dick."

"Glad to see we're on the same page there."

"But you didn't give me a chance not to be," Grant pointed out, a lick of fire entering his eyes now. "Didn't give me a chance to change my mind."

"I was supposed to think I had a shot at that? You were firm as hell, Grant. You made your position on family life abundantly clear."

If humans could have huffed steam out their noses like cartoon bulls, Grant would have. But he stayed his course, God help them both. "Maybe so. But you didn't even try, and that makes *you* kind of a dick."

"Bite me."

"I did. Not half an hour ago. I ran till I was out of breath and I still couldn't catch up with. Not sure how I got here ahead of you, but I did, in time to meet Wardo and your son. Your kid -- Hadrian -- took one look at me and thought I was the funniest thing he'd ever seen."

Zane's mouth twitched without his permission. Yeah, he'd just bet that, too.

"And then he took me by the hand, dragged me inside, and shoved that homework at me and demanded I help. He is *so* your kid, Omega. Didn't ask, didn't make nice, just took what he wanted. Like father, like son." Grant's grin widened. "And if the run didn't give me a heart attack, that will. You wait and see. That ought to comfort you whenever I piss you off, yeah?"

Zane's mouth twitched again, and he only just barely got it under control. "Don't make me laugh, asshole. I'm mad at you."

"Why do you think I'm trying so hard?"

Fair point. But, and -- Zane gave in to the urge to rake his hair up. "I don't understand."

"I know." Grant hitched himself a few inches closer, near enough for Zane to feel his body heat. His own traitorous body responded, the first stirrings of heat making themselves known again. "That's partly why I'm here. Well, mostly it's to make sure you didn't throw all your shit in the back of a beat-up VW and take off for the border before I had a chance to see you again, but explaining, that's the main point. Explaining, and… making sure I didn't lose you."

Zane's heart gave a great, painful *thump-thump-thump* and he lost his breath. Trying to cover it, and in a vain effort to recover some distance, he sat back on his heels. It didn't help.

Grant watched him as calmly and patiently as he'd watched Hadrian, and just as inexorably as he had when he'd sworn up and down he didn't want kids, didn't want a family, only had room in his life for the shop and what it took to get its door back open.

Which meant…

But Zane couldn't hope for that. He didn't dare. Even if *trying* was what he did, he… he… He gave up. Just a little, but an important little. "What are you trying to say, Grant?" he asked, throwing his hands in the air. "You're acting like things are different. Are they?"

Grant said nothing. Just watched him, with things in his face that Zane didn't know how to interpret. Were they good things? Zane hesitated, his heart in his throat. "Are… are they different? And seriously, don't fuck with me. This is too important."

"Yeah, I get that." Grant took both of Zane's hands and held them loosely. "See, when you ditched me down by the river, I had what they used to call a come-to-Jesus moment."

"A what, now? No, don't explain, I get the idea, I just never heard the phrase before."

"Eduardo would be ashamed."

"Eduardo hasn't darkened the door of a church since he was a teenager."

Grant accepted that with a philosophical shrug and blazed right on. "So, come-to-Jesus moment. I realized a few things, right there, right then. Things I should have seen all along. Like how important you are to me and have been from the start. Just like you hired yourself, you fit yourself into a place at the shop, you slid right into my life like you belong there. No, that's not quite right." He took a tighter hold of Zane's hands. "Like you should have belonged there for a long time, only I was too much of a dumbass to realize I had a big empty hole in my life. A you-shaped hole."

Zane snorted.

"Hey now, don't you make *me* laugh. This is my important shit." Grant stroked Zane's hands, not gentle, but nice and firm and comforting. "You are everything I never knew I wanted, Zane. Everything I was too blinded by my own drives to realize I needed. You are all I could ever hope for, and my only wish right now is that you'll give me a second chance to prove it."

Zane would have answered. Really, he would have, only the knot in his throat was too big to speak around. He tried to swallow and that didn't help -- but he could take hold of Grant's hands in return, and he could squeeze them tight. And at that, his vocal chords let go just enough for him to whisper. "You mean that. You promise."

"I do."

It had the ring of a wedding vow. Zane heard it, and knew Grant heard it too. He swallowed again, with more success this time. "And kids? You don't mind kids now? You won't resent Hadrian? Wish he wasn't part of this? Because he is, Grant, and he will be. He's my son."

"Didn't I point that out a time or two?" Grant's grin softened, as did his massage of Zane's hands. "I like Hadrian. He's a little firecracker, and I do well with firecrackers. And you know what, Zane? That's been bugging me all along. Every time I looked at you, every time I was with you, something in the back of my mind started ticking over, saying *what-if, what-if, what*-if."

And there went the lump in Zane's throat again.

"I like Hadrian. I could be part of his life, if you'd let me. Try to earn myself the title of -- what's Spanish for father?"

"Padre. You idiot," Zane rasped. "You really want to be 'padre'?"

"Okay, I could be Da instead. If you don't mind some Irish in you." Grant waggled his eyebrows. "I kinda have proof you haven't minded it so far."

He did make Zane laugh this time, and if it was a little watery, Grant was kind enough not to point that out.

"And if there are other kids?" Zane pressed. "That happens, you know. I'm fertile as hell if I don't take precautions, Grant, and I *did* take precautions with Hadrian. He was just too stubborn not to bull his way into the world. What would you think about that?"

"I'd think a good few things," Grant said. He lifted Zane's hand to his cheek and held it there. "But here's what I think most. I love you."

Zane gaped at him. "You what?"

"I love you," Grant said again, steady and true. "I think I have for a while now. I just needed a good smack to the back of the head to figure it out. If we end up with another kid, I'll love him, too. If we end up with a houseful, even."

Zane stared at him.

Grant pressed his cheek into Zane's palm, but there was a challenge in his body language, his face, that hadn't been there before. A dare. "So, what do you say, Omega? Give us another shot? Let me prove myself?"

Because doing things, proving himself, was what Grant did. And once he'd made up his mind, stated his purpose, hell itself could not bar his way. And nothing except Zane could swerve him. He meant it. He really meant it.

Zane took one deep breath to center himself, made sure he was sure of himself, gave up entirely on speaking, and leaned forward to press his mouth to Grant's. Not a deep kiss, but a passionate one, a kiss that he put his whole heart into, betraying every vulnerability and hint of hope just for this moment.

When he let go, Grant looked dazed, but delighted and growing ever more so. "That's a yes?"

"Yes," Zane said, kissing him again, this time finishing with a nip to his lower lip. "And as soon as Eduardo's gone and Hadrian's asleep -- with earmuffs on and the bedroom door closed -- you're going to put your money where your mouth is."

Grant was the one to give him the third kiss, and said with a grin, "Oh, Omega. You just watch me."

Epilogue

Not long after midnight, and all through Zane's house -- though it wasn't Christmas and wouldn't be for a few months yet -- not a creature was stirring, not even a four-year-old. Or the Alpha who'd gotten so pooped wrangling said five-year-old out of the bath, into pajamas, and into bed that he'd sacked out not long after, fast asleep on Zane's couch.

Zane chuckled to himself as he padded barefoot through his apartment. He hadn't felt the need to check his perimeter and make sure the house was safe and sound since Hadrian was a newborn, but it made sense to him that he'd feel the urge tonight.

For one thing, once again, it wasn't just him who needed the security of locked doors. He had a family resting with him tonight. And what else should the resident night owl do?

His memory hadn't tricked him. Doors were secure, windows closed, Eduardo paid for the night and sent home, still wearing a shit-eating grin that Zane suspected someone would have to surgically remove from his face. He'd never let Zane live this down.

Zane decided he would be surprisingly okay with that.

Perimeter, check. Zane turned on his heel and made for Hadrian's room next. Grant had promised to paint a mural of rolling hills and stone walls on there, which had made Hadrian scowl until Grant also promised to paint dinosaurs ravaging the countryside. *Then* he'd gotten a soon-to-be gap-toothed grin and a fist bump.

Grant hadn't done a bad job of tucking Zane's son in. Sure, the covers were lopsided and his pillow on the floor, but Hadrian had curled up with his head on his teddy bear instead and plugged his thumb in his mouth. He slept peacefully, limp with the boneless looseness only little kids seemed to manage, not a care in the world. Back when he was a teenager and just coming into his own as an Omega, Zane hadn't ever imagined he'd be the kind of parent who'd tiptoe into their kid's room and kiss them goodnight.

Yeah, well, what had that teenage punk known? Zane walked as silently as he could to Hadrian, rumpled his hair with the lightest touch, and bent to touch his lips to his son's forehead.

Hadrian, check.

Zane retraced his steps back to the living room and sank to a crouch in front of the couch, taking the rare opportunity to study Grant at peace. He could see the little boy Grant had once been -- only glimpses, mostly subsumed by the man he'd become -- but there was an innocence and sweetness to Grant when he slept that never showed when he was awake. He sighed and turned more deeply into the couch cushions, almost like he was moving instinctively closer to Zane.

That, Zane didn't need to decide he could be okay with. He was sure of it before the question even occurred to him. "You weren't the only one who fell in love," he said, reaching out to brush his fingertips over Grant's forearm with all its bright colors and inked patterns. "Just in case you needed to know. Or even if you didn't, I still wanted to say it."

Grant huffed again, but his eyes drifted open. He blinked at Zane, who grinned back. "I fell asleep?"

"Like a rock, like a log," Zane confirmed. "It was downright damned cute, Alpha."

Grant scoffed and turned with a flop to lie on his

back. "'M not cute. 'M never cute. 'M an Alpha."

"And don't we all know it." Zane stood, considered his options -- he hadn't planned to wake Grant, but now that he *had* -- and, what the hell? He threw one leg over, planting his knee carefully between Grant and the couch back and then one on the near side to the couch edge. Poised there, not yet sinking down, he reached to cup Grant's cheek. "But still cute. Sorry, I don't make the rules. It is what it is, Alpha."

"This feels familiar." Grant batted his hand away, but caught it in the next second and brought it to his lips. "You don't want me to go home?"

"Nope," Zane said cheerfully. He had the feeling he and Hadrian would be the ones moving to Grant's home soon enough -- Grant wouldn't leave the apartment over his shop, and why should he? -- and besides, there was plenty of room for more than one man up there. Whereas he and Hadrian would burst this place at the seams before much longer. "I want you to stay right here."

"Oh yeah?"

"Mm-hmm." Zane eased himself down and kissed Grant, light but with plenty of promise, his hips moving in much the same way. "You promised me another seeing-to tonight, Alpha. In case you forgot."

"As if I could." Grant put his hands on Zane, stroking his chest, his hips, kneading his ass. He breathed in deep and let his air out in a sound of pleased satisfaction. "You're mine, Omega. Just so *you* know."

Oh, Zane knew. He let his eyes go half-lidded in enjoyment and satisfaction at least equal to Grant's. Because there was something more Grant didn't know. To be fair Zane didn't know himself, not for sure, not yet, but there was nothing wrong with his memory or his understanding of his own body. They'd been careful earlier when Grant was inside him, sure. As careful as he and Hadrian's father had been the night Hadrian was conceived.

And he felt the exact same way now. As if he wasn't alone inside his body. There was someone else within him, someone so new they weren't really even a clump of cells yet, but some*one* all the same.

Grant's firstborn. Forming, becoming, making himself known. *Like father, like son.* Zane wondered if he might be just a little too fertile for his own good, then figured he was the most okay with that of anything else that'd happened this night. He'd get confirmation soon enough, and so would Grant, and then the three -- four -- of them would make a family. They'd tuck themselves in above the tattoo shop snug as bugs, and their kids would grow up rough and tumble, surrounded by the sharp smells of ink and disinfectant, and they'd be fed, taken care of, *happy*. What more could an Omega ask for?

Zane laughed suddenly, making Grant stop the important work of kissing him and look up with a patient scowl. "What's funny?"

"Nothing," Zane said, then amended, "Everything. Life's funny, Grant. Don't you think?"

Grant's scowl faded to a grin. He drew Zane back down to him, getting back to work. Zane went happily, but he kept the thought that'd made him laugh in his mind. *Marshall is going to hold this over our heads for the rest of our lives.*

Let him. After all, it'd be his turn soon enough.

So thinking, Zane let everything else go and melted into his Alpha's arms. Safe. Loved. *Mine. Mine, mine, mine, and forever mine.* And *that* was what Zane called a happy ending.

Will Okati

Will Okati (formerly known as Willa) has lived through a few Interesting Times, but come out the other side a little grayer, a little wiser, and ready to get writing. Still as passionate about coffee, cats, and crafts as ever, but knowing that to your own self you must be true. Also still one of the quiet ones to watch out for, but life -- like storytelling -- is always a work in progress.

Will at Changeling: changelingpress.com/will-okati-a-213

Changeling Press E-Books

More Sci-Fi, Fantasy, Paranormal, and BDSM adventures available in e-book format for immediate download at ChangelingPress.com -- Werewolves, Vampires, Dragons, Shapeshifters and more -- Erotic Tales from the edge of your imagination.

What are E-Books?

E-books, or electronic books, are books designed to be read in digital format -- on your desktop or laptop computer, notebook, tablet, Smart Phone, or any electronic e-book reader.

Where can I get Changeling Press E-Books?

Changeling Press e-books are available at ChangelingPress.com, Amazon, Apple Books, Barnes & Noble, and Kobo/Walmart.

ChangelingPress.com